BLOOD IN THE STREETS

DION BAIA

A POST HILL PRESS BOOK
ISBN: 978-1-64293-063-4
ISBN (eBook): 978-1-64293-064-1

Blood in the Streets

Cover design by Cody Corcoran

Post Hill Press
New York • Nashville
posthillpress.com

Published in the United States of America

THE END

"ONE..."

With so much rage locked up inside, Frank was deranged, driven crazy by an unfamiliar psychotic madness. Every option seemed rational, even the irrational. What was more, he couldn't control it. He literally saw red. He sensed all the blood in his head flowing straight into his temples and forehead, causing his mind to almost boil over, like it was about to explode and spew out into the air all the anger, desperation, and revenge he wrestled to keep locked away deep inside of him. The cold steel of his .357 service revolver did not give as he squeezed the handgrip harder than he ever thought possible, desperately trying to vent some of the fury out of his body.

Yet all it did was transfer the pressure out and down the long barrel and make the kid's sweaty forehead he had it pressed up against turn bone white.

In the background, the needle of the record player skipped around at the center of the LP that spun lazily on the turntable's platter, projecting a crackling static of mechanical white noise into the sonorous, dingy, pre-war apartment. So many thoughts bounced around like tennis balls in Frank's head, questions:

What should my next decision here be, really? What then, if I choose to let this kid go, and then this savage subsequently slips through the cracks and escapes justice? Can I live with that? Live with myself? And honestly, should I even bother to care about my own wellbeing at this point? Every time he closed his eyes it all returned to haunt him.

Frank was on the dark side of the moon now, his mind set to autopilot.

"Two..."

What now, asshole?

The answer to that question may determine if Frank lived or died tonight. Or if the kid on his knees in front of him kept breathing after the count of three, or if the back of this cunt's head would add a little color to the wall of this shitty little apartment.

Frank's life no longer mattered. He knew that, and it didn't bother him; he just didn't want this little mope here to hire a fancy lawyer and get off unpunished. It was more than this piece of shit deserved. But if he didn't get the answer to where this murderer was right now by the count of three, well, he was going to ventilate this asshole in a heartbeat. Full stop.

The broken glass shards in the shag rug from the shattered coffee table crunched underneath his dress shoes as Frank shifted his weight. It was the rage guiding him now. The blind fury, the hate, the loathing for whoever did this, and their complete lack of empathy, even now at this late stage in the game, when they were called on it. Someone with this blatant disregard for life didn't deserve to live.

Frank's grip tightened on the weapon, his trigger finger danced on the lever, testing the play that the apparatus had within its action.

"Three."

Could he do it? Should he do it? COULD he really do it, though, really?

Frank closed his eyes, exhaled, and calmly unloaded the .357, unable to escape the deafening successive reports confined inside the large room.

SEVEN DAYS PRIOR

Saturday, October 11, 1976

Dawn

THE BRIGHT, SOBERING sun shone down upon East Rock Mountain in such a way that it perfectly silhouetted the city of New Haven in a warm orange hue directly below, making the harbor and Long Island Sound that lay just beyond glimmer as though millions and millions of tiny diamonds had been tossed across her choppy waves for all to see. Frank Suchy gazed out from the parking lot of the observation area down at the autumn foliage which camouflaged and hid the city and suburbs below, thinking to himself how tranquil it all looked. It made him think of when he came up here with his mother as a boy. How fun life used to be, how none of the real world was known to a child. Oh, how he envied those days. As fast as one of the twinkles of light reflecting off the water in the harbor faded, though, so did those memories leave his mind.

Frank was in his late thirties, and as he liked to say, his body was starting to 'creak.' That was the just deserts of being active and athletic in his youth. Frank wore his light brown hair long nowadays, just beginning to curl over his ears. He frowned, and his hand instinctively went to stroke the bushy moustache that used to inhabit the space below his nose, which he momentarily forgot he'd shaven off the night before.

His eyes wanted to shift their gaze toward the park and river that was at the southwest base, bordering the suburb of Hamden. He never drove past there anymore and had completely erased it from his mind, but being this far up the mountain, that particular wooded area was kind of hard to ignore. It was one of those things where, the more he tried to remove it from his head, the bigger of a black dot it was on the landscape, beckoning him to look over. It took all of his strength to instead ignore that little voice that was in the back of his head, *daring* him to gaze over. Much like it did with him and the old *bug*. But alas, a noise brought his mind back to why he was now up here on such a beautiful morning. It was his team's turn to be up.

Frank turned back to the small row of parking spaces that abutted the lookout area and his eyes found the dark lime green Ford LTD Country Squire. He bent over and stuck his head into the car via the passenger-side window, the broken glass of which littered the pavement below and crackled under his feet. What was left of the victim's skull on the passenger side was starting to attract the nighthawks of the insect world, looking for a quick meal. The shotgun blast took off about three-quarters of the young man's head, leaving the bottom jaw, the right cheek, right eye, and ear, and what looked to be maybe his medulla oblongata. Everything else now decorated the vinyl back seat and ceiling liner of the LTD. A glance at the tableau was all Frank needed. He removed his head from the window and looked over the scene.

Pellet marks were present on the shattered windshield as well as on the front hood and right fender. Frank stepped back, trying to gauge how close the gunman could have been to inflict so much devastation on his victim. He peered over to the driver's side and at the open door. A trail of blood slithered away from the Country Squire, toward the mountain's towering bronze and red granite Soldiers and Sailors monument, erected to honor those local residents who fought in the country's early wars of the seventieth and eightieth century. The blood trail reached thirty feet, where it halted in the two-lane road and connected to a much larger pool of dark, coagulated blood.

Even as high up on a mountain as this one, maybe the most remote place in New Haven, a crowd could still be attracted. People were already two deep behind the yellow police tape, smelling out the crime and looking on at every movement the New Haven Police Department made. It could make a man nervous being under a microscope like he and the force were these days, but Frank was used to it now and in some weird way, after all these years, he was still fascinated by it.

"Gun wavin' New Haven," he muttered to himself.

A young uniformed officer, or blue suit, as they were called, crossed into his line of sight, blocking his view from the gathering crowd. The rookie looked down at his notes, like he was gathering the courage to brief a superior for the first time.

"Talk to me..." Frank's eyes darted down to the officer's nameplate that glimmered in the sun, "...McCurdy. Whatcha got?"

The officer nervously flicked a page. "Well, um, Sergeant," he hesitated, "a radio car pulled through here at about five a.m. and found the driver, a male identified by a Connecticut State license on his person as Matthew Hallwell, lying about thirty-six feet from the car. He'd passed out after dragging himself away from the scene. He was taken to Saint Ray's and is reported to be in critical but stable condition, suffering from multiple laceration wounds from the buckshot he received from a shotgun. We have not been able to get a statement from him thus far. The vehicle is registered to a Louis and Debra Brighton of Hamden." The officer unconsciously gestured with his pad north, toward the bordering town of the same name which was visible from their location. He then pointed with his pencil to the occupant still in the car and continued, "And we haven't touched this fella yet to see if he has any ID on him."

One of Frank's partners, Graham Birdsall, a dusty-haired detective who had been with Frank since 1972, walked around from the back of the car with his notepad in hand.

"You think they were up here in lover's lane necking or something?" Graham inquired. Frank glanced back down to the victim in the car and at the guy's black leather pants which were unbuttoned, exposing his genitalia.

"Whatever gave you that idea, Graham?" Frank asked rhetorically.

"I guess the fact this has been a hangout after dark for all kinds, queens included, for years now really kind of gave it away," Graham answered back, half grinning.

"The victim who was taken to the hospital," the rookie said, "his pants were undone and his joint, um, penis was exposed as well."

Frank smirked. "Well, there you go, Officer, you got this thing half solved." He winked at Graham.

McCurdy chuckled to himself and glanced back down at his notes.

"You may be right, though," Frank said. "Their sexual preference could very well be a motive here. It looks like the

VIC here took the brunt of the impact, judging from the damage on the windshield and fender of the Ford." He took a step back. "It would appear our killer was standing about here, and it looks as if our victims had no warning, so maybe the perp watched for a little while before taking it to the next level."

Frank looked around on the ground. "No shell casings," he muttered. "Why haven't the lab guys arrived yet?"

The officer stole a glance at his watch. "Last we heard they were stuck in traffic up on the Wilbur Cross Parkway, near Oakdale, sir. That's why we didn't touch John Doe here, we were waiting on them."

"What are they doing way the hell up there?" Frank snorted. "Taking in a seminar?"

"I don't know, Sergeant," McCurdy replied. "Hopefully they'll be here any minute now."

"Okay. Go make sure the perimeter is secure. When they do get here, have them check those bushes over there for any signs of disturbance. Maybe our mope likes to watch first. Graham, you were up, so you take the lead on this one."

"Okay."

"I think you and I are gonna have to carefully move this body to see if he's got any ID in his back pockets, which will be fun with rigor set in," he said to Graham.

Frank looked down at the body in the passenger seat, wondering if the guy even had back pockets with leather pants.

"Get Joe and Randy into the loop too." Frank started around the car toward Graham, speaking about the two other detectives that filled out the five-man unit.

"Joe's already on his way to the hospital to sit with the victim, in case he wakes."

"Wow, Spinall's up early today then?" Frank said with a smirk. "Great." He looked over to the young rookie. "And good job, McCurdy."

McCurdy smiled at the compliment before turning away and starting to leave. Graham grinned at Frank and nodded as if to tell his partner to watch.

"How long have you been out of the academy, Officer?" Graham queried.

"Um, about a month now, Detective, uh, sir," McCurdy answered with the respect one gives to a commanding officer.

"Remember the three rules they tell you as a rookie?"

"Oh shit, I know this," the Youngblood said, stumped.

"Check the receivers on the call boxes when you use 'em, 'cause kids like to put dog shit on them. Don't let children wear your hat unless you wanna run the risk of getting lice. And don't walk too close to the buildings in the projects because people sometimes like to drop bricks on our heads. Okay?" Graham smiled at him.

"Thank you for the advice, sir."

Frank put a hand on the rookie's shoulder. "He's no 'sir.' And good work, officer."

The Youngblood put his pad in his pocket and headed toward the police tape that was dragged over the bushes disguising the entrance to a footpath.

Frank turned toward Graham. "They didn't tell me that in the academy."

"Well, times are a-changing."

"Fair point." Frank sighed. "Okay, Graham, let's see if this guy has back pockets and pray he hasn't been incontinent yet."

FRANK SUCHY

Sunday Morning, October 12, 1976

A MIST HUNG low on the grassy hills. The wet dew gave the slanting terrain and surrounding forest a glossy sheen, provided by the glare of a low-hanging morning sun that lingered just above the tops of the trees. Gradually, the far-off purr of an engine came into earshot long before a vehicle was in view.

A Ford GT40 Mark 3 shot around the corner and started up the long straightaway at lightning speed, the biggest one at the racetrack. The hammer was slammed to the floor and the metallic baby blue car was temporally shielded from view by the sloping hills, popped up again, then vanished a moment later. When the GT40 rounded the corner, the driver shifted gears and the tires skirted the track's slick edge, audibly making itself known as the rubber hit the dirt and zipped back onto the asphalt. The Mark 3 again shifted in a loud protest into the next gear, sending it dangerously fast toward the upcoming curves. Yet the car was kept on the road and expertly controlled.

It came around the last turn and hit the straightaway that led to the finish line. Within seconds, it sailed across and decelerated.

An older, bearded man who was watching the exhibition checked his watch, put his hands in his pockets, and shook his head disapprovingly. The Ford slowed and made a U-turn and lazily started back toward the finish line. The gray-haired man combed his beard with his long, bony fingers and walked out from the pit to meet the baby blue Mark 3. The vehicle coasted to a stop.

Stepping out, Frank removed his black helmet and unzipped his leather racing jacket. He frowned again as his bottom lip instinctively still went to touch the bushy moustache he'd shaved off. He tossed the helmet on the seat and greeted his mentor, Vincent Channing, ex-NYPD Homicide Detective First Grade, five years retired now. Along with sharing a career, they both were fascinated with fast cars. And they both shared sobriety. Vince was Frank's sponsor and the man who taught Frank how to navigate through the world in which he now lived. Racing had become an outlet toward which they could concentrate their energy. Since Frank was blessed to own such a rare vehicle as a GT40, why not put it to good use?

The two stood in silence for a moment before the older man finally spoke.

"There's no point," Vince blurted out finally, cleared miffed. "I said, if you're gonna get killed while trying to beat a record, there's no point. And if you keep on doing it like this," he said, raising his long finger toward Frank, "Lime Rock's liable to kick you off the track, which I would half agree with them about, in principle."

"Gotta have something to look forward to accomplishing," Frank retorted after some thought.

Vincent answered with another shake of his head and turned away. His Santa Claus-sized beard distorted as he curled the side of his lip. "Well, I won't be the one using a can opener to peel you out when you wrap yourself around one of them trees out there!" He knew there was no talking to his younger friend.

Out of the small wooden shed popped the head of Don Gordon, an old man who oversaw the track on a weekend. In his hand, he held a phone receiver, which he raised in the air. "Suchy! Hey, Frank! *Work*!" the old grease monkey yelled.

Frank took off his gloves and squinted. "See, Vin? The world keeps going around."

Frank hoped he'd get a day off to be able to get his mind off the job. He'd found that was what he needed these days to keep a comfortable balance between everything. But that wasn't to be. The detectives worked in five-man squads, four detectives under a sergeant. Frank oversaw his team, and he and Graham spent the majority of yesterday, basically all afternoon and Saturday evening, processing the East Rock scene and running down any friends and relatives their victims had. The survivor, Matthew Hallwell, was still under sedation post-surgery, after the doctors cleaned out as much of the lead as they could from the shotgun blast and stemmed the bleeding from the excessive damage. Some of the pellets were too dangerous to remove, so they unfortunately had to be left alone and, sadly, would become morbid keepsakes for the kid if he pulled through.

With nothing for them to do at the hospital, Detective Joe Spinall, with the help of their fourth partner Randy Jurgens, drove out to Hallwell's home to make the notification and necessary inquiries. Their murder victim, Joshua Brighton, had been currently living in New York City. They'd notified the 13th Precinct in Manhattan, whose territory was where the VIC resided, and a lieutenant at the station house was kind enough to dispatch two detectives to search the VIC's apartment and maybe talk to a roommate or neighbors, if possible. Randy and Joe also took a ride to the DOA's parents' residence in the upper-class end of Hamden where the car was registered to get what they could from the parents. Saturday night's fun ended with everyone anxiously waiting for the M.E.'s primary on the victim, and for Graham's journey back up from forensics downstairs, where they were going over the Ford LTD Country Squire with a fine-tooth comb.

The team met back up before quitting time on 'the floor' as they called it, the major crimes division, located on over half of the third floor of the New Haven police station. It was the hallowed ground where all the detective bureaus covering sex crimes, robbery, homicide, and the like, occupied a big open expanse cluttered with desks, filing cabinets, and chairs, and often could be as busy as the floor of the stock exchange.

The call that had brought Frank in on his day off, on this Sunday, ended up being quite a sad one to boot. He was snagged to give an opinion on two bodies that were found, to figure out if it was a case of foul play or, as it initially appeared, a joint suicide. A married couple discovered by a black and white that was dispatched, because neighbors hadn't heard from their elderly friends that lived at the lone residence at the back of Evergreen Court off Legion Avenue for a number of days. The house was buried within a block with backyards facing it in all directions, situated on a dirt and gravel road that terminated on their property, a spacious, somewhat isolated plot of land where 17 Evergreen was located. It turned out the couple had used a long bathrobe belt draped over the bathroom door in the master bedroom and positioned themselves on either side of that door, tied the belt around each other's necks, and sat down, each using their weight to hang the other. It seemed to be an increasing trend by how some elderly couples were deciding to end their lives, this way or the other 'fad', if you wanted to call it that, which was sitting in the car together in the garage with the engine running.

When this couple's son arrived on scene after the anxious neighbor finally got ahold of him, he confirmed that the mother had been recently diagnosed with pancreatic cancer. The couple then must have decided they would go out together on their own terms. Of course, the M.E. would have final say, but Frank's learned opinion was that it was suicide, pure and sadly simple.

The record player was still on and Frank was the one to finally click it off. The needle had been scratching away at the end of side one of an old 78 RPM of Kay Kyser and his Orchestra's single, *The Old Lamp-Lighter*. Whatever significance the "Ol' Perfessor's" song was to Mary Louise and Marvin Wessell would now be forever lost in the abyss of time. Yet this was the selection the married couple of sixty-one years decided to fade out together with.

Frank opened his sleepy eyes only a crack, but enough to see Fred dancing up the ceiling. He struggled to open them more, still exhausted from his day, and could barely concentrate on the scene that was playing out on the small thirteen-inch black and white television that he had balanced atop a TV table on the other side of the living room. The last he remembered, he'd just sat down and taken his shoes off, planning a momentary rest before starting dinner but struggled against the eternal battle with the Sandman. When he opened his eyes again, it was nearly one in the morning. Mr. Astaire's singing and tap dancing must have stirred him. It took ages before he'd finally had the energy to fight off the great, long numbness of sleep and reopen his eyes.

Tired and disoriented, Frank laid on his old beat-up recliner cuddling his afghan, like a child would his baby blanket.

It took a second to realize this was indeed a movie he was seeing and not his imagination that had propelled Fred up the walls, onto the ceiling, and back down again in one fluid dance. He'd fallen asleep watching a Lon Chaney, Sr. movie, one where he actually spoke. Maybe the only one. Frank opened his eyes a little more and reached for the Jerrold channel changer, the lap-sized, piano-looking, wood-paneled device that was tethered to the television.

He flipped the channel, landing on a rebroadcast of the late-night news. A news anchor introduced a young reporter's pretaped package of yesterday's commission ceremony for newly completed additions to the New Haven Coliseum.

"Yes, Barbara. Along with the mayor and much to the delight of the crowd, Councilman Theodore Pregosin was also present, and they officially christened these expanded storefront locations down here at street level of the Coliseum, and more importantly, by having this event, city bureaucrats are essentially now waving a green flag to businesses to get them to come back down and make a home here in downtown New Haven, and help generate some much need tax revenue to help pay for our newly remodeled city."

Frank thought that would be a huge feat to accomplish. The New Haven Coliseum was the new modern 'super venue' which replaced the aging New Haven Arena in 1972. The christening of this expanded storefront section was part of the mayor's new campaign to keep New Haven the 'de facto' showcase in this era of the redeveloped city. Revitalize her image and hope to combat the over twenty-year mass exodus to the suburbs which started after the war and get foot traffic back downtown.

Easier said than done, though, Frank thought.

"Sadly, what has also become a reality is New Haven's historical image being severely marred," the reporter continued. "*In the last ten or so years, by incidents such as the 1967 summer race riots that occurred on Congress Avenue and ongoing racial tension in some communities with local law enforcement. Or the onstage arrest of rock singer Jim Morrison and near riot, and alleged battery upon a* Life Magazine *reporter the same night; or the internationally famous trials of the Black Panthers' co-founder Bobby Seale and member Erica Huggins for the brutal 1969 murder of Alex Rackley."*

Frank had worked the massive May Day protest rally that resulted. The National Guard was even deployed for that one, and the Elm City nearly plunged into martial law.

"Yet now, twenty years into its urban renewal, New Haven has been coined the 'Model City.' It has been adopted as the country's poster child, and spawned exposure in periodicals like Harper's Magazine, Life, Time, *and the* Saturday Evening Post, *putting us on the international stage and exalting the work that city officials did to bring New Haven's Urban Renewal Program to fruition and completion. But we nearly had all the accomplishments marred by an unfortunate series of events. New Haven almost failed its own people, but as Councilman Theodore Pregosin explained, the city was fortunately brought back from the brink."*

There was a delayed reaction as the young, bushy-haired, mustached Latino reporter paused before grainy, underexposed B-roll footage of yesterday's ceremony appeared on the small screen, and then he continued.

"Along with his Downtown Urban Coalition coordinating between the local government, local businesses, and New Haven's biggest single occupant, Yale University, he singlehandedly kept this city on course to its destiny. Councilman Pregosin focused his speech on how, in his mind, the potential businesses that will come flocking to this brutalist-styled Coliseum's storefront real estate, and open the flood gates that will bring businesses back downtown to aid in a recovery of this ailing, stagnant local economy. Here's what the councilman had to say..."

The reporter waited uncomfortably for more time than it needed to take before the segment cut to a sound bite of impeccably dressed Theodore Pregosin behind a lectern.

"New Haven has a legacy and history that we must reaffirm in the eyes of America. Dignitaries from major cities all over the country have come to consult and view our improvements, so they can take them back and possibly adopt them in their own native metropolises. Achievements like the Chapel Square Mall, the massive Oak Street Connector, which lies right behind us here, that gives travelers a straight line right into the downtown area from Interstate 95 or 91, for people to patronize our local businesses or take in a show at the Shubert, or even perhaps our lovely Coliseum here this weekend, for example, when Stevie Wonder is scheduled to arrive and raise the roof high above us." There were audio hoots and yelps of excitement from the crowd from the plug for the upcoming performance.

Boy, he was good, Frank thought through the fog of sleep. This guy was a born politician. He knew how to rile up a crowd.

"The revitalization of the downtown area, along with the numerous other smaller programs, where we focus specifically

on individual neighborhoods, like in struggling minority communities to combat poverty. The Community Q House in the Dixwell Avenue area and Congregational Church, for example. We believe these new projects have already started to benefit New Haven's citizens." The film cut to a close-up of a young black couple in the audience who listened intently and nodded in agreement. It cut back to Councilman Pregosin as he indicated over his shoulder. *"And here today, with this brand new street-level portion of the Coliseum dedicated to commerce and, eventually, an exhibition hall, is the spearhead in New Haven's future, a figurative example of her dogged determination, proudly living up to her nickname: America's City—A Model City—that will inspire people internationally for generations to come."* That was met with a loud applause from the large group gathered.

The report cut to B-roll of the mayor shaking hands with the various philanthropists present onstage and other attendants in the crowd, while the councilman followed suit. A shot appeared of the mayor, Councilman Pregosin, and another city official cutting the ribbon and officially opening this street-level area of the Coliseum. Behind them lay the vast eternity of cement steps leading up to the entrance of the enormous cement and brick structure.

Frank was one of the public masses that couldn't make heads or tails of what the designers were going for with the inside-out-looking mega venue. After the initial plans had been drawn up, the builders were forced to progressively draw back and cut down on the costs of the building, since the money was coming from government funding. Even now, it still had an unfinished look to it that made it literally look like a child's Erector set, due to a design that featured the skeleton of the faculty truly on the outside. The entire edifice was of steel and cement with the parking garage physically above the arena itself, so as to conserve the much-needed downtown real estate, among other practical concerns. On either side of the structure were two quarter-mile-long winding helical ramps that led cars up to the overhead parking area. They were unpopular for motorists to say the least, especially if you were stuck in traffic going up and driving a stick-shift.

How this city even arrived at this massive, highly controversial reimagining called Urban Renewal was a long and bumpy road that would surely be studied for centuries to come for its broader social implications. But Frank sensed the Sandman swinging around again, and his eyes felt like heavy lead.

Fuck it, he thought. He didn't need to eat right now. He couldn't remember if he'd even eaten lunch today. He'd already missed *Kojak,* which really upset him.

Maybe if he ventured back to the Land of Nod, he may, just *may*, get some much-needed rest.

Maybe this time it would be different...

MONDAY

October 13, 1976

FRANK STARED OUT the windshield of his brand-new Dodge Monaco undercover unit at the early morning downpour, lost in a daydream. He left his house just as the bad weather arrived by sea to unpack. Now, the conditions outside matched some of the season's colorful autumn foliage and sporadic Halloween decorations.

He sat parked outside the house of his other partner, the fifth, waiting for him to join in on whatever adventures this day would bring. It was pelting down and the canopy of elm trees that skirted the side street shielded enough daylight from above that the whole morning looked and felt a whole lot grayer than it actually was.

Frank sat with the engine idling, his hands firmly gripped on the steering wheel. Currently, he was listening to the city's very own The Five Satins, singing *Downtown* (where they even namechecked New Haven), on Frank's small, portable AM/FM transistor radio he always had on him while in the radio car. The continuous tinny chatter of the dispatcher and officer replies on the Motorola police radio unit became a mash of garbled white noise when mixed with the music after a while. He found that a mind quickly got used to deciphering the competing signals and, before you knew it, you were comfortably listening to each simultaneously. He needed the music, though. He always needed the music. Ever since he was a little boy, he was fascinated by it and always regretted not learning to play an instrument because he had such a love for the art form. He studied all forms and styles. Aside from his car, music was his other real passion. It comforted and soothed him. It was like a buffer and he self-medicated with it, keeping that annoying mind of his occupied.

He sat, contemplating nothing in particular, only random memories that came and went from his head like the raindrops on the glass outside. The shadows of the rain on the windshield slowly made their way down on his face, looking like tiny tears.

The front door to the small colonial home he was parked in front of opened, and Detective Tom McHugh popped out with his wife and daughter. His wife handed him his leather messenger bag and he kissed her goodbye. Tall and slender, with thick light brown hair that he wore slicked back that fell to either side, Tom always looked perfect and immaculately styled. Frank always thought Tom's wife must help him pick out his wardrobe every morning. The whole scene was reminiscent of the opening to *Hazel*, with Don DeFore and Bobby Buntrock waving goodbye to wife and mother, Whitney Blake, while their maid, Shirley Booth, handed out umbrellas. The perfect family portrait.

Tom's little girl was dressed in a red raincoat and had a tiny pack strapped to her back. They both dashed out into the rain hand in hand, Tom's tan Burberry jacket flapping in the wind. By the time they got to the car, Frank had already reached over and popped open the back door so little Grace could jump in. Tom shut the car door behind her and jumped into the passenger seat. Mrs. McHugh watched until they were all in, waved at the car, and then shut the front door.

Frank and Tom had been working together for almost a year and a half now, after Tom had made detective. Frank was only five years older and got the impression Tom looked at their partnership as a big brother relationship. Frank never had a younger brother and embraced the idea. Tom was a good cop and a very good detective, and with Graham, Randy, and Joe, Tom was the much-embraced young blood of the group. And the ladies' man.

"'*Rainy days and Mondays always get me down*, huh, Frank?" Tom joked. "You don't mind if we take Grace to kindergarten over at St. Michael's school, do you?"

"Sure." Frank smirked. "Hey, Grace!"

"Hi, Uncle Frank!"

"Why are you all wet?"

She giggled at the question. "Because, silly! It's raining outside!"

"Oh yeah, so it is! Ha!" Frank shot her a wink in the rearview mirror.

"Make sure you buckle your seatbelt like Mommy showed you, okay, baby?" Tom reminded her.

"I will, Daddy."

Graham was pushing the witness as hard as he could without crossing the line. They were trying to get information and felt he was still withholding. Tom and Frank watched from behind the two-way glass, chain smoking, tired and bored.

Graham's dirty blond hair parted down the side and formed a kind of bowl haircut, just covering his ears and a tad longer in the back. It made him look like the typical vice cop. He had fair skin and freckles, with a huge moustache that Tom used to joke looked like those in the adult "avant-garde" films everyone used to go to that were now branded "XXX", like *Deep Throat* and *Behind the Green Door.* Right out of their central casting.

The man being questioned was one of the homosexuals that cruised East Rock Park after dark. It was a scene unto itself that only the nighthawks of the world and people of that sexual persuasion even knew existed. Sparkles, as he called himself, was a legend on the scene, known from here to New York City, and everywhere in between. He had a good rapport with the police department, meaning he had an ear to the street and a mouth that liked to do more than just satisfy men up on the mountain on a Saturday night, so they hoped they could get a lead on their double shooting. So far, the only thing they were getting from him was a shitload of attitude. Sparkles was infamous on the Conrail line between here and New York City because, as a six-foot-six, two-hundred-and-fifty-pound plus black man, he would take the local train down to the city dressed in complete drag, which consisted of mesh half-shirts, bright red hot pants and six-inch clear heel platform shoes. Quite the gentle giant. Conductors found him so odd that they eventually stopped collecting a fare from him altogether and instead just smiled, waved hello, and let him ride for free. He had balls, though, for wearing those outfits night after night, riding with all the young kids too. As soon as a cross word was said his way, he'd give it right back, never afraid to stand up for himself and put a foot up some fool's ass if he needed to. He was a veteran of the New Haven gay community, a staple in trending clubs like The Snow Chicken, which last year had changed its name to the Neuter Rooster, back when the place was still exclusively gay-only. Sparkles knew just about everything there was to know about the New Haven scene.

Right now, however, he wasn't in any kind of giving mood.

The problem was his stories weren't exactly matching up when Graham had him repeat and repeat what he'd heard about the night before.

"So you say the two fellas probably didn't know each other?" Graham inquired yet again.

"That's what I said to you the first seventeen times, moustache man," Sparkles quipped. "You know, I've seen a lot of stag films that star guys with cum-catchers smaller than yours on your top lip. That thing there could be legendary."

That made Frank and Tom both smile and it broke the monotony.

"I told him he'd get shit from Sparkles going in there with that thing on him," Tom said to his partner.

"Let's not start talking about your personal fantasies, okay?" Graham shot back on the other side of the glass.

"I guess it's the danger that comes along with the job," Frank said with a half-smile to Tom. "Shit, Sparkles was one of the reasons I shaved mine off!"

Graham shot a glance at the two-way glass and rolled his eyes. He could only guess what the other two were saying on the other side of that mirror.

The door to the small viewing room opened, and Detective Jurgens entered. He was a tall, lanky, dark-haired detective who'd survived Korea only to be nearly beaten to death by a fifteen-year-old in the summer of '71 with a mop handle in the Newhallville section of town.

"Well, boss, Joe got a line on the murder victim's ex from pressing the parents who live up in Hamden. A black man named Irving Skippermeyer, local, 'Nam vet. Red flags went up with Mr. and Mrs. Brighton because they said he had some sort of mental condition, like came back from the war shell-shocked, and his not staying on his meds and not seeking therapy made the relationship too volatile. This is coming from two of the most 'traditional' parents you could meet. According to Joe, we're talking Robert Young and Jane Wyatt types here, so it got us thinking. On a lark, Joe made contact with a relative at the ex-boyfriend's last known address and they say they haven't seen Mr. Skippermeyer for over a week now. They confirmed he served, came back and had some issues, and got testy when the conversation got to his sexuality. They wouldn't let him enter the house. Spinall thinks they could be feeding him a yarn. He's chatting with the neighbors to see if he can get anyone to keep an eye out for us."

"Skippermeyer's relatives may be feeding us a yarn?" Frank clarified.

Randy nodded.

Frank looked back over toward the two-way glass. "Okay, great, Rand. Maybe we'll get a break."

Sparkles' bald head shined from the overhead lights in the interrogation room, having a sheen that made him look like he'd polished it.

"Don't flatter yourself, Marlboro man," Sparkles answered with a grin to Graham. "I prefer dark chocolate," he finished with a wink. That got an audible reaction from Tom, Frank, and Randy, who all laughed.

"Jesus, the abuse we have to go through on this job," Tom remarked with a smirk.

"Alright, alright, let's keep on task here," Graham urged, "Why don't you think they knew each other? Your gut feeling." At this point, he was just looking to wrap this up for the day and head straight for bed. It had been a long day for them all.

"Well, Sapphire would get off on giving strangers a mouth-ride and was into everything, hips or lips, and went anywhere. He fell down the rabbit hole of that leather bar scene you get in the Meat Packing District in the city, which he got exposed to while cruising. He liked the thrill of it all. Up in town here, he liked to hang out nights in the men's room under the Memorial Rotunda in Woolsey Hall on campus, looking for young Yalies to please. You know the spot. He was notorious."

"Sapphire?" Randy said.

"That's Matthew Hallwell, our survivor," Tom answered.

"Ah."

"Falling down a rabbit hole is an interesting way to put it," Randy said to no one in particular.

"So he found someone cruising the scene there on East Rock," Graham speculated out loud to Sparkles.

"Or they could have met at a bar just as easy."

Frank turned to his partner. "Tom, let's start checking the hot spots to see if they were seen out together Friday night before this. Get a timeline going. Maybe we can place them at one of the clubs and see if he's as promiscuous as we're being told."

Graham turned away from Sparkles "Okay, and who do you think now would want to hurt Sapphire?"

"Take your pick, Sunshine. With all the haters out there nowadays, we're not exactly the most popular people around this town. It's tough out there for people like us," he said. "Look, I'm done talking. Like I've already said twenty times, go check out the crazy, obsessed ex-boyfriend for a start."

"The murder victim's, the guy from New York? His ex?" Graham looked at the mirror, to his partners on the other side.

"Yes."

Tom said to his partners, "We need to corroborate this. We get ahold of this jealous ex-Army boyfriend fella and toss him as soon as possible."

"But why this song and dance with not knowing who these fellas were to begin with?" Graham said with slight defeat.

"Jesus! Why do I even bother with you oinkers?"

That was about all the noise Frank was going to deal with this early in the week. Today had already turned out to be a long day. He turned to the other two in the dimly-lit listening room. "All right, you bright boys seem to have this under control at the moment. I've got someplace to be and I'll leave it in your capable hands."

"Thanks, Skipper," Tom shot back sarcastically, smoothing everything over with a grin.

"Throw it all in the report and we'll reconvene in the A.M., savvy?"

"Sure thing, Frank. Have a gay ole time, my friend." Randy winked.

"Now that's not even funny. Give moustache man in there my regards."

It was late afternoon when Frank pulled up in his baby blue 1967 Ford GT40 Mark 3. Christopher Wallace lived in an airy cape on a nice piece of land off the Boulevard. Frank loved the area, and when he was a child, he and Chris aspired to live there. Luckily, the modernization hadn't affected the area, and it hadn't really changed much, which Frank found comforting, like it resided in a *Twilight Zone* episode. He'd always thought Chris had lucked out in finding the house;

a perfect place to raise a family. They'd grown up together and lost touch when Chris went to college and Frank the Academy, but fate brought them back together on Chris' first night out as a probie in '68, when Frank was still living out his punishment for his behavior at the incident at the New Haven Arena the year before, back when he was still a rookie himself. The country was in turmoil amidst riots in practically every major city. Fires had broken out on Congress Avenue, in a housing project that was so dilapidated it was a surprise it hadn't been condemned years before. It was one of those huge relics of a building, all made of wood that still didn't have indoor plumbing, even in the 1960s. It reminded Frank of the wooden row housing that had lined the sides of the old Oak Street neighborhoods, before they broke up the area in the name of urban renewal.

That night so long ago was still as vivid as if it were yesterday. The over one-hundred-year-old structure went up like kindling. Frank's was the first prowl car on the scene. The Fire Department and their big white bullet-nose Seagrave trucks had already arrived, and the crowd was unruly and on edge. They saw the New Haven Fire Department as the way to vent. Chris' truck was rocking like a buoy in the ocean when Frank rolled up. What was the best way to quell dozens of rioters before they tore some poor firemen to shreds? Emptying his service revolver into the air and hoping for the best. It was directly because of that incident that the New Haven Fire Department went on to only employ closed cabs for all the fire trucks like the ones New York City used, so as to protect their brigades while out responding, and also standard operating procedure became waiting for black-and-white radio car units to assess the safety of a scene before fire trucks and ambulances would be allowed to arrive.

After that, Chris and Frank became inseparable. Chris and his wife Rhonda had dated since high school, and had their first child, a daughter, Arianna, shortly after graduating. Frank and Chris were then the best man at each other's weddings and godfathers to each other's daughters. Arianna was turning sixteen now, and like her old man, had developed a great affinity for sports cars and music.

What better way to treat his goddaughter on her birthday than to let her take a spin in his little baby blue Ford GT40?

Chris was tinkering underneath his '49 Merc that was up on two jacks in front of the garage when he noticed Frank slumping up the driveway with two pink balloons and a birthday card in hand.

"You brought the Mark 3?" Chris got up off the ground and wiped his hands on his pants. "You never take the Blue Boy out." They shook hands and hugged.

Chris' body was built more like a weightlifter, and his dark black skin glistened with sweat from working under the car. He kept his hair in a small, tightly kept afro and was always clean shaven, with Frank being one of the only people outside of the family that knew Chris was always shaved because, even at his age now, he still really couldn't grow a complete moustache or beard. It was something Frank joked with him about from time to time, that he forever had the face of a child and never seemed to age.

"It's been a minute, my brotha."

"I know. Just been working is all," Frank replied.

"Arianna's gonna love that you brought it."

Frank shrugged. "She's always askin' to ride in it and I figured on her sweet sixteen, why not bring Blue Boy over and have her take a spin?"

Chris put his hand on Frank's shoulder. "She just got her license today. Passed this morning. She's already asking to borrow the car tomorrow, just to drive to school!" Chris let out a laugh that came from the gut. It made Frank laugh too; if for nothing else, it reminded him of the old days, the fun days, when they were young. "How is the young princess doing nowadays?"

Keeping the smile on his face, Chris looked down but did not answer Frank's question with words. After a moment he raised his left eyebrow slightly and looked back up to his friend. "She's growing up I guess. C'mon, let's go inside. I gotta shower and change before we head over to the party."

Arianna was the spitting image of her mother, already appearing like she could pass for eighteen or possibly twenty. What always impressed Frank was the intelligence she had for a girl her age. Arianna excelled in school and was in the top ten in her class. She was politically active within her high school, her tastes and interests echoed that of a woman in her twenties, all of which manifested itself outwardly in the maturity she exuded. He even saw shades of his own daughter in Arianna, and often wondered if this is how Katy would turn out when she got older.

Frank downshifted and hung a left as he turned east onto Whalley Avenue. The large group was caravanning over to where her birthday party was being held, Arianna, of course, hitching a ride over in Blue Boy with Frank. She definitely shared a passion for cars like her father by how she paid attention to the engine's growls and grunts. Her captivated eyes darted all around the car's interior, taking in every detail of the experience driving inside a GT40, while Queen's *Somebody to Love* filled in any dead space in the conversation.

"This is *soooo* groovy, Uncle Frank, thank you so much!"

"You're welcome, kid. You deserve it."

There was an uncomfortable pause and Frank felt it was his duty to keep the conversation going.

"So do you still play with your Barbies or read your Nancy Drew books? Gosh, you loved Nancy Drew."

Arianna giggled in mild embarrassment. "Uncle Frank, you're kidding me, right? I don't play with Barbies anymore and I've moved on from Nancy Drew." She began to play with the long silver necklace she'd worn since she was a child, and turned her head to look outside. "My teacher let me borrow her Bronte sisters' books. I really like the Brontes. You know, I originally only got into Nancy Drew because you were a detective. I thought that was so cool." Her silence continued for a long moment before she went on, "Life is just weird, huh? I mean, do you find it weird that, out of the Bronte sisters, say, the only one to live the longest of the sisters died at age 39, Charlotte, but in that time they all accomplished so much? Charlotte wrote *Jane Eyre* and other stuff and was a poet. Emily, who wrote *Wuthering Heights,* died at age thirty, and Anne, another writer, was dead by 29. Can you believe doing that much in that time? I can't even make thirty with my wo-pm."

"Wo-pm?"

"Words per minute," she said. "Just makes you think."

"That's a tad morbid for a sixteen-year-old who only stopped playing with Barbies and reading Nancy Drew two years ago. Should I start calling you Wednesday Addams?" He smiled, and she reciprocated.

"I don't mean it like that, Uncle Frank, it's just mind-blowing. How much someone can accomplish in so little time. Or what people *don't* accomplish in a lifetime. Or how fast you can grow up."

"I know what you mean. Look at Jim Morrison. He passed away at age twenty-seven and look at how prolific he was. Or James Dean, at twenty-four, Hank Williams senior, say, who was only thirty. Heck, Alexander the Great was only thirty-three and he conquered the world. Ha. It does really put things in perspective, especially when you get to my age." Frank cracked a smile and looked over at her. "And for the record, Ari, I was still playing with my erector sets and Army men and reading my EC comic books at fifteen!"

"Sixteen!" she protested with a laugh. They shared a chuckle. "Well, since you brought it up, is it true? Did Jim Morrison actually buy you this car?"

"That's right. Got it for me in 1969." Arianna had a half smile on her face that told Frank he hadn't answered the question enough for her and she wanted more. "We were friends and he used to give his friends presents. He just happened to give them expensive things, like cars. He knew I would never have been able to afford this old boy on a policeman's salary."

"How the heck did you ever become friends with Jim Morrison?"

"His band played the old Arena back in December of '67, and we met then and became close friends. Shortly after, I started working in my off time for him for some extra money."

Arianna leaned in excitedly. "You played in the band?"

Frank laughed. "No, no, as security. After he was arrested downtown, he asked if I'd be interested in being his bodyguard so—"

"Wait, he got arrested here, in New Haven?" Arianna unconsciously twirled the solitary skate key on her long silver necklace.

"Yes, he did, at the Arena. Hence the line, '*Blood in the Streets in the town of New Haven.*' You didn't know that? You seem to know everything."

"I don't listen to them, that's all. They're a little too old for me. I'm more of an Elton John, Bowie, ABBA, Kiss, Bee Gees kinda girl."

"'Dancing Queen,' eh?"

"That's right, full on disco and glam rock. That's my bag."

"Ah."

"So what did he get arrested for?"

Frank looked at Arianna out of the corner of his eye, trying to figure out how to proceed. "Before the show that night, he'd met up with a girl from Southern Connecticut University and they were in the locker room area chatting. A policeman walked in on them and thought they were just two kids who got backstage. He told them to leave and they got into it, and before you know it, he got maced."

"They maced Morrison?" Frank nodded. "What happened then?"

"Once they realized that NHPD had maced the lead singer of The Doors, who were about to perform, nobody was happy."

Arianna giggled.

"They apologized, the powers that be let him go on, and the band went onstage." Frank's eyes moved over around the dash and then to the radio, still cautious about how to say it pleasantly and apolitically. "Once they were performing, Morrison still was pretty upset, so he told the crowd what just happened, venting. But it was a tad antagonizing, and he had some blue language in there. Well, that was it. They put the lights on and Lieutenant Kelly came out and they escorted him offstage, citing state obscenity laws and breach of peace. It was a tense night, to say the least, and a near-riot ensued. Tempers were already high, and some of the officers lost their cool a little bit. Which, I would like to emphasize, is *not* the norm, mind you. That was the mindset of the old guard, you know? Not usually condoned nor tolerated. So I stepped in and stuck up for him."

They both sat there, maybe uncomfortable about the subject of police brutality and Frank being a cop, or perhaps because of the social pleasantries they both were used to. "The charges were eventually dropped after it gained national attention, and he and I became friends and he never forgot what I had done."

Frank turned into the parking lot and started to look for a spot. "And that's how I came to know Ole Blue here." The radio segued to Syreeta's *Black Maybe*.

"Crazy story."

"Just for the record," Frank clarified, "enjoy your youth now because once it's gone, you don't want to be one of those people who looks backwards and longs for yesterday." Frank smiled warmly and winked. "Take it from me."

Roller Haven was one of the modern juvenile discotheques that had sprung up in recent years with the resurgence of roller skating. It catered to families, young kids, teens, and everyone in between. They'd taken a long-ago defunct dance hall that been vacant for years and had turned it into a black light, psychedelic-colored, flashing strobe light mess, giving the American family the romanticized and commercialized experience of the free love movement, with fun for all ages. They had a deejay booth on one end, and a beautiful hardwood dance floor laid so long ago so people could 'swing the night away,' which now had a large scribbled circle carved out on the wood by the constant repetition of the little wheels going round and round, accented with thumping bass and a disco ball. The coat room had been gutted and a wall knocked down and turned into a video game arcade filled with the latest pinball machines and stand-up consoles religiously patronized by adolescent boys into which they dropped their weekly allowances. That room was still adorned with posters celebrating the country's Bicentennial, which had occurred the past July Fourth and would probably stay up well into 1977.

Donna Summers' extended version of *Love to Love You Baby* belted from the speakers, another entirely different irony lost on those kids here today to skate. While they travel in a slow circle, they got to listen to Donna moan out a ten-plus-minute orgasm.

Frank sat at the nearby table the Wallaces had rented for Arianna's sweet sixteen. Rhonda, Chris' wife, had made her famous barbeque ribs, which everyone at the party was currently devouring. The aroma of dinner being roasted for hours had permeated the entire dining area. Besides the naked body of a beautiful woman, Frank was sure the smell of Rhonda's cooking was the only thing that would make a man resort to the intellect of a Neanderthal.

He hadn't eaten anything all day aside from drinking black coffee, so he was worried his eyes betrayed his primal thoughts. Rhonda, a gorgeous Black woman in her mid-thirties, sat at the end of the table next to Chris. Frank had always been a huge fan of hers and believed she truly leveled Chris out and complemented him as a person, the two making a great couple. You could also see where Arianna got her striking features from. Frank sat on the end next to their middle child Tyrell, diagonal to their youngest daughter Mina.

"This spread looks so amazing. Thank you, Rhonda," Frank said.

Rhonda grinned coyly. "I don't know who you're trying to butter up over there, so just eat what you can, because whatever you don't is going home with you."

Frank smiled. "Thank you."

Arianna was the first to finish the feast because she hadn't touched her food and took to the dance floor to skate the afternoon away with her best friend, MaryAnn Decan. The two were inseparable and both were now enjoying themselves, acting silly together, like two kids should. Frank realized he'd answered his own question from the car ride. Arianna had always loved to skate, ever since she could stand up and walk. That was something that still made her a kid, at least in his mind.

Frank bit into a piece of heaven and rolled his eyes in bliss. "I'm serious though, I think you've outdone yourself tonight, Rhonda."

"We got plenty more. Eat up, so you can get some meat on your bones there."

That made Frank smile. He hadn't felt cared for in a long time and it made him blush. Frank saw Rhonda quietly tap Chris' hand and nod toward the dance floor, toward Arianna. Warm smiles appeared on their faces as they saw their daughter laughing and having fun. Chris glanced over to Frank, realizing he'd seen the shared moment. He beckoned with his head to have Frank lean over and they met over Tyrell's head so Chris could speak into his ear.

"It's just really good to see her happy. We haven't seen her smile or laugh for a long time. You know, she's a stroppy teenager now." Frank looked back at the dance floor at the two young girls moving in and out of the small groups of people, and nodded.

"I understand," Frank said, wiping his rib sauce-stained fingers after he'd succeeded in clearing his plate. He flushed his mouth out with some water while Chris and Rhonda shared another moment, seeing how happy Arianna was at that instant. Frank grabbed his pack of smokes and lit a cigarette. He leaned over and moved a red plastic ashtray closer and moved Arianna's large keyring with Disney's Tigger attached over to her seat place. His gaze was now filled with the various roller skaters on the dance floor who happily grooved around to the disco pop. It brought a grin to his face to see how much fun everyone was having under the mellow flashes of the dance lights that flickered through the nicotine-filled and fog machine-enhanced haze.

Seeing her from a distance forced Frank to step back and take it all in. It was only then that it occurred to him how MaryAnn's very short shorts—hot pants as they called them—were a tad inappropriate for a girl her age. Along with her half shirt that showed off her stomach and chest area, it seemed on one hand quite innocent, but on the other, something that quite quickly would become sexualized on a young woman in her middle teens. Arianna's outfit seemed quite tame at first also; tight jeans with bell bottom pant legs and a half shirt, but stacked up next to MaryAnn's, it fell under the same realm of ambiguity that seemed to inhabit MaryAnn's, though to a much lesser extent. It was unclear without talking to MaryAnn which side of the proverbial fence she was conscious of and what she, if anything, was striving for in her stylistic choices at such an impressionable age. Either way, in his professional opinion, the makeup they wore made them look like women, not girls.

After two revolutions around the immense dance floor, Arianna and her friend rolled over to the partition next to where Frank leaned his elbow. He mashed out his Marlboro Red into the crimson colored, cosmic-shaped ashtray while the girls gripped the little wooden partition wall for stability.

"What do you think, Uncle Frank? Is it too childish to have a sweet sixteen in a roller rink?" She looked to her friend. "MaryAnn seems to think so," Arianna admitted with an embarrassed smile. "She thinks we should have gone for a proper club to have it in."

"Naw, this is perfect. Great music, great atmosphere, and the most important thing, conversation. A place like this, you can hear yourself talk." He looked over at MaryAnn. "And there's even boys to poke fun at, if one wanted to."

"Not the kind we like," MaryAnn said under her breath. Her face formed a forced smile across her lips. She already was developing frown lines. "This place doesn't even serve alcohol." She genuinely grinned then, embarrassed, realizing she'd misspoken.

"That's not necessarily a bad thing." Frank said in a parental tone. "Especially since the drinking age is still eighteen in this state."

MaryAnn's smile strained.

"Frank's a cop," Arianna said with a grin to MaryAnn. "A detective. Detective *sergeant,* actually." MaryAnn nodded uncomfortably. Arianna looked back at Frank. "I just want to make sure everyone is having a good time, because I'm the first one to admit that these kinds of places can be pretty *fucking* lame sometimes."

The sentence and swear were loud enough to be heard by her mother, who wasn't until then paying attention to the conversation.

"Arianna! Watch your mouth!" Rhonda shouted. She rolled her eyes at her parents.

"That better not be how you talk around your friends," Chris said in an authoritative tone, also only now just entering into the fray.

Arianna looked down toward Frank's terminally crippled cigarette butt in the ashtray that still smoked, trying to subdue the frazzled child's reaction to the public parental chastising. "No, Dad, that's not how I talk. I wanted to make sure everyone was having a good time because I know how boring these kiddy places can be for some people…" She trailed off, barely making eye contact with her mother. Rhonda purposely ignored her and continued to eat. It was obvious that Mom had organized the party and even if Arianna had initially agreed or even wanted this venue, the peer pressure to show her contempt for 'childish' ways had to be put in check in front of her best friend.

Frank refrained from adding his opinion as silence swept over the dinner. "How's school going, Ari? Everything well?" he finally said.

Arianna answered without looking at him, "Yeah, everything is okay. School's just school." She stared down at the scarred white rubber stoppers on the toes of her roller boots. Her mood had clearly changed. Must be a sore subject.

Frank reached into his inside breast pocket and produced a card in a fancy pink envelope. "I know you haven't had your cake yet, but I will have to go soon. As you can imagine, my job never stops." He handed it to her. Arianna tore open the envelope and retrieved the pretty pink card. She read the loving words, opened the card, and finished the poem. Inside the sleeve where money would sometimes be stowed was instead two tickets to the upcoming Stevie Wonder concert at the end of the week at the Coliseum.

Arianna's eyes widened and she screamed. "Oh my God, Uncle Frank, I can't believe it! I thought this had been sold out for weeks!"

"It has been, but your uncle still has some connections in the music industry," he said with a wink. Frank knew she loved the music.

"Thank you, Uncle Frank. Oh my God! Thank you!"

MaryAnn whispered something into her ear and Arianna laughed, and in an instant, they were together back out skating around and holding hands to Vicki Sue Robinson's *Turn the Beat Around.* Frank recalled later on, whenever he heard Vicki Sue turn that beat upside down, that this was the moment when Arianna grew up in his eyes and was no longer a little girl. No longer his *little* goddaughter.

The last of the sun's rays outlined the clouds and streaks in the sky, and a warm orange glow in the twilight emanated from just over the horizon. Chris walked Frank out to his car to say a final goodbye before they parted.

"You remember what it was like being a teenager, Chris, especially how boys are at that age. I'm sure there's a lot of pressures coming down on her and could be contributing to her moods and attitude lately, that's all."

"I know. I figured you getting those Stevie Wonder tickets for Saturday would have lightened her spirits, but it did for only a few minutes before she was back inside herself again.

She's just been so sad and glum. And her friend MaryAnn just feeds into that misery."

They reached Frank's GT40 and Chris gave Blue Boy's curves a onceover while gathering his thoughts. "She's been down these past couple of weeks," he said. "Not wanting to be hugged or even touched. How you said she was on the way over here is the brightest she's been in almost a month."

Frank leaned back against his car and peered back at Roller Haven. He could tell this was something serious for Chris and his wife. "What do you think it is? Guy problems? Maybe just getting older and becoming a woman? Both boys and girls around her age start to face a level of depression and probably, anxiety. I know I did, right?"

Chris hesitated before he answered. "I know she and her boyfriend, Albert, have been fighting. I heard her on the phone with him the other day, and it made me want to pick up the extension and hear what all the fuss was about. Everything is drama nowadays, and she puts him through the ringer. Notice how he wasn't here today? She probably uninvited him and his friends. I remember how *girls* were, too, at her age."

Frank smiled and looked over at the final parting moments of the setting sun. "Ha, yes, I do too."

"Probably looking for attention, I would think."

"Yeah."

There was a moment of silence and Chris noticed Frank's mind had wandered. Chris had an idea why, and after a moment of silence, drummed up the courage to ask.

"Sorry to talk about all my family stuff. How's everything going with you?"

"Okay," he replied automatically without thinking.

Chris put his hand on his best friend's shoulder. "You been alright lately?"

Frank instantly came back down to Earth. "Yeah. Keeping busy. This job is around the clock, it keeps my mind occupied. I try to get Blue Boy here up to the Lime Rock track too, whenever the weather permits."

Chris was satisfied with the answer but finally asked the question he'd been trying to work his way up to. "You still off the sauce, brother?"

Frank stared at him for a moment, knowing the question came from his friend's heart and was seeded in a deep concern, and he didn't mean it to be nosy.

Frank tried to frame his answer in the politest way he could. He deliberately blinked slowly, lifted the corners of his mouth and replied, "Going on three years now."

"Well, I know you're busy, but I don't like not seeing you. Now that winter is around the corner you should come over and we can do game night or something. Rhonda's a nasty hangman player. She just bought the Vincent Price Edition in a Halloween sale. It would be fun."

Frank laughed and slowly made his way around over to the driver's side. "I've been looking to polish up my hangman skills."

"The kids would love to see you too," Chris urged. "It would give us all a reason to spend time together as a family. It would be great to have an excuse to keep Arianna in to spend some time with the family once in a while."

"You got me. I'm sold. We'll have to work a night out soon. Thank you. It was good seeing you, brotha."

"You as well, Frank. Thank you for today, for making Arianna happy."

The sun had completely gone down by the time Frank pulled out onto Elm Street, heading back downtown. The stars were beginning to come out and were shining clear and bright, pulsating so far up above, thousands of lightyears away.

It really reminded Frank of how wonderfully small life's problems ultimately were, in the grand scheme of things.

TUESDAY

October 14, 1976

HE WAS JARRED from sleep by the loud, reverberating ring of his telephone. He glanced at the clock and realized that it was close to six thirty. Wow, hadn't it just been 1 a.m.?

He leaned over and, after fumbling with the receiver, brought it up to his ear.

"Frank Suchy."

The man on the other end of the line started rattling off sentences and sounded much more awake than he was.

"Say that again? Councilman Theodore Pregosin? Yeah, of course I know who he is. I saw him on TV at the Coliseum ceremony thing. Yes..." His eyebrows rose. "He wants to meet with me? This morning?" Frank shot up and rechecked the clock. "He wants to meet me when? Okay."

Frank spotted the car about a block-and-a-half away from his brownstone. He leaned back against the large stone banister of his front steps and used the curved right angle to try to crack his back. He felt the little rocks mixed in with the cement that comprised the railing area poke through his blazer and tickle his back as he stretched. He had another drag of his cigarette and felt the smoke expand his lungs. He loved the taste of the nicotine-filled air.

The jet-black Cadillac Fleetwood was next year's model. Its extended back seat must have been the reason it was classified as a limo. With the skirts on the back tires and tinted back windows, Frank thought it all looked very slick. Screw wood-imitation station wagons; this would be a great family car.

He took one last drag and tossed the butt out. Without making a sound, the Caddy zoomed up and, as if on cue, it came to a halt and, in one fluid motion, the rear door opened. Frank stepped in, pulled the large bulky door shut, and off they went.

Across and facing him sat Councilman Theodore Pregosin. He was in his early sixties, dressed in a fresh Italian suit, and had dark olive skin—the kind that was perpetually tanned even in the winter—black hair worn slicked back, and a matching trimmed moustache. By the appearance of his physique, he appeared quite fit for his age. He topped it all off with large gold-rimmed glasses with auburn-colored lenses that covered his pronounced cheekbones. Frank had to admit, in person, he looked pretty slick.

Next to the councilman was an even smarter-dressed man, in an expertly tailored J. Press three-button, button-on-center "crash linen" suit and big, loud-looking alligator shoes. He was around the same age and appeared just as affluent. Slightly aloof, he didn't act at all bothered or concerned that someone else had just entered the car.

Next to Frank, he surmised, was an assistant to the councilman: a man in his twenties who wore round, wire-framed glasses and dressed just as stylishly in a loud Brooks Brothers three-piece suit, to the point of flashy and pompous annoyance. He had his head buried in a large leather itinerary that he thumbed through with a fancy pen. He did not bother to acknowledge Frank's presence.

From what Frank had read about Pregosin and seen on TV, he seemed like an okay guy. He came across like an idealist. He'd made a name for himself by taking over where the last mayor had left off, basically now sewing up the city after it received one of the biggest cosmetic and reconstructive surgeries the country had ever seen a metropolis have. Urban Renewal, they called it. Whether New Haven even needed to undergo this massive retrofit in the first place was still a *highly* contested topic between the city's bureaucrats and its residents. Even after everything was said and done, it was still being debated.

Like other northeastern cities, New Haven prospered in the second half of the nineteenth century, due to the Industrial Revolution. She was the home of prestigious carriage and couch manufacturers, firearms factories like Winchester and Mossberg, Stanley Hardware, clockmakers, and numerous other large name-brand factories making all kinds of goods. It was also the home of the first commercial telephone exchange in 1879 and the birthplace of the master builder, Robert Moses. At the dawn of the twentieth century, New Haven began a slow decline in industry. As the century wore on, like other post-industrial cities, the Elm City began feeling the effects of deindustrialization.

After World War II, soldiers returning home wanting homeownership, with help from the G.I. bill, moved their families from cramped downtown areas out into the spacious and newly-expanding countryside of the suburbs. A tremendous housing boom occurred outside of every major municipality in the United States. Commercial commerce followed their customers, lulled by the open space to stretch their legs, culminating with the advent of the strip mall. Now, many cities had to figure out ways to stimulate local economies in urban centers. In contrast, a massive influx of Blacks migrated north, looking to escape oppression and the shrinking farming jobs in the south, hoping to try their luck for work in the northern industrialized factory cities. Except they were too late to the party. Replacing the escapism of Whites moving out, Blacks, for the most part, found no work in urban centers, and were forced to live in the low-income housing consolidated around the downtown areas that was left, alongside other struggling minorities like Jews, Latinos, Italians, and the Irish. Then the concept of Urban Renewal was born. The basic idea was to make the downtowns in urban areas more attractive to a middle class now out in suburbia with disposable income, to come back and spend their money there once again.

The Federal government, along with its spearhead program, the American Council to Improve Our Neighborhoods, or ACTION, by way of new urban renewal legislation (which was fancy speak for eminent domain), started giving huge subsidies to cities for the purpose of redeveloping its business districts and revitalizing its central areas. This made it possible for New Haven to buy and/or seize and bulldoze whatever land it deemed slums and resell it to developers, Yale University, or other businesses to build skyscrapers, department stores and shopping centers, stadiums, convention centers, and expand college campuses. New Haven's plans were so ambitious it was considered the ideal example, hence it received the moniker 'The Model City' to show America what was possible through Urban Renewal. To put it into some historical context, by 1972 in its per capita grants—

that is, money it got from the government—New Haven was the largest in the nation; bigger than New York City, Boston, Chicago, or Newark, receiving something like a thousand dollars for each citizen, compared to four hundred-fifty dollars by its closest competitor.

To ride the coattails and now oversee New Haven's Renewal Program to its complete fruition and resolution, the renowned Councilman Theodore Pregosin was appointed.

There was a moment of awkward silence, and Frank wondered if the men seated around him were waiting for him to say the first words. He hoped they weren't taking notice of his reasonably cheap, off-the-rack Sears and Roebuck suit. Only cops on TV wore Botany 500. The problem was, homicide detectives, in particular, always went through a lot of suits because of the job, ruining them by getting blood, flesh, brain matter, trash, dirt, mud, or whatever else all over them while on the job. Frank learned early on you couldn't be Kojak on this job; you had to buy cheap to afford the wardrobe changes.

"Frank Suchy, my name is Theodore Pregosin." They shook hands and the councilman gestured to his left, "This is Edward Gladstone, New Haven's biggest philanthropist, head of the Urban Coalition, and sits on the boards of Redevelopment Committee, Community Progress Authority, and Board of Education. He has been indispensable with Yale, being a member of their Endowment Foundation. Have I forgotten any, Ed?"

"I don't think so, Theo."

"And he is probably the biggest reason New Haven's finally been able to see this urban renewal project through to its natural end so successfully."

"How do you do?" Frank nodded politely to Mr. Gladstone.

"I do it well, Detective Sergeant."

"I'm so glad you were able to squeeze us in," the councilman continued. "I'd like to start out by apologizing to you."

"Why, sir?"

"I've heard a lot about you. I'm shocked that I haven't yet had the pleasure of complimenting you on the excellent job you're doing for this city." The councilman and Gladstone smiled.

Frank politely returned the pleasantry. "Why, thank you very much, sir, for all you've done."

"Your record speaks for itself." The councilman gestured to his counterpart on his left, who acknowledged the motion with a nod. "You've been part of some of the key events and cases in the past ten years that have defined this city and held it together, Mr. Suchy. Very admirable. I'm even curious why you haven't yet been recommended for a commendation."

As they continued past the picturesque outskirts of Wooster Square, they hit the remnants of the Oak Street area, most of which had been demolished to make way for the massive Connector, which Interstates I-95 and I-91 drained into. Frank's mind wandered thinking about this, and the lull in the conversation gave him a bit of confusion.

"I'm sorry," he said, "I was on second shift last night and I'm still half-asleep. You're going to commend me?"

That got a chuckle from all the occupants in the Caddy. Even the aide looked up from his itinerary book for the first time and shared the laugh with the councilman and Gladstone, still never making eye contact with Frank.

"Well, why not? I think you deserve it. Men like you are few and far between in these times." The councilman gestured out the window. "You're the future."

As they passed Yale New Haven Hospital and continued on North Frontage Road, the neighborhood took a turn for the worse. The empty inner city blocks which had been leveled had yet to be rebuilt. The redeveloping of the Connector and neighborhood had only gotten as far as the hospital, and though land had been acquired, seized, and cleared, the few miles of vacant blocks that lay west all the way down the 'The Boulevard' were now just empty plots of grassland, dry dirt, and knee-high weeds, with broken glass and bricks covering the bulldozed land. The once-bustling commercial district of lower Legion Avenue, which lay parallel to this area, now was completely gone. Lost were scores of family-owned businesses, including restaurants, markets, delis, stores, and bakeries, all erased from existence. The people that lived to the north and south walked the neighborhoods as though the buildings and businesses were still there, while the empty lots had become playgrounds for the local children. The surrounding neighborhoods also saw a gradual decline and an uptick in crime and the like. Homeless people and addicts staggered across the empty sidewalks, some squatting in the large empty buildings like the old high school, places that had been closed and evacuated, but never torn down because they were not yet in the immediate way of the progress that, in this area, and at this stage in the game, may never come.

Pregosin leaned in. "This kind of segues into why we are having this meeting of the minds here today." The councilman pointed out the window with his thumb and Frank followed with his eyes. "There are certain sections in New Haven we are trying to reinvent so they can better serve the public, and more specifically, the family unit. The parks, beaches, and such. You live here, patrol its streets. You understand?"

Frank nodded. "I think I'm following."

"Let us get to the point," Mr. Gladstone injected.

Out of nowhere, the aide seated next to Frank looked up from his work and focused on the conversation.

"You responded to an incident that occurred at the observation area at the top of East Rock yesterday, correct? Two homosexuals, was it?"

Frank looked over at the aide and forced a polite smile. "Yes, a couple of kids necking. One shot fatally, the other is still critical."

"You are quite confident they didn't shoot each other? Lovers' quarrel?" Gladstone probed.

Frank cleared his throat and looked over to the public official. "Um, quite confident sir."

"Do you have anything to go on? Any leads?" the councilman asked, lighting a cigarette.

"Nothing solid yet, only speculation."

The councilman having a smoke relaxed the atmosphere for Frank, and he went for his own in his breast pocket, grabbing for one out of his crumpled soft pack. "The relatives of our murder victim said he supposedly had an overly jealous ex-boyfriend who is now currently MIA. They say this individual has a history of psychological problems. Two tours in 'Nam. Came back from the war with a party in his head. Hasn't shown up to the V.A. in about two months. We're also talking to any other friends and family. Starting today, my team is gonna be sitting on his last known residence to see if our person of interest makes an appearance."

With a cig in his mouth, Frank searched his pockets for his matches but Pregosin, like he was showing off a sleight-of-hand trick some boardwalk confidence man once taught him, had his lighter in hand and a flame ready. Impressive.

Frank leaned in, lit his smoke, and nodded his thanks.

As soon as Frank was done speaking, Gladstone and the aide simultaneously let out a collective sigh of relief, like they both had been holding in some hidden, bottled up feelings of resignation. Gladstone looked at Pregosin and filled with excitement, tapped him on the thigh.

"That's a huge relief, Theo."

The aide nodded with an arrogant *I-told-you-so* look on his face that made him fall even further in Frank's estimation, if that were possible. The councilman, still not breaking a smile, held eye contact with Frank.

"So a 'one-off,' Sergeant? Nothing more?" the councilman said, his brow raised in a way to also betray that he too might be looking to let out a sigh of relief.

The overzealous Gladstone interjected before Frank could say a word. "Clearly, this guy is the perpetrator. Nothing to be concerned about then." The public official didn't bother to glance at Frank when making the proclamation; his focus was on the councilman.

"Well, first we have to verify all that, of course," Frank cut in. "In these very initial stages, I'm still concerned about the man in ICU and being able to see if we can get a statement from him. It's too early to rule anything out. His ex-lover *also* hadn't been seen for two weeks prior to the incident. We've been known to have random acts of violence on both East and West Rocks, especially against homosexuals, so it may have just as well been a prowler. Sadly, the world has a lot of sickos out there. East Rock's particularly known in some circles to be a gay hangout for Yalies or the like after dark, which could be debatable, but it is something some in the broader community might find objectionable. So all you need is some wacko with spare time on his hands to want to take some sick fantasy to the next level, and Bob's your uncle.

But I guess from your end of things, you can take comfort in the fact that a good portion of the public is oblivious to the whole after-hours hideaway, and all this would be completely lost on them."

The councilman listened intently as the smiles disappeared from the other faces.

"To play devil's advocate for a moment, I'm just saying we can't rule anything out because it sounds plausible. That's why we must *investigate*," Frank enunciated with a smile but realized his joke didn't take. "The lead on the case, Detective Graham Birdsall, has up-to-the-minute details, if they are needed."

Gladstone seemed to take issue even before Frank finished his sentence, looking away, sighing to himself, and fixing his cufflinks and tie. "Detective, this seems like an open-and-shut case. No need to drag East Rock Park through the mud any more than it has to be. I know for a fact the Urban Coalition, meaning the various businesses and local city organizations that I represent, especially don't want to showcase to the public at large the fact that gays like to congregate in groups anywhere, let alone on a mountain that overlooks the city after dark. Let them party the night away at the Neuter Rooster Go-Go Club on Hamilton or in the shadows in the locker rooms on the third floor of the Payne Whitney Gymnasium."

The limo continued past the strife-filled neighborhoods and entered into a new section, an area off the Boulevard where construction was rabid, and new modern condominiums were going up.

The councilman looked at his colleague next to him while digesting the last remark, then focused out the window to the expanding progress. "You see, Sergeant, areas like

East Rock need the resurgence the people of this city can bring. We would like East Rock to, once again, be known for its breathtaking vistas, grand parks, and impressive trails, all recreation that's family-oriented," he looked back to Frank, "rather than splattered across the tabloids as an after-hours hangout, no matter who is there."

Gladstone then added a last thought, laid in with a thick layer of condescension. "Christ, this isn't The Rambles in Central Park. We're Democrats, but we don't want Sodom and Gomorrah here."

Frank could tell, out of all of them, Pregosin was the most reasonable. Still, it did not stop him from having a colorful agenda.

"Sir, we're doing the best we can." Frank used caution in choosing his next words carefully. "But we still need to remind the public that these places can be dangerous at night, no matter which way they may lean politically. We remind them there is a reason these areas are closed after dark and could be dangerous to, as you said, sir, whoever may want to venture up there. Maybe that point alone might caution anyone wanting to loiter or congregate anywhere to rethink it."

He could see this did not sit well with Gladstone. "Please, do not mistake our intentions. We are here to help, and we care about every demographic that makes up our community. We're only trying to step back and view the whole picture. I think we can assume, at this point, that it was an isolated incident. Likely a jealous ex-lover. It's a horrible tragedy, which we will hope to avoid in the future. But there's no need to frighten the public anymore." He said these last few words with as much breath as he could muster; making sure to lock his eyes with Frank so there would be no misunderstanding their intentions.

"We just ask you act as discreetly and quickly as you can, so not to stir up the pot." The councilman gestured to the construction that they passed and added, "The people have to know that New Haven is safe and that we are entering a new era of security and freedom for all."

"Well, give us more manpower, and funding, if I may be so bold as to say, sir."

The councilman appeared genuinely concerned. "We are *trying* to bring relief, but it will take time. I know how hard it is for your people, Sergeant, the man out pounding that beat. I was there for the riots on Congress Avenue and saw the abuse your men took. I think one of the biggest blunders cities across the country implemented was taking the officer off the beat, off the streets and away from the community and its citizens and putting them into the police car. That's how you lose the trust of a community, by making the police look like the faceless oppressor. I want nothing more than to be able to support and provide for Elm City's police department as best I can. Believe me, we're working toward the same goal in New Haven, as we are in Hartford or Bridgeport, and down in D.C. I am working toward that goal with my agenda. We want to continue the previous administration's pioneering strides in civil rights and anti-discrimination legislation. We ultimately have the same goals in my mind, Suchy."

Gladstone smiled. "We just don't want people thinking we have monsters aimlessly roaming around the countryside. We spent the last twenty years doing things to draw people *back* into the city. Headlines like this would destroy all we've built up, overnight."

"This city is safe, Sergeant," the councilman felt required to say for all to hear, as if to reassure the group. "That is because of men and women like you."

"Thank you." Frank paused. "We just don't want to shield them from the reality that sometimes the wolves will stray from the forest and stroll onto the prairie."

That drew a collective silence and even the aide raised his head and looked at Frank.

Boy, he could use a drink.

♦ ♦ ♦

By the time Frank unlocked his front door and stepped back into this house, the phone was ringing off the hook.

He leapt at it and caught it before the ringing stopped. He put the cold receiver to his ear. "Frank Suchy."

It was his partner Tom. *"We got work, Frank. I need you downtown at the Temple Street Garage, the big one connected to Macy's and the mall. And I need you here now."*

What immediately troubled Frank was his partner's tone.

"Yeah, I know where it is. What we got?"

"Frank, uh, just get down here now. It's a bad one…."

DOWNTOWN

IT TOOK ONLY minutes with his party hat blazing to get on scene. A radio car was set up at the main entrance and exit to the Temple Street Garage, which serviced the entire Chapel Square Mall. This was one of the first modern touches of revitalization brought to fruition by the previous mayor, who conceived and oversaw the urban renewal project that started in the late 1950s. An overbearing cement monster—designed by Paul Rudolph, who would do another six structures in the city that would be praised by Yale and city officials alike, but what residents would call *interesting*, at best—it was designed in a post-modern style, with little to no forethought of how it may be viewed within the context of the community's architecture in twenty years.

Frank pulled his undercover Dodge sedan up to the entrance. A uniformed officer was trying to wave him away and tell him the garage was closed. It took two steps before the officer realized that Frank was on the job and riding in an unmarked cruiser. He embarrassingly stumbled back over to move his black-and-white so Frank could proceed.

The Monaco climbed up to the ninth level where all the action was happening. A small crowd of curious shoppers gathered, watching near the police tape that stretched out on the far side of that parking level. A couple of uniforms leaned up against a prowl car, just in case the unruly crowd of mall dwellers threw down their shopping bags and made a run for the crime scene. Frank parked as close as he could and made his way over to the officers. They nonchalantly nodded and motioned toward the stairwell that led to the lower floors. He gestured in return, giving them the same casual interest they showed him.

He entered the stairwell, nodded at another officer, and headed down toward the landing in between the ninth and eighth floors. Completely cut off from natural light because of the concrete silo they were now in, long pairs of flickering and humming florescent bulbs lit the stairwell from overhead, tinting everything a synthetic nighttime blend of orange and yellow. Tom was on the stairs, close to the middle landing to greet him. Frank saw the worry on his face, something that was not common for his young partner.

"Thomas."

"Frank, about ninety minutes ago we got a call from a couple coming back from getting coffee after shopping."

They continued down to the landing, rounding the wall that obscured the view and entered the crime scene. Frank's eyes picked up the body on the floor and he stopped in his tracks. It took a moment for him to fully register what he was seeing.

It was his goddaughter, Arianna Wallace.

She lay sprawled out like a ragdoll on the stairs, surrounded by the discarded scraps and plastic wrappers from the paramedic's disposal equipment from when they attempted to save her. Frank could already see the lividity forming around the back half of her body that lay against the floor as the stagnant blood inside settled in the lowermost area. There was heavy bruising and swelling around her neck and face, her eyes almost swollen shut and her nose broken. Her complexion was now becoming a ghostly white-purple blend, and Frank could tell the back of the head was split open because of the large amount of dark blood pooled up around the cranium, now slowly starting to make its way down to the stairs below. But what made Frank collapse to one knee was her face. One eye was open, the other half closed. Frank recognized the gaze because he'd see it hundreds of times on the job. It was the glazed look of someone who no longer had concern for the world.

Frank stared at her for a couple of moments, completely unprepared for the discovery. He closed his eyes, stood up, and tried to clear his head, before letting out a long breath. "Oh my God." His comment was barely audible, but Tom heard it.

"I'm sorry, Frank."

"Does her family know yet?"

"No, I recognized her and rang you immediately."

Frank paced, trying to think. He checked his watch: 2:03 p.m. He grabbed Tom by the elbow and led him away from the body. "How many people have you told about this?"

"Only you."

"Are you sure?" Frank asked pointedly.

"Yeah." Tom looked puzzled, as if maybe he should have answered differently.

"Okay, good, good…sorry. Um. I don't want it to get out at the moment how close I am with the family or I might be reassigned. This is my goddaughter for Christ's sake, Tom." Tom nodded in understanding, almost searching Frank's face for their next move. "Okay, I'm up, so I'll be the lead." Frank studied Tom's eyes the entire time, looking for any indication he disagreed with Frank's requests. But Frank's young partner was one hundred percent behind him.

"Understood, Frank."

"Okay, talk to me, Tom. What's the absolute latest?"

"At first, it was thought to be an accidental fall. Looks like blunt trauma to the skull." Tom knelt down and used his pen to point at the back of Arianna's head. "Looks like the cranium was repeatedly slammed into the concrete, I'm speculating. She had a very weak pulse when the couple found her, but by the time the bus got here, at least 1000-1500 CCs of blood loss had occurred here on the scene." He indicated to the blood with his pen, stood up, and turned to Frank. "They called her at 12:38. I was on scene by 12:55. Joe's interviewing the young couple who found her now."

Frank was in a daze, and the color had drained from his face.

"I'm still debating whether it's a robbery or not. Her pocketbook is missing, but all her jewelry is still on her, and so is her watch," said Tom. "Um, also no signs of a sexual assault, thus far."

Frank knelt down to make a close inspection himself, looking for any injuries that could have been inflicted in the attack. "It could be a botched robbery," he considered out loud.

He could barely think right. It reminded him of when he would be on duty with a mean hangover and how hard it was to think and function. *Drinking*. Boy, he suddenly was engulfed with that old feeling. *The bug*. He could use a drink right now. But it was just enough to get *the bug* out of his head and to deal with the task at hand. The world had suddenly fallen in around him. He felt short of breath, a tightness in his chest. It was a feeling he'd hadn't felt, well, since....

It was all he could do to get it out of his mind, slow his breathing, and continue on with the crime scene.

Her necklace remained around her neck, the one she'd played with only eighteen hours before in his car, but this time, the skate key was covered in coagulated blood, which Frank quickly scanned past as he continued to look over the body.

"Any witnesses?" he asked.

"I've got Graham and some uniforms looking into that right now, and Joe's with the one who stumbled onto her."

"Do we know why she was here? Why she wasn't in school? Shit, wait, she just got her license and I think was borrowing the family car today, a Pontiac Grand Ville. Did she plan to take the day off or was she taking it to school?"

"I'll get someone on the car."

Frank stared down at the once-beautiful face. Blood had begun to dry in the hair. His hand unconsciously moved to fix the hair that was stuck to the face by dried blood, but he stopped himself once he realized what he was doing.

"She had a job here at Malley's Department Store, I think maybe in the perfume department. Could she have been working?" Frank thought aloud. "Do we know which way she was traveling?"

"I initially thought up, by the position of the body."

"No bag or keys makes me think robbery." Frank thought for a moment. "You call the lab guys and—"

"All called, and on the way."

Frank scanned the area, looking over the body and surrounding area. "Make sure they bag the buttons and necklace to check for prints and check for anything on the dress before they move her too. And bag the hands as soon as possible so we don't lose anything under the fingernails okay?"

"Of course, Frank."

"I want this garage, Macy's, Malley's, and the entire mall shut down now, if it hasn't been already. I want to run every plate in here. Have a man positioned at every exit, getting the names of everyone at this mall who is leaving. Someone could have been a witness to something."

An officer walked over to Tom and gave him a word. Tom looked over to Frank. "Patrol found an empty Pontiac Grand Ville on the top level, with the engine still running." They looked over to the uniformed officer who began his oral report.

"Doors open and keys in the ignition. Her license was in a handbag on the passenger-side floor, so we got an ID of an Arianna Wallace. Just issued too. Some money was also present."

Tom nodded a thank you to the blue suit. "Maybe we can rule out robbery at the moment." He took a breath between scribbling down what the uniformed officer just told him.

"So she was traveling down the stairs then." Frank looked back down at the body. He tried his hardest not to look at the face.

Frank knelt down and took a pen from his breast pocket and used it to lift her arm, just enough to look at the concrete underneath. Something caught his eye and he rose to one knee to look down the flight of stairs to the eighth floor. "Tom, you said the car was found upstairs, meaning she ran down to where we are now." Tom nodded. "So who does this blood trail belong to that's going to the lower levels?"

Tom looked down and saw the blood drops that Frank was referring to on the steps, which blended in with the dark shade of the concrete. He whipped his head around to the uniformed officer who was closest to him. "Officer, who *cleared* this scene?"

Before he could respond, Tom barked, "And before ya start picking things up, you're gonna fucking put gloves on when you're on my crime scene, understand?"

The flustered officer was barely able to stutter back a response, "Uh, yes, sir. Sorry, sir."

Frank stood and motioned to another officer. "Seal this stairwell immediately until the lab gets here. We already have people walking through evidence."

"Yes, sir."

Frank ran down the stairs with Tom on his heels, following the trail of the dark, elliptical-shaped blood droplets. "Looks like our guy might have gotten cut."

In one fluid motion, Frank slammed open the sixth-floor stairwell door with his elbow so not to touch it with his bare hand and continued forward with his head to the floor, following the trail of droplets. "Please see that that door is dusted as soon as the lab shows up."

The trail continued about thirty yards on that level, abruptly ending next to an empty parking space with some skid marks in front of it.

"Well, fingers crossed, we got the perp's blood." Tom jotted down another note. "Maybe he had a vehicle too?"

"Yeah. Let's go look at her car."

The sounds of the city were noticeably louder on the completely exposed top outdoor-level of the garage than they were on the other only partially-enclosed floors. The day was chilly, and a strong wind blew off Long Island Sound. The

Oak Street Connector was next to them down below with traffic thundering between the downtown and the adjacent I-91 and I-95 highways with unending regularity.

The lab teams had arrived and were setting up, while Frank and Tom, along with other officers assisting, searched Arianna's parents' car. The Pontiac's passenger door was partially ajar with the warning chime still going, indicating that keys were still in the ignition. Tom used a handkerchief to turn the engine off and pull the ring of keys with the Disney Tigger figure attached out just enough to stop the chiming, and Frank opened the opposite door all the way to get a better look inside. He immediately saw her handbag and pack of smokes on the passenger-seat floor. Outside the car window, there were numerous cigarette butts visible on the cement. They all had the same color lipstick Arianna was wearing.

"They knew each other.

"How's that?" Tom replied.

"Her pocketbook, here? I'm thinking she was sitting here, on this side."

"She wasn't in the driver seat?"

Frank motioned to her cigarette pack and open bag. "She sat here long enough to open her bag, maybe reapply some makeup and have a few cigarettes." He indicated to the pile of butts outside the car door. "They've all got her lipstick on 'em." He pointed to the side where Tom stood. "Which means our perp probably sat on the driver's side."

"Maybe he didn't want her to leave?" Tom speculated.

"They then sit here and chat for a while until the conversation goes sour?"

They began a onceover of the car, and the first thing that caught Frank's eye was a crumpled piece of paper lodged in the seat on the driver's side of the bench seat, next to a zippo and some loose change. He glanced over to one of the officers.

"Mike, bag that zippo for prints. Grab the change too. This all could have fallen out of our boy's pockets. Lend me some gloves." The officer pulled out a pair of plastic gloves and handed them to Frank. He put them on and slowly pulled out the crumpled piece of torn-out notebook paper and carefully unfolded it. On it, was scribbled a note: *We need to talk.*

Frank was handed a bag, put the note inside, and sealed the top, then handed it to one of the lab technicians.

Spinall came from out of the stairwell doorway and walked over to Frank. "Skipper, I spoke to her manager down at Malley's. She was due in today at noon. According to her friend and coworker, a MaryAnn Decan, she—"

"MaryAnn's there now?" Frank cut in. "Working?"

"Yeah. You know her?'

"Yeah. I know the vic too. Sorry, keep going."

Joe took the time to carefully remove his dark yellow-shaded glasses that hung between the top buttons of his shirt and re-placed them on his face to stop the sun's glare. "The two had a half day at school today and came over here together, both due in at noon. The vic received a call shortly after and told the manager she suddenly wasn't feeling well and asked to take her break then. No one saw her after that."

"Did you—"

"Yeah, got a call out to Ma Bell for the numbers that rang the phone extension that was in her department."

"Okay, good work, Joe. Thanks. Stay on top of this car search here and see if they come up with anything else." Tom tapped Frank on the shoulder and indicated behind him. Frank turned to see 'Cleveland,' his boss's 1974 Ford

Torino undercover unit, coming up the ramp into view on the top level.

The department had gotten Cleveland from the Ford Motor Company in '73 as a prototype to test and see if the department wanted to implement the model the following year. Even though the force ended up declining, Ford never followed up to get the car back, and after sitting as an oddball in the motor pool, Frank's boss, Lieutenant Michael William Warner, deemed the 'boat' his ride and adopted Cleveland as his own. He called it Cleveland because of the big Cleveland 351 V8 engine under the hood which had been manufactured in the Ohio city of the same name.

The cruiser quickly sped over the top level to their side, slowed down, and jerked to a halt with a bounce on the suspension when the massive vehicle was put into park. Lieutenant Warner, a six-foot, two-inch tall, lean black man stepped out. He was fit and toned, as if he had a propensity to work out, which he did not. Some on the force thought he secretly might even be a vegetarian. He wore his hair long on top and slicked back, and it shined gold in the sunlight.

He closed the massive car door with a thud, and in two or three strides, Mike was standing in front of Frank's team. As detective sergeant, Frank reported directly to his lieutenant, who in turn reported to the Assistant Chief of Detectives, which in New Haven was a position usually held by a captain.

Lieutenant Warner was Frank's buffer and helped field all the bullshit that trickled downhill that was supposed to be passed on to each lower in command. Mike was a no-nonsense and standup guy, and Frank and his squad were very loyal to him because of that.

"Is it as bad as I'm hearing?" he asked, brushing the front of his blazer to the sides so he could put his hands on his hips.

"I'm afraid so. Vic's a sixteen-year-old girl who vanished from work in the mall and was found by a couple coming back from shopping in the stairwell, barely alive. By the time the bus got here, she was gone, so they called her about an hour and fifteen..." Frank stole a glance at his watch, "... to an hour and a half ago. Looks like maybe strangulation, as well as blunt force trauma to the head. They beat her up pretty bad."

"What motive we running with?"

"That's currently the sixty-nine thousand-dollar question. Doesn't look to be robbery, and we think by what we found so far, they probably knew each other."

"Dum dee dum-dum," Joe added.

"Why don't you go look at the scene and get caught up there. Tom and I are going to where she worked."

"Sounds good," replied Lieutenant Warner.

"Joe, take him down." Frank motioned over to Tom. "C'mon."

It was all Tom could do to keep up with Frank as he followed him back into the stairwell, and if anything else was said at that point, it was drowned out by the loud downshifting of a Freightliner semi-tractor trailer passing on the highway down below.

The two detectives walked across the second-floor enclosed glass bridge that connected the Temple Street Garage to the massive Malley's Department Store. It had three levels above ground and two below, and showcased a bakery, post office, beauty salon, and 300-seat restaurant among its notable amenities. Arianna worked on the store's second floor, near the children's shoe department, right near the store's exit and within sight of the immense eight-foot tall and four-foot wide birdcage out in the mall, which usually attracted a crowd to view the parakeets that lived within. Music was piped in and made for a very tranquil environment to shop within, as you listened to such soothing sounds as the Captain and Tennille's *Love Will Keep Us Together.*

Past the shoe department, behind the huge mirrored support columns and before the restaurant, was the store's perfume department. Tom spoke with the overly dramatic department manager who looked a lot like Jack Cassidy's twin and dressed just as loudly, which let Frank quietly confer with the visibly shaken-up MaryAnn. She held it together a hell of a lot better than Frank would have thought for a girl her age. She appeared rather guarded and only reiterated what Spinall had learned earlier. She and Arianna had a half day at school, and when they got to work, they separated to do their duties. MaryAnn had seen Arianna receive a call, and the next thing she knew, she'd disappeared. When he compared notes with Tom moments later, he corroborated what Ari had told Jack Cassidy, that she was ill and asked to go on her break. The manager was unaware that she'd had a phone call. Frank used the extension she'd received the call on to ring the phone company. Frank spoke to the operator as Tom took the notes.

"Detective Sergeant Frank Suchy, here. Yes, between noon and 12:30. Thank you. Okay, two calls from a number originating from Hamden, one from Concord Street and Third? What's that?" Tom finished writing that down and made eye contact with his partner, waiting for the relayed information.

"Here? What is the number to that exactly? Really? Where is it located?"

Tom frowned as he tried to discern what was being said. Frank jerked around with the receiver in his hand and switched ears, so he could fully twist his body in the other direction. For Tom's benefit, he pointed out of the department and across the floor, toward the restaurant on the other side.

The detectives examined the payphone that was on the side wall of the restaurant. From there, one had a clear line of sight to the perfume department counter, and even to the area where its phone extension was located. They learned the eatery had been open since 10 a.m., and no one saw during the busy lunch rush who had used the payphone. They got all the employees' names, and Frank decided to go back and touch base with the other officers in the garage, then decided to pay the parking attendant a visit.

The parking attendant's office was small, and the cold concrete that was used to produce the entire structure made everything appear quite grungy. Tom spoke to the teenage attendant who, seated in a swivel chair, kept slowly twirling from side to side, unconsciously conveying his nervousness to the detectives. Frank had seen this a hundred times before; he wasn't on edge because he had anything to do with the crime; he just wasn't used to being questioned by the law, let alone being questioned while high as a kite. It must have never occurred to the boy to at least try to disguise the smell, even if he was going to do it right before he went to work.

Tom also smelled it and used the boy's paranoia against him. "So you don't remember seeing or hearing anything?"

The teen's acne-covered face turned red. "Naw. I-I'm only responsible for getting the ticket from them and buzzing the cars out after they've paid." Frank started to inspect the office and moved a few paces behind the boy, settling down against the window, facing the boy's back with his ears perked. "You see a lot of cars and, after a while, they all start looking alike, you dig man?"

"I dig," Tom replied. "I guess it doesn't help coming to work blasted, does it?"

The boy's eyes widened. "W-w-what do you mean officer?"

Tom ignored his question. "How about this: Did you see anyone come through here recently that looked like they had an injury of some sort?"

The boy took a moment to think, then his eyes lit up as his neurons fired. "Someone did pass through who was a little weird. Handed me his ticket with his left hand that was bruised and swollen."

Behind the teen, Frank made eye contact with Tom and wiggled his left hand and pointed to it with his right, and Tom nodded.

"Bruised and swollen? Like he had just been punching something?"

The boy shrugged. "Maybe."

"What about the other hand? Was either of them cut?" Frank chimed in.

"His left wasn't, but I couldn't see his right, he had his hand between his knees, like he was hiding it."

"But you didn't see if there was any injury on it?" Tom confirmed.

"I couldn't tell."

"We'll need that ticket."

With how Frank was standing, he faced the lane that allowed for cars to enter into the garage. Though the structure was supposed to be closed, Frank saw a long sedan coming up the lane from the entrance, obviously let in by the guard posted out front. He recognized it as the Cadillac Fleetwood belonging to Councilman Theodore Pregosin, and as it passed the booth, Frank recognized the valet. Why would a murder like this interest Pregosin and his ilk, if only to show up and observe an investigation up close? Then it dawned on him. Downtown. Negative exposure. He felt an unsettled feeling in his gut. This added a whole new dimension to the investigation, and not for the better. He wanted to wrap up the questioning here as soon as they could.

Frank finally spoke up. "You get a look at what he was driving?"

The boy peered back over his shoulder at Frank. "Maybe a green Chevelle, or a GTO?"

Tom finished a notation in his pad. "Can you remember the plate perhaps?" The teenager turned, and a look of surprise and incomprehension crossed his face, which completely negated a response. Even though Frank was behind the attendant, he could guess by Tom's reaction, the "*you-got-to-be-kidding*" look that his partner received was the only answer to the question they were going to get. It was worth a try, though.

The two detectives walked out of the small concrete office and stopped at the curb to consult.

Tom was a little irritated. "That kid was flying high in the friendly sky—"

"Without even leaving the ground," Frank cut in. "Yeah, I know."

"Well, it's a wonder he was even able to tell us his name."

"So his hands are swollen and bruised from punching her or missing and hitting the floor, and maybe he got cut in the struggle." Frank held up a torn parking ticket stub with a smear of blood on it inside an evidence bag. "At least we got this. Hopefully we can get a print off of it that's not our mate's in there." He handed Tom the evidence bag and looked down at his shoes. "Did you see the Caddy that passed when we were in there?

"Yeah, why?"

"It's the brass."

Tom grimaced. "Ugh. That's never a good sign." Lieutenant Warner exited the stairwell doorway and walked over to them. "Well, fellas, this balloon is starting to expand real fast. Now we've got a very important person holding onto the end, not wanting to let the air out."

"Hopefully we'll have something up and running by the end of the day," Frank said.

"Okay. We need to get around this as soon we can. This heat we have here because of this murder scene's location, is gonna boil over *very* quickly, dig?"

"Understood." Frank nodded. "We'll get back to you. C'mon, Tom."

They walked toward the sidewalk, away from the garage. Frank looked down at Tom's shoes and said, "This is gonna get bad, very fast."

Tom looked down at Frank's dress shoes. "Of course. Can you image how this looks to the big shots to have a young girl murdered in broad daylight, downtown, at the goddamn brand-spanking-new Chapel Square Mall?"

Frank stopped at the sidewalk. "Yep, not good." He looked up Crown Street. "Okay. Start a timeline. Make sure we didn't miss anything. And I know this might a sound a bit odd, but could you make sure the body is taken care of and, um, just make sure everything is taken care of and handled properly?"

"Of course, Frank."

"I'll be back soon."

"What are you going to do?"

Frank looked back at his partner. "I have to go tell Chris and Rhonda Wallace about Arianna."

Tom looked away and frowned in understanding.

Frank pulled his unmarked Monaco up in front of his best friend's house. He paused for a moment before exiting the car. It was less than twenty-four hours ago that he'd parked in the exact same spot and was showing his goddaughter how to drive his sports car.

What a difference a day makes.

He took some more time to gather the strength to exit the car. He'd been on the job ten years now, a homicide detective for more than half that, and nothing had prepared him for what he was about to do. He built up the nerve to exit the Dodge and walked up the driveway.

Chris and Rhonda were in the backyard, busy covering their above-ground pool. Chris told him the night before they'd gotten a tear in the cover and were going to have to put a new one on before the winter set in.

They were both on the deck, Rhonda unfolding a new cover, while Chris dragged the wet leaves off the older one, which had a fresh hole in it. Frank passed the family's youngest child, Mina, who, along with her male friend, were busy playing with their *Emergency!* TV show toys. In the distance a loud air raid horn started to howl. It was common on a Saturday at noon to hear it be tested, but not at all usual on a Tuesday afternoon. Frank made it to the deck before the Wallaces noticed him, just as the horn increased in volume.

He climbed the wooden stairs and all he could think was, *Why is that horn blowing on a Tuesday?*

He put on the best face he had for these situations, for this was something he'd become accustomed to, telling New Haven's mothers that their children were now dead. Overdoses, shootings, stabbings, rape, murder—any violent crime you could think up, or accidental deaths, and he thought he'd gotten used to it. At least he'd been able to be that far removed because it was part of the job. Not this time. He remembered what the old-timers used to say: *If you walk onto a crime scene and what you see doesn't affect you, then you're gone, brother.* He wondered how his stone-cold façade would hold up for the ultimate test of breaking the news to his closest friends.

Rhonda quickly rose to her feet to greet Frank. Feeling there was no way around it, with as much calm as he could muster Frank told them the horrible news.

He didn't hear the words actually come out of his mouth, all he heard was the air raid horn blaring miles away. He knew it was only tested for sixty seconds but it felt like it went on for an eternity.

Has there been a nuclear attack? he thought idly.

Frank knew what he needed to say had come out, because he saw the reaction on both their faces. He wanted to run away. The anxiety bottled up inside made it like it was the first time delivering the news of a death. Rhonda fell silent and her arms fell to her sides; Chris unconsciously dropped his rake and it bounced off the deck floor, falling onto the pool cover. Frank just stood there. What could he do? He'd gone through this a hundred times before, but never needed the words that he felt he couldn't find now. The two children on the lawn had stopped playing by this point, knowing something serious had occurred, though unaware of the gravity of the situation. Frank's mind screamed to get far away from there, to run and hide away from the world.

Rhonda was frozen. She did not move a muscle, not comprehending the impact of what Frank had said. At first, she thought it was some cruel, sick joke. But she knew Frank too well, and after her initial reaction expressed by a frown and half smile, it sank in. Her eyes filled with tears and her lower lip quivered. She screamed, a terrifying wail that probably would have the neighbors calling the police.

She lashed out, taking Frank by surprise. Nonetheless, he stood his ground and refused to flinch. She jumped at him, hitting him about the face and chest. Frank took it, thinking he somehow deserved it. Chris snapped out of his daze and jumped to her side to stop her. He yanked her hands off of Frank and pulled her into his arms. They collapsed to their knees, Rhonda breaking into an uncontrollable wail of pain.

Frank stood solemnly, having not moved a muscle, unable to determine what to do next. By the time he realized the air raid siren had ceased, it was now only an echo vanishing in the silence.

Upon leaving the Wallaces, Frank glanced at his watch to see what time it was. Nearly five o'clock. It hadn't dawned on him at the time how long he'd been with them; he just felt like it was his place. He glanced up at the sky, which had turned noticeably dark. Gray clouds loomed in the distance and a crack of thunder echoed into the air, reverberating between East and West Rocks, into the valley in which New Haven and its immediate suburbs were situated.

About halfway down the front path, he slowed to a halt. It wasn't necessarily a conscious action, more like his body and mind agreed that they both needed a rest. He wanted to give up. He stood there in front of his best friend's house, as though his batteries had been completely depleted.

This is the bad one. This is the case that will do me in.

Frank dealt with almost every conceivable horror in his line of work. Horror knocked on his doorstep nearly every day. However, with Chris and Rhonda, he found it different. Technically, it shouldn't be. He'd been dealing with scores of homicide cases a year, on which he was lead investigator. If you combined his team's cases that they'd triaged together, he'd surely given his fair share of bad news to victims' families. This was different for him. He couldn't bear seeing his close friends having to deal with this.

And the worst kind of death...*murder.* He was jolted out of deep thought by a raindrop that exploded atop his forehead. It made him open his eyes. The menacing thunderclouds seemed a lot closer than before. Or had he been standing there longer than he thought? It was time to move. Like it or not, he had work to do.

Yale New Haven's morgue really hadn't changed in fifty years. Back when, it was still called Grace New Haven Hospital or even just New Haven Hospital. It was a relic, much like the old police station they occupied before moving over to the new concrete mass that now sat across the street from the city's train station, built next to the Oak Street connector. The morgue's equipment looked older than Frank, and he wondered if the old tiles on the walls had actually once been white instead of the yellow-brown they were now. He made his way down the dark corridors and found the door at the end of the hall marked "Pathology."

It was a full-house today with every gurney filled, all patiently waiting to go under the knife for that final cosmetic job. Bill Sanders, the head Medical Examiner was in the middle of a session. The place gave Frank the creeps. He eased past each body and glanced at the toe tags to see if there was anyone there he knew. Bill was doing his post-mortem at the end of the room. As Frank got closer, he could see it was Arianna.

"There are multiple contusions on the left side of the face, the left side of the neck at about the upper thorax... there's bleeding and trauma in the neck muscles, and both the hyoid bone, and thyroid cartilage and cricoid cartilages are broken." Bill took a breath and wiped his brow with the back of his gloved hand before continuing his dictation to the microphone that hung over the table from the ceiling. "The trachea is also fractured. There are shallow lacerations in the anterior belly of digastricus and hemorrhaging in these tissues. There are scrapes atop the jaw, and similar wounds are found on the left upper clavicular head...period."

Frank stared into Arianna's face. That lovely, beautiful face that would never get a day older, never see another sunrise or snowfall. A face that was now swollen, broken, black, yellow and purple in color. It was around this time Bill decided to take a break and stopped the recording. He walked over to Frank and the two stepped out into the hallway to talk. It was odd, but they felt like they'd have more privacy out there. Besides, it was more respectful.

Tom was just arriving as they exited into the hall. Bill nodded at Tom and adjusted his glasses on the bridge on his nose. "Well, guys, on the outset, it looks like a strangulation, but there seems to be hernia of the brain due to an intracerebral hemorrhage."

Frank nodded. "Blunt force trauma to the head."

"Yes. I *think* that's what technically killed her, despite the massive damage to the throat area and the one helluva beating this guy gave her: broke her nose, left zygomatic-huh-cheek fracture, temporomandibular joint and mandible fracture, left orbital fracture, among other things. And with the posterior cranium fractures of the occipital, and what looks like the parietal bones injuries, she then bled out, the heart still active, not knowing that the brain had been affected."

"Any prior bruising on the body or contusions to indicate a history that you can see?"

Bill shook his head and scratched the back of his neck. "Nothing really superficial. Most of the trauma was to her head and neck." He took another breath, masking a burp that was a remembrance of his late lunch. "But in my opinion, it does not seem to be a random attack. I can't see a mugger or potential rapist staying around this long to inflict this amount of damage. I mean, beating, strangling, and bashing her head open on the concrete, or vice versa. Call it speculation on my part, but in my humble opinion, the excessive injuries seem to indicate it was personal."

Frank nodded, not bothering to lift his eyes from the floor. "Overkill."

"Usually stemming from a vendetta," Tom chimed in, to reassure himself as much as his colleagues that he knew their terminology. "Or something along those lines."

"Yes," Bill said. "So much rage and anger has built up and this was the breaking point."

Tom noted a slight excitement in his own voice which he quickly muted, as not to come off as too happy with himself. "It would make sense. We've been working with the idea that it was someone she was acquainted with, because they were so quickly able to lure her away from her job and then have a heart-to-heart with her, while driving *her* car."

"There is also bruising on her forearms from self-defense," Bill said, "but no cuts on her arms or hands. We did find a little blood on her hands and clothes that were not consistent with her injuries."

"We think it was from her assailant," Frank offered.

"I won't know until the lab work is done to see if it's another blood type. We also found skin and a few hair follicles under her nails. I'm sending them all over to be analyzed. But your guy should have some significant injuries to his knuckles and fists from this barrage."

Frank nodded and glanced over to his partner. "We found a blood trail leading away from the body. We think it's the killer's from injuries sustained in the attack. We got the lab on it. Maybe we'll get lucky."

Frank nodded. "Anything else you can tell me?"

The M.E. shifted his feet and sighed. "Not until I'm finished here. Just about to make entry into the cranial cavity and have a mosey."

That was the last thing Frank wanted to hear, but he had to shore himself up and remember he was here as a cop, and this *was* what a cop saw. He saw a look of interest pique in Sanders' eyes, picking up on Frank's uneasiness. Frank chalked it up to on-the-job experience, along with how far back he and Sanders went.

Frank went on, not missing a beat. "Just make this the number one priority, William. This situation is ripe to explode because of the circumstances, and to be honest, I—"

The sergeant's voice was cut off by a noise at the other end of the corridor. That wasn't abnormal; this was a busy hospital on a weekday. But it was enough to make the three stop what they were doing and look down the hall. Two people opened the double doors at the far end and made their way down the dimly lit corridor. They were embracing, as if one was using the other to stand. Frank knew who it was before he could confirm it with his eyes: Chris and Rhonda.

When they reached the end of the hall, they looked up from the floor, making eye contact with the three who huddled next to the morgue entrance. Chris' eyes were bloodshot, and Rhonda didn't look like she was even aware that the three men stood before her. Chris cleared his throat and rallied the courage to speak. "We've come to see our daughter."

There was a long silence while everyone processed the request.

"That may need to wait at the moment, Chris," Frank said sadly.

"Yes, this may not be the best time to see her," Bill said. "Maybe it might be good to wait until arrangements are made with a funeral director has been able to take her and—"

Frank broke in, "This really isn't the time to view the body, as it is now. It's not how you..." he fought for the right word before he continued, "...want to remember her, and this is part of the journey where the funeral director has an important job to fill—"

"I want to see my daughter," Rhonda said. "*Now.*"

"We've talked about it," Chris said, as if to soothe his wife's tone to the other men, "and we'd like to see our little girl and see what this monster did to her."

Frank glanced over at Bill, and the seasoned M.E. could read the detective's mind.

Bill sighed. "Well, please just give me a moment before you come in, then."

Chris nodded while Rhonda stared at the tiled floor, as if she hadn't even heard the request. Sanders disappeared back into the morgue. The two detectives and the Wallaces stood in silence within the hall. Frank glanced over his shoulder and through the window that had the word '*Pathology*' written below, and watched Bill quickly cover a couple of bodies before going over to Arianna. He hastily discarded any surrounding equipment and grabbed a sheet to drape over the body, so only her face was visible.

"Are you both absolutely sure this is what you want to do? This really could wait." Frank asked the couple. "You must remember, what you see now isn't how she looked… before."

"Usually, a funeral director has some time beforehand to aide in the presentation of the body…to benefit the loved ones…" Tom tried to be as soothing as possible.

"We're ready to see her now," Rhonda said calmly.

Frank checked back over his shoulder and Bill nodded. "Alright, please follow me." They went in behind Frank. Tom remained in the hall.

For the first time, Frank felt embarrassment at the state of the pathology room. He didn't know why exactly; he just thought they deserved a prettier or more comforting place for this moment.

He led the way with the two parents behind. They passed all the death that rested on the many tables until they reached the one that was their own. Frank stopped about ten feet before the gurney, carefully moved out of the way, and waited. The parents passed him and got closer to the table. Bill stood behind the body, and when Frank nodded, the M.E. gently uncovered Arianna's face.

The couple took three halting steps toward their daughter. Looks of unimaginable sorrow appeared on both their faces. Tears rolled down Chris' face. He tried to silently let out a breath but instead released a moan. Rhonda broke away from her husband and took a step forward. Her already bloodshot eyes again filled up with an uncontrollable fury, and Bill Sanders did his best to keep his composure, respectfully looking down to the floor.

Rhonda stood in silence, sizing up the life that should have surpassed her own. Dozens of thoughts passed through her head all at once; her daughter's birth, memories of her childhood, early adolescence, and teen years, all the elements that turned someone into the person they would become in life. Arianna had been robbed of that in the most brutal and selfish way. She was intentionally beaten to a pulp and murdered by another human being. Rhonda could no longer take it.

She raised her hand and slowly reached over and stroked her daughter's hair. Her eyes filled up with tears and the shell-shocked mother broke down again. "My baby. My sweet little baby."

Her sobs echoed through the cold, sterile, practically antique room. Rhonda's glare immediately darted over to Frank's, and the unexpected direct eye contact made him jump.

"You find out who did this, Frank. You find the bastard who did this to my little baby. My poor baby." She petered out, collapsing into Chris' arms.

Detective Sergeant Francis Pasquale Suchy had nothing to say, he just stood watching, lost in mindless thought.

♠ ♠ ♠

Frank had lost track of how long he'd been sitting there in the dim light, staring down at the sweet golden-colored temptation in a glass.

He'd driven around as much as he could bear, sometimes down the same street twice, maybe three times, trying to clear his head.

Then he'd drifted in here to try and put his head back on right. He looked down at the little shot glass. The shiny liquid inside appeared to groove along with the bass sounds and rhythm around him.

His left hand was in his pocket, his fingers digging through the change, trying to find *it*.

Such a small, cute, tiny glass.

Frank didn't like calling Vince from here, of all places, but felt like, since it was such a pressing matter, he had to get it off his chest so he could concentrate on the case at hand. He packed into the phone booth in the back of the discotheque and tried his best to sound convincing about why they couldn't meet up and blow out the GT40's engine tomorrow at Lime Rock. Even over the music booming in the background of the club, Frank recognized the subtle charge in tone of Vince's voice while they spoke. Frank assured him it was only work, which it was.

Basically.

Vincent Channing had been there and done that with the NYPD, putting in his twenty up in the 2-8 in Harlem, or as they called it, the Murder Factory. It was the smallest precinct in the entire city of New York but was the most violent precinct in the entire country. Vince was on the force back at a time when the blissfully ignorant 1950s *Car 54, Where are You?*-era police officer of the 1930s, '40s, and '50s watched as heroin came on the scene and first rotted out the heart of inner city neighborhoods, gradually spreading out to society as a whole. Vince had a front-row seat to witness the world completely lose its mind in the late 1960s. Amidst the turmoil and almost losing his own sanity, he retired up here to a family farm in Connecticut in 1971 and decided to give back to his fellow officers and counsel those who need it. Subsequently, he helped Frank through some of his worst days.

Now Frank was lying to him. And he felt horrible for it.

Still, Frank didn't have the patience or the courage for lack of a better word, to tell him how he really felt. Frank felt like a failure, to himself and to his friend. To have someone like Channing, who'd seen it all while pounding the arches and still came out the other end okay, only now for Frank to have what should be a routine murder, something that *should* be normal because of his job, tear up the calm that Vince had helped Frank rebuild. He couldn't bear it.

He avoided as much as he could and just told Vince it was the job. He'd understand. Besides, he didn't want to worry him. His car was just the last thing he needed to be thinking about now.

However, Vincent was too good of a man to be openly lied to. To hear himself try to make some stupid, bullshit excuse would be a slap in the face to the trust they'd built over the years. He tried to make the conversation as short and sweet as he could, so as not to insult the man's intelligence.

Frank's left hand was in his pocket, turning *it* around and around in his hand subconsciously.

What now?

Frank knew simply going home would do nothing for him. Sleep was the last thing his mind could do right now.

He no longer found solace and rest in slumber. When Frank closed his eyes now, the day's latest victims would show up on the back of his eyelids to do their grim dance and remind Frank of their fate. It had gotten worse in recent years. There was a time he could come home, let the evil out of the car a block away, and arrive into Audrey's arms. She would have everything ready for him. A smile, a hug, and a face filled with such joy and love he would be able to forget the most horrible, terrible things the streets decided to leave on his back to carry that day.

That had all changed now.

He was no longer able to escape the demons; even his old friend sleep held no comfort for him anymore. He felt so alone. And he'd learned the numbing effects of alcohol or things much worse were the only way to ensure a night of dreamless sleep.

He felt it turn around inside his fist, his hand clenching it tighter, feeling the hard metal press into his palm and fingers.

He'd given up alcohol because of the *bug,* and because of his lack of control while he was feeding it. How he resented that, and himself most of all, that he'd let it get to that point.

He'd worked with boatloads of seasoned detectives who made it seem like the most stressful thing they did was direct traffic, and here Frank sat day in and day out, trying as desperately as he could just to keep the demons away for one more night. It appeared drinking was part of the job; a required level of self-prescribed medication if one wanted to stay sane in the world they inhabited. The booze acted as a buffer, because what really frightened him these days was the job.

There was a time a few years ago when it all happened that he thought he'd end it. He'd hit a wall. He couldn't take the job any longer. He'd seen it happen to others, like with Nick Camputaro in Narcotics. The hole freshly dug out by the horror of the job would then start to rot and turn your insides into a stinking bile of diseased filth. Above all, the death. How do you sanely deal with all that death? Like people who went to war and saw the worst humankind had to offer, came back home, and then were expected not to be affected and adjust on their own back into daily life, to just be okay and not take it back home and have it repeat in their head, over and over again, on an endless loop.

It turned quicker and quicker in his hand inside his pocket, his fingers acting as an autonomous entity, pressing it tighter and tighter, feeling the increasing pain from it inside his palm.

How was what happened to those who served in war different from those who served daily on the streets? Of course, war was war, and being in a ditch in Europe or in a rice paddy in 'Nam was not comparable to working in a civilized society on the street, but in a kind of war to keep the streets and people safe, to be the first line of defense against the evil that preyed on society, how was the horror that he and his brothers in blue and red dealt with every day—murders, the cheapness of life—supposed to be forgotten after work, as if taking off the uniform?

That was never taught to the police.

And that was how alcohol came into the picture for many. The ultimate daily eraser.

For Frank, that was how the *bug* first took over, helping to fill that hole and compensate for the emptiness, acting as a buffer against what he saw on the job. Soon the *bug* overpowered him and he lost control of it. Miraculously, with the help of his sponsor Vince, his friend Chris Wallace, and Chris' family, he was somehow able to cope and somehow, some way, he was able to go on and survive.

But only being able to cope isn't enough in my job.

That made him laugh because he sure as hell knew there were plenty of men on the force, or probably in life in general, that were only just coping with the day-to-day of life. Deep down inside, and maybe he wouldn't even admit to himself, this was why the job frightened him. When would the job truly become *too much*? When would *he* finally be gone?

Gone.

He'd heard it from the old timers on the job, stories of the guys who entered a scene and the job wouldn't affect them because they'd become numb to it all. To the beatings, violence, murder, rape, ODs, abuse, the filth, seeing the dregs of life, the animal abuse. When you'd walk onto the scene of such horror and desperation and feel *nothing,* then you were *gone*. That was his biggest fear, something he worried more about than getting shot or being killed in the line of duty. The biggest fear he had was the day he walked onto a scene and what he saw didn't affect him.

Then he'd be gone, brother. Bye bye.

His fingers tightened around it and it dug deep into his palm, the pain intensifying with every beat of his heart.

Frank kicked himself to get back to reality. His mind wandered, and he now realized he'd staring down at the glass of bourbon for nearly an hour.

It was the *bug*.

It took all the will he could muster not to immediately shoot the liquid down his throat and achieve that satisfying burning sensation, knowing the task was getting done. Knowing the *bug* was being fed. This day had taken all the courage he'd been able to muster for the past few years of sobriety and thrown it all into the wind. All the walls he'd erected to protect himself were tumbling down. It was like Irwin Allen himself had created the ultimate disaster flick, all just to destroy Francis Pasquale Suchy.

Yet that was part of the agreement, the deal he'd reached with himself, that if he wanted to keep going and make it in this thing called *life* and have something to show for it, he'd have to give up the hooch. Say no to the vicious *bug*.

All of this was bouncing around his head as he stared down at that heavenly liquid.

His hand clenched it so hard in his palm that he wouldn't be surprised if he was bleeding.

Frank realized what jogged his mind back to reality was hearing The Shangri-La's *He Cried* start, which changed the pace of the music from the forever-blasting disco. The clubgoers on the dance floor loved the old throwback and slowed their groove along to the seductive rhythms. The song had broken his train of thought and made Frank look up. He gazed into the mirror behind the bar to view the dance floor.

It was a humid, foggy mess of multi-colored flashing light reflected on sweaty bodies, everyone grinding away, like at a Roman orgy. Boy, what it was like to be young! His gaze shifted to his ratty reflection in the mirror in front of him, and it may have been the first time in three years that he sized himself up. He wasn't happy with what he saw.

His right forearm on the bar felt a sensation he'd forgotten even existed. The woman next to him was speaking to a male friend and her back was to Frank. She had long, dark brown hair that was down to her mid-back, the tips of which danced and teased his naked forearm, her head moving while she spoke, bringing back memories he'd long forgotten. He stood there motionless taking in the moment, wondering if this was the norm in a place like this and if he was discovering what he was missing by not frequenting these places in a non-professional capacity anymore. Or if this was a bit perverted.

These were thoughts his wife wouldn't care for.

He tuned into the conversation next to him.

"...my brother got him and his wife one of those new video/recorder players," the man was saying. "VCRs, and from what I seen, it's pretty neat."

"Really?" the woman asked, intrigued. "They're pretty expensive, aren't they?"

"They're coming down in price. But, baby, imagine being able to tape *Columbo* and, instead, watch *Kojak.* You can go back and watch *Columbo* whenever you like! Or if the late movie is really good but you can't stay up, you can just tape it and watch it the next day. I mean, can you dig it?" The man shrieked out a laugh. The man piped up next to him.

"To hell with those clowns, how about stag films? Being able to watch those fuck films at home without having to set up a screen and projector, and by yourself?! Ha! They're gonna put all the picture houses outta business!"

Frank's left hand inside his pocket squeezed so hard he surely was bleeding by now.

The woman continued to move her head, chuckling at the crudeness over her companion while her hair continued the ritual-like dance on Frank's skin. He just couldn't bear it.

He withdrew his right arm from the bar. His hairs were on end, which made him glance down at his arm, and that was when he first noticed it.

His right hand was trembling. He didn't feel it moving though. He had never noticed that before, and it really frightened him.

Frank looked back at the glass and then at his hand, and without hesitation, threw back the drink, downing the stinging liquid in one fell swoop. The forgotten taste caught his throat by surprise and embarrassingly, he coughed before finally swallowing it all and feeling the burn in his gullet. He felt betrayed by his body. How many times had he finished an entire bottle of this stuff only to gag now because he had forgotten the sensation?

Just outta practice, is all.

That was the last straw.

He threw down a tip and walked out into the brisk night. On the steps outside, he dug into his left pocket and finally took his hand out and opened his fist to look. It still dug into his palm. It hadn't drawn any blood, but it sure felt like it had.

He held it up into the light to inspect it.

The bronze sobriety coin he kept on him at all times signified his three-year stint off the booze. On one side of the coin, it marked the length of sobriety, and on the other it had the serenity prayer. It had kept him strong and kept him sober for three years. In an instant, lost in thought and even while it rolled around in his hand, he'd broken his pledge.

Now it was useless.

He cocked his arm back like an outfielder would when trying to get a ball back into the infield and threw it as far as he could down the street and into the gutter.

He turned and walked off.

When he pulled onto his street, Frank could make out Cleveland parked out in front of his brownstone. He deposited a stick of gum into his mouth and pulled his car up behind it. By the time he got his stuff together and closed the Monaco's door, Mike was already out and leaning against his trunk.

Frank crossed in front of his car and stepped next to Mike, leaning his butt back on the Dodge's grill.

"Hope I haven't kept you, Skipper."

"Not at all, Frank. Only been here about two minutes. I wanted to catch you before it got too late tonight. Long day today?"

"Yeah, very long." Frank hesitated to see if the lieutenant would speak up first. When he didn't, Frank asked, "What can I do for you, Mike?"

Mike crossed his arms. "You didn't tell me your best friend is the victim's father."

"Yeah."

"Well?"

"It's not gonna be a problem."

"Are you damn well sure?"

"I am, sir."

"I'm sure you know Councilman Theodore Pregosin by reputation. He's taken on this entire urban renewal fiasco as some kind of legacy that Mayor Lee started. He and the entire Urban Renewal Council, or whatever it's called, have got a lot riding on the downtown area. That's the heart of the whole project. Can you imagine the implications if this garage today or the mall became stigmatized and people suddenly feared going down there? Going downtown? Do you know what can happen?"

"I do, Mike."

"That's heat that ends careers and cracks the department right down its back, so I need to hear it. From your mouth."

"I am completely fine to handle this case. No personal feelings will, in any way, hinder this investigation. I give you my word."

Mike eyed Frank for a moment. "Okay, Sergeant. You've got my full, complete support."

"Thank you, sir."

Later, Frank mulled over and over in his head what he'd said to Mike, his friend and boss. From the bottom of his heart, he did believe his statement was the truth. He really did. Maybe it was the buzz he'd gotten from the shot of hooch.

He entered his apartment and saw the kitchen light was still on from this morning. He'd left it on.

Before everything changed again.

He walked over to an end table and one by one removed everything from his person: his wallet, watch, note pad and pencil, spare change, jacket, his stainless steel .357 Model 66 Smith and Wesson snub-nose service revolver, waist holster and belt, ending his daily ritual with two spare reload cylinders of bullets. He looked over his place, deciding that the dishes could wait until tomorrow.

He proceeded down the hall toward his bedroom, but only got as far as his daughter's room. Her door was covered in children's drawings with the words "KATY" written out in colorful cardboard letters. He stood there thinking for a long time, raised his arm and placed his hand on the knob, turned it, and with not a sound, the door opened. It cracked about a foot or so. Frank carefully shut it again, making sure to be as quiet as he could.

He stood reflecting in front of the door, not wanting to make a sound. He leaned against the wall, completely lost in thought. He pulled the pint of liquor he'd acquired out of his pocket, cracked open the seal, and threw his head back, finishing it in one long gulp. When it was emptied he stuck his tongue into the opening to get every last drop, all to satisfy the *bug* that had been released from its deep, dark hole once again. He didn't care. Not now. He knew he'd need it to sleep tonight and kill the thoughts in his head. He didn't want to have to knock a liter back, say, because he needed to be functional tomorrow, so he'd shown considerable restraint in his mind. He'd purposefully only bought enough to drink tonight, knowing he couldn't trust himself with having extra in the house. He was worried what would happen once he sat down and closed his eyes.

He hoped, he prayed for a dreamless sleep.

DECEMBER 9, 1967

FRANK WAS BACK in the old downtown headquarters. The old station house dated back to the turn of the century. Its old and weathered lead paint covered the walls, its asbestos covered pipes leaked, and the steam heat in the building made everything unbearably hot and dry in the cold winters because there was no way to shut the damn radiators off except to open the windows, which were mostly painted shut.

The furniture scattered about was as old as the precinct itself. Ancient wooden chairs, benches, and desks with huge antique Underwood typewriters atop so one could slowly, so very slowly, type out a report, as long as you found one where all the keys still worked. The one Frank used was over by one of the holding cells on the first floor. It was his favorite because only the letter "Z" didn't work, and how many times did you need to use the letter "Z" in a police report?

Boy, this was something he hadn't thought about since about 1967.

That night had been a rough tour, one that could have potentially and prematurely ended his, as of then, very short and uneventful career as a police officer. His conscience had gotten in the way of his job that evening, back when that sort of thing mattered to any younger, idealistic kid who wanted to change the world. He became the Henry Fonda in the *Oxbow Incident* posse of other uniformed officers, the only one with the balls to step in and announce enough was enough. For that, he'd incurred the wrath of some of his fellow officers, vocally and physically. It was spreading through the station house like wildfire.

Frank had been standing inside his sergeant's office, an old weathered Irishman named Sullivan who used to excrete Guinness stout from his pores, receiving a verbal dressing down chock-full of 'son of a bitches' and 'your man(s)', due to Frank's "lack of cooperation and cohesion" with his fellow uniformed officers, for causing a rift within the department, and most of all, because he stepped in and didn't allow his colleagues to continue to 'tune up' a suspect. This was unheard of by a rookie. Sullivan could completely understand and agree with an intervention because of, say, excessive force or a racial component (as he often stood up for because of his own minority status), but this kid, this "rock-and-roll hooligan" from what he'd heard, completely deserved what he got. Mocking the thin blue line, the men who put themselves on the line for the public every day, in front of a packed arena of people from their very own town? That was intolerable.

But even a couple of punches was completely uncalled for in Frank's mind. He had to step in and stick up for what he thought was right.

If only the younger optimist Frank Suchy could meet who he'd grown up to be.

Standing in that office, Frank knew nothing else could be done or would be done, aside from a chastising by Sergeant Sullivan, some dirty looks from co-workers, and maybe desk duty for the next year or so. Frank knew he was right. Deep down, Sullivan knew Frank was right too, and in the years past, nothing did happen to him for going against the grain. He actually garnered some lasting respect in the years to come, once the new generation of guys came to replace the older guard. It set Frank on a path that would eventually lead him to detective sergeant, in charge of his own squad of the best homicide detectives around. All because of that cold, snowy night back in December of 1967.

Frank recalled the man who'd been the center of attention that night sitting just outside the sergeant's office and well within earshot of Frank's berating. He sat handcuffed to a large wooden bench, in the poorly-lit hall that was covered in years of dust and grime. He angled his head back, staring up at the ceiling, a tissue pressed against his face and nose to stop any bleeding. He was dressed in black leather pants, cowboy boots, a black shirt, and black denim jacket. His hair was down to his shoulders and his face was slightly swollen.

After the yelling stopped in the office, the door opened and out came a young Frank Suchy in a wrinkled patrol uniform, sporting a crew cut. Frank had a swollen eye himself on the left side of his face and was holding a bag of ice up on it. The young rookie officer carefully shut the door to his superior's office and planted himself on the bench next to the detained suspect. After sizing up the situation, Frank handed over the ice to the handcuffed man next to him.

The man nodded in thanks and they both sat silent until the man finally spoke up. "Gun wavin' New Haven, huh?" he said with a smirk.

The comment took Frank by surprise and he laughed. "I haven't heard that one before."

"Really? I heard that upstate in Troy the other night. Frank, isn't it?"

"Yes, Frank Suchy. Jim?"

"Jim Morrison, pleased to meet you." He tried to smile but pain flashed across his face. "Thank you for intervening with your fellow co-workers."

Frank laughed at the remark.

A dream perhaps? Morrison has been dead for five years now...

"Don't mention it." He looked at the singer's face. "How are you feeling?"

"I'll live. You?"

"Gonna be doing parking tickets for a while, but okay."

A silence fell over the two until Morrison said, "You should bodyguard, man."

"Ha, I can dig it." Frank thought about all that had happened that night, and a wave of embarrassment came over him. "Sorry about all this. They get frustrated and don't know how to vent; to have to take so much crap from these college punks and the like, antagonizing and calling us pigs and the other abuse nowadays, day in and day out. I think you just made them feel like assholes for doing their job in front of half of New Haven's young adults."

Frank couldn't quite remember if he'd tried to justify it more for himself now, or if he'd gone that far in rationalizing the behavior that cold night back in '67 and actually spoken those words aloud to Morrison and all these thoughts were coming back to him now.

"Well, I do tend to get carried away at times, but I thought I had the point." Morrison finally said. They both shared a laugh.

Morrison glanced at Frank's ring. "You married, Frank?"

"Yeah. And got a nine-month-old little girl."

"Living the American dream. Congratulations," Morrison said sincerely.

"You?" Frank now knew the answer, all these years later. Poor Pamela, passing that way in '74.

"Me? No, I got a woman, but we're not married. I'll probably end up marrying Pam but not yet. Can't seem to hold onto much of anything, I'm only barely able to keep her."

There was another long silence while Frank's thoughts bounced around in his head.

"Must be real exciting to be on the road in one of the biggest bands around, to be famous and everything, huh? Kinda like the old vaudeville days, touring all those cities?" Frank smiled now at his own naïve comment.

Morrison shook his head. "It's not all it's cracked up to be. Hell, look what happened tonight. Especially if you like to indulge in exploring the limits of your vices, like I tend to do."

"I guess you've got a point there."

"I went to film school. Wanted to explore the 'mise en scène' of life. Now I'm here, sitting on a police bench, waiting for my bail to be processed, all 'cause I sing music that is controversial...today's modern art, you know? I only want to create." He looked over to the young officer. "How about you? Is this what you wanted to do with your life?"

The question had never been asked of him. "No. Honestly, no. I'm a motor-head, gear-head. You know? I would have loved to have been a racecar driver like Steve McQueen or something. I race cars in my free time upstate and on Long Island, and one of these days, once I get the bills paid off, I'm gonna buy myself something nice and sporty."

"Well at least you have it all planned out."

Morrison looked back at Frank.

Frank was no longer the young uniformed cop but the present day, weathered homicide detective he was now in 1976. He sat there staring at Morrison with his hands cupped between his legs.

"Yeah, but it never goes how it's supposed to go, does it?"

That's the understatement of the century, Frank thought.

He glanced back at the singer, who was now a rotting corpse. Frank's eyes widened at the image now seated next to him.

What did you expect? He's been in the ground over five years now.

♦ ♦ ♦

Frank awoke startled, his eyes frantically scanning the dark room until he realized where he was. His gaze found the electric alarm clock. 3:13 a.m. He could hear a freight train passing off in the distance, with its air horn blowing and the clanking of the wheels as each car went over a crook in the tracks. It *had* been a fucking dream. Back to the old days to compound it, when he was still in uniform, and *a patrolman* at that. And that night too, an entire lifetime ago.

Was it the drink? Had the drink caused this…this fluke? Behind the clock on the nightstand was a picture of his family. Gradually, his eyes unconsciously gravitated toward the framed memory. Frank was covered from head to toe in sweat but felt hot. It was the middle of October and he was sweating like it was the dog days of summer. He rolled over onto his back.

"The nightmares are starting to come back, baby," he said aloud, half asleep, to his wife.

There was a pause.

"Don't worry, poppet. Just go back to sleep now," said Audrey's low, beautiful voice coming to his left ear like a dream.

The repetitive sound of a needle in the center of a record became audible when the far-off train finally passed and silence again blanketed the room. He eventually got out of bed and crossed the darkened threshold into the shadowy living room. The soft ambient glow of a streetlight shone through his venetian blind-covered windows, creating the ultimate nightlight while also painting film noir-ish shadows upon the walls. The massive wood shelves Frank had added the previous year covered the entire living room from floor to ceiling with hundreds, if not thousands, of LPs on them, all compulsively alphabetized, to Frank's liking. Occasionally, there was a gap of space in the shelving where a framed picture was positioned on the wall, randomly breaking the visual monotony. Marvin Gaye (leaning back in close up with his hands behind his head in thought), The Doors (from the *LA Woman* sessions, signed), Chet Baker from his *Chet Baker Sings* album, a rare theatrical poster of *Bullitt*, and his family's photo from Sears, all decorated the walls.

Frank stepped into the living room as if sleepwalking, scanned the walls, and impulsively grabbed an LP off the shelf. In one fluid motion, he took out Sinatra's *No One Cares* record, carefully dropped the cover, and replaced Johnny Ace's *Anthology* on the turntable with the wax in his other hand. He then spun around, carefully dropped the old one on the couch, and hurried back to the bedroom.

Mr. Sinatra's *When No One Cares* began.

Frank jumped back into bed, assuming a fetal position, hugging a pillow. It didn't take long before he fell back to the dreamy sleep that he knew now would plague him once more.

WEDNESDAY

October 15, 1976

IT WAS ABOUT ten in the morning before Frank and Tom finished their breakfast at the diner on Long Wharf. Long Wharf was a neighborhood east of the New Haven train station and railyard, stretching out to Interstate I-95 along the coast line. At one time, the area had been the harbor and marshland. It was filled in with what was dug up when they deepened the harbor the same time the Interstate had been laid, part of the country's bigger Eisenhower infrastructure projects to connect America in the '50s. Maybe in another twenty or thirty years the entire harbor would be paved. Who knew? Still, a very profitable meat and fish-packing district had been developed. In the middle of this hustle and bustle was the Long Wharf Theatre, a black box venue that had already become almost as famous as New Haven's prestigious Shubert Theatre. Next to the diner was a large marquee sign visible to the passing travelers on the Interstate, promoting the upcoming production of *The Shadow Box*, starring Geraldine Fitzgerald.

Frank and Tom walked from a booth to the counter to pay the check. When they stepped into the parking lot, the two detectives were going over everything they had after the first twenty-four hours. Frank squinted in the morning sun reflecting off of Long Island Sound, and he had to raise his voice to be heard over the loud traffic that flew past on the adjacent highway. He'd forgotten how bad a hangover could be, but kept that thought to himself.

"So the prints on the zippo and on the parking ticket stub isn't hers and aren't in our records?" Frank asked.

Tom nodded and patted his pockets to see if he had the keys. "Of what we've been able to check, correct. They're still searching our print records, so maybe we'll get lucky."

"Got a list of her friends?"

"Yes. We've got MaryAnn Decan, her best friend. We've got her boyfriend, um, what's his name..."

"Al, ain't it?" Frank took the keys from his pocket and tossed them to Tom.

"Yes, Albert Fisher."

"I seem to remember they had a fight a couple of nights ago."

"That a fact? Which could lead to motive?"

"We'd have to see."

Tom looked down at his notes. "He works for Sikorsky out in Stratford, does engine work."

They got into their undercover Monaco.

"Makes great helicopters, that Igor Sikorsky," Frank commented.

Tom put the car in gear and they drove off.

Sikorsky Industries was a vast factory that manufactured helicopters for both private and government firms and had been doing so since Igor flew the first helicopter on the same land back in 1939. The factory spanned city blocks, and once inside, one almost forgot they were in an enclosed building. In the distance, helicopter bodies, prototype Blackhawk chassis dangled from tracks on the roof, swaying back and forth, while enormous machines inhabited the floor. The floor of the plant was noisy, and the men who worked the assembly lines wore ear protection, and different-colored hard hats to denote rank.

Coming down the main walkway was a supervisor in an orange hard hat who passed other workers wearing blue and green. He went up to a young man working on the line and yelled something into his ear. The kid removed his ear protection and replied with a questioning mannerism. The foreman nodded, and they both started their way back up the walkway.

High above the floor, a huge corner office overlooked the massive plant. The wall facing the factory floor was made entirely of glass, providing a clear view of the daily operations. The flashy office that encompassed the clerical side area of Sikorsky was the size of a large boardroom and used to show off the work assembly area to visitors and potential clients. Designed with the once-hip "Retro Modern" flair that was in vogue over fifteen years before, the walls, curtains, and shag carpeting were done in early 1960s lime green, yellow, and orange hues, all of which seemed quite dated now; even if paired against the hugely extravagant styles of 1976.

Frank stood, leaning against the glass, watching the young man and the supervisor walk back up the walkway toward the office area. Behind him, Tom stood chatting with the general manager of the factory, answering the normal, concerned questions. Tom gave the generic answers that a policeman does when they don't want to be too specific about what they were doing there, and really meaning to find out.

Al Fisher was brought into the office and the employees kindly left Frank and Tom alone to question the boy privately. He sat down in front of the desk, while Frank lingered by the window. He was about six feet tall, and thin. He had long black hair that he wore spiked, and appeared to be cultivating a punk rock look, the soon-to-be next trend. He didn't seem that bothered or concerned to be speaking with the two officers, even at his place of employment.

Tom handed him a glass of water and sat on the edge of the desk in front of him.

They both noticed a bandage on Al's left hand.

"Cigarette?" Tom asked, holding out his pack, after grabbing one for himself.

"I don't smoke," Al replied coldly.

Tom put the pack back in his pocket and lit up. He could already tell how this was going to go. He produced an evidence bag out of his jacket and dangled it in front of Al's face. It contained the one-sentence note found in Arianna's car.

"So this isn't from you?" It took a moment for the young man to register the question and he squinted to read the writing through the plastic.

"No, it's not. Did you find that on her?"

Tom disregarded that. "You see or speak with Arianna yesterday?"

"No, haven't talked to her in days, after she disinvited me to her sweet sixteen at Roller Haven." Al shifted in his seat and looked over his shoulder at Frank, who stood silently with his arms folded over his chest. "Why? You think I had something to do with what happened to her or something?"

"Where were you yesterday?" Tom dutifully pressed on. "Your boss says you weren't at work."

"I was off sick."

Tom shifted his head in a questionable way. "Off sick? I'm glad you're feeling better. You don't seem to be too broken up about what happened to your girlfriend. I mean, 'off sick' yesterday, and then after she is killed, you come into work today."

Al's mouth creased up into a ball with a flash of anger, then sadness, and he looked away from Tom's glare. "Some people take it in different ways, I guess."

Frank had enough of this parlaying. "Where were you yesterday and what happened to your hand there?"

Al turned in his chair to see him. He seemed irritated. "Wasn't where you're trying to say I was."

Tom jumped back in. "Her parents say you both weren't talking. You two were fighting?"

"Nope."

"You guys were together for over a year, and you're tellin' me you didn't check in with each other every day?"

"Wasn't that kind of relationship."

"Wasn't that kind of relationship? What's that supposed to mean?"

"It's self-explanatory. We would talk every few days."

"You got a girl on the side?"

"No."

"You go fag?"

"What?!"

Tom leaned in, trying to put the pressure on. "You got a drop-dead gorgeous girl on your arm and you hardly saw her. You say you weren't fucking around with some skirt on the side, so what's the deal?"

"We just had our differences."

"So you guys were broken up?"

"No."

Frank chimed in. "So you guys were on the outs then?"

"Not exactly."

"She was seeing other people then?" Tom asked.

Al nearly jumped out of his chair. "Look, I don't have to talk to you. Someone has fucking *murdered* the girl I love and all you can do is point fingers at me? Why don't you talk to MaryAnn? She hung out with her more than anyone, going to those fucking discothèques."

"Look, no one's pointing fingers," Tom said, annoyed. "We're just trying to run down all the angles."

"Then why don't you fuzz lay off me and go find the son of a bitch who fucking killed Ari and leave me the fuck alone? Dig it?"

Tom looked up at Frank as if to say it was his turn up at bat. He'd gotten annoyed at the kid's dodging and wanted to wrap this up. Frank walked over to Al's chair, swiveled it around, and carefully took the water glass out of the boy's hand. He leaned in until their noses touched and kept his voice barely above a whisper.

"That's what we're trying to do here, dig? So work with us and let us in on what the deal is, and we can move on and leave you the fuck alone, okay? 'Cause right now, this hard little attitude you're copping ain't impressing anyone, understand? I don't know if you're tryin' to be tough to impress us or what, but yesterday my goddaughter was murdered. I watched that girl grow up, gave her presents at Christmas, and played in the pool with her during the summer. She was like my second daughter. As of right now," Frank pointed a finger in his face, "you are the number one suspect, so until you level with us, you're gonna be the son of a bitch I'm gonna focus all my rage and aggression on." He paused briefly for affect. "Dig it?"

There was a long silence. The boy fought back his emotions. Their needling had made a crack. Al finally let loose. "My father's illiterate. I was working at his garage, helping him keep up the books for his landscaping business. I've been having to take a lot of time off lately 'cause of that. His regular accountant, an older Jewish guy named Leonard Kaplan, dropped dead of a heart attack a month ago. I was helping my dad fix a lawnmower engine yesterday when *this* happened." He pointed to his bandaged hand. "Sliced it on the inside of the blade."

The two detectives glanced at each other, then Tom asked, "Anyone else other than your father present there to see you?"

Al broke eye contact with Frank and looked up at Tom. "Marvin and Glenn, two of my dad's employees."

"What about Arianna?" Frank asked. "Anyone new she been hangin' with?"

This looked to be a touchy subject for Al. "She was out with MaryAnn all the time."

Frank added an air of sympathy to his tone. "C'mon, why weren't you two talkin'?"

Al debated a moment what answer he should give but apparently decided to lay it all on the table. "She was tellin' me she was too young and wanted to live her life and not be committed. Honestly, I think she is seeing somebody else. She and her friends kept going out to party at the discos. I hate those places. And she's changed. Ya know? She doesn't want anything to do with me anymore. Really closed herself off. Doesn't wanna be close to me or even let me kiss her or anything like that anymore in the past couple of weeks. My friends kept telling me I should drop her 'cause she was..." Al looked uncomfortable and leaned in toward Frank, his voice changing to a whisper, "…'cause she was a prude. You know? We haven't even done it yet. Which is fine by me 'cause she wanted to keep the moment special, but something changed about a month ago. Makes me think she is maybe two-timing me. You know? And I love her."

Frank looked away as if he empathized with him and put his hand on the boy's shoulder. "Okay." He grabbed the glass Al had used off the table and stood up.

They exited the factory and crossed the parking lot. A handful of helicopters came into view behind them and one took off as another approached and landed.

Frank tossed the water out of the glass, retrieved an evidence bag from his pocket, and carefully put the glass in. "Get in touch with Dad's business to see if his alibi jives."

Tom adjusted his butterfly collar from the wind of the choppers leaving. "I'll get Graham on it. You believe him?"

"I think I do. He referred to her several times in the present tense, like a lot of next-of-kin dealing with a sudden loss. Not in the past tense, as someone who actually perpetrated the crime might. And if we take the parking attendant at his word, that cut on Al is on the wrong hand. His was on the left, and he also had no bruising or anything on his hands and knuckles. Take that sample of handwriting you got from his boss and give it to the lab to check against the note. Give this," Frank handed him the glass in the evidence bag, "to them too and see if any of his prints match up with the ones we got. I doubt they're gonna match up to the ones on that zippo or letter we found, though." Frank stood by the car before getting in. "No signs of a sexual assault yet. Any signs of prior sexual abuse?"

"I'll inquire with the M.E."

Frank opened the car door. "It's interesting that he said she closed off from him because that's how she was acting with her folks too. As if something did happen to her."

♠ ♠ ♠

3 p.m.

In a daze, Frank stared up at the drop ceiling of his office. He'd been nodding off all afternoon. He reckoned he'd need something to put him to sleep tonight again. He gazed intently at the millions of holes in the ceiling tile, picking out faces like one would do while lying on a hillside looking up at clouds. This new station had been built some years ago, and even though he'd complained incessantly about the previous ancient building, he missed the old place. His eyes started to close but he forced them open again. This new concrete-and-steel structure they called headquarters was tailored after the trend for the modernist designs he'd seen culminate in the past years, especially around here. Now he felt like he was in *Logan's Run*, and he had New Haven and its leaders to thank for that.

Darkness. His eyes were closed. Someone in an adjoining office slammed a phone down and it snapped him back to reality.

Frank jumped up to pin the autopsy and crime scene photos on a large bulletin board. He stepped back to take in the whole board, studying the series of photos and his notes. He glanced over the evidence that was on Arianna's person: necklace with skate keys, and shoes, and the keys with Tigger, her cigarettes, and handbag all found in the car, all of which were in separate bags. He concentrated hard to see if anything popped out at him, before sitting back down. He studied the collage. Something wasn't right. In his gut he knew something was up there. Before long, his arm was being used to keep his head supported and his feet were up on the corner of the desk. Maybe he should nip out now for something to help get him through the afternoon, some sauce. No, that was crazy.

No, no, no. You're not a kid anymore. You need to fight the bug.

His eyelids were heavy. It felt like trying to keep the Titanic from dropping under the waves of the Atlantic, never to be seen again, except in a Clive Cussler novel.

Ha, Clive Cussler. *You need to stay awake.* Frank loved Clive Cussler. *Iceberg,* great novel. *Keep those eyes open.*

His lids were so heavy. He was going again…heading toward the darkness.

Right on for the Darkness, as Curtis would say. *Why fight it?*

Before he knew it, he was gone…

Frank heard the noise of a crowd in the eternal blackness. What was he remembering? *Holding a crowd back*? A hostile crowd, yes. Was he at a crime scene? Were these crime-scene gawkers?

No, these were the wails of excitement, joy, and youth.

Youth.

These were fans.

It was the noise of Frank opening the handle to a large car door. He remembered positioning himself against a pressing mob of spectators, blocking them from the limo door that was propped open. He was bodyguarding again, back before the Sullivan Detective Agency had been hired to do that work for the band.

Jim Morrison, along with a television host and a small film crew, jumped into the back of the car, followed by Frank, who slammed the door shut behind them. The limo quickly pulled away and a couple of the people from the huge crowd tried to run after it. The interviewer was a local television celebrity, a husky man in a trendy jacket and fancy haircut, complete with a vampire cape. He crossed his legs and went right in as if he was the singer's best friend.

"So where do you see yourself and The Doors in, say, a year, and how do you like being called a celebrity?"

"Well, we're kinda off playing concerts..." Morrison looked out the window deep in thought. "No one enjoys the big places anymore, so we may take a break from touring for a while. The band has projects they'd like to do more independently, you know." He glanced over at Frank, who kept an eye down the block on the crowd they'd just evaded and on the upcoming streets.

"As for your second question, I despise the fame aspect. I'm just an artist, trying to create. Who knows if I'm a very good one? That's what fellas like you like to do, judge. I just want to contribute. I'm actually working on a film right now called *Highway,* spelled H-W-Y. Have you heard of it? It was featured at various festivals, Toronto and the like. Getting good reviews so far. That's what I'd like to get back to, my filmmaking."

The interviewer stared at his notes and didn't really pay attention to the last part of the singer's response, too busy searching for his next question. "I have not seen it."

This isn't real. Morrison is dead. Is it a memory?

The interviewer finally looked up from his notes. "Do you have any predictions for where you can see music or the music industry going in the coming years?"

"Well, I think you have to look back to look forward," Morrison said. "For example, I think the two basic types of music that are indigenous to this country are black music—

blues or jazz—and the folk music that was brought over from Europe, I guess they call it country music, or the West Virginia High & Lonesome sound. Those are two mainstream root American music styles. There might be others, but ten years ago what they called Rock & Roll was a blending of those two forms. I guess, in four or five years, the new generation's music will have a synthesis of those two elements and some third thing, maybe it might rely heavily on electronics. I can kind of envision one person with a lot of machines, tapes, electronic setups, singing or speaking using machines."

All sound suddenly stopped. He was no longer in the back of a limo.

Was he asleep again? Was he dreaming? He must have been. *Jim was dead.*

Frank was alone on an empty city street on a foggy and overcast night. He swung his head around, but not a soul was within sight. Only the isolated downward spotlights from antique lampposts that appeared to have been converted from the gas-fueled original installations made the empty street visible. The area was reminiscent of the old condemned Oak Street neighborhood, with its wooden and decaying row houses, interspaced with ancient walkup apartment buildings. These structures once housed ground-floor mom-and-pop businesses that had long-since gone belly up, and now, the entire area seemed abandoned from any kind of residents. Everything was bathed in a thick, heavy fog that had drifted off the Sound, making visibility exceptionally poor, like some antiquated London street on a studio backlot.

Wait, this is the Oak Street neighborhood.

He could have sworn this neighborhood had already been torn down years ago. Frank looked around him, but only found a loud silence.

Yes, I must be dreaming. Of course, this is a dream.

He glanced down and spotted a little girl standing beside him. She looked up at Frank with affection and held out her hand. He took it and the young girl smiled blissfully. They started down the sidewalk. He recognized the girl but couldn't place her.

Why don't I remember her name?

Frank was wearing a bulletproof vest with a large gold policemen's star embroidered across the front. It was extremely shiny, and the reflection of the streetlights made the little girl squint when looking up at him.

They continued down the block and rounded the corner. Out of the pea soup fog, they came across a crowd lingering on a street corner. They all were disheveled, like they were wearing rags that were once great gowns and suits. The crowd staggered around in a daze. Frank instinctively grasped the child's hand tighter, and when he looked down, he recognized her as his daughter, Katy.

KATY. My God, why have I forgotten her name? Why couldn't I place her face?

Almost on cue, the crowd turned toward Frank and his daughter. Instantly, the detective recognized them. They were the victims of all the murders he'd investigated, rotting corpses staring back at him with black, empty sockets where their eyes used to be. The ghouls staggered around as Frank looked from face to face, taking everyone in. He knew them all intimately: Antwon Silver, the five-year-old who was used as a punching bag by his dad and as an ashtray by his mother, who couldn't take the abuse any longer and died while being scalded alive in a bathtub; Mitchell Livingston, all-star at Hill House High School until he got mixed up with the wrong crowd and overdosed in a hazing; Margaret Brewer, eighty-seven years young, didn't look a day over seventy the night she was taken, grandmother of ten, local good Samaritan until a gang of kids took advantage of her good nature and mugged her as she returned home from church, hitting her head repeatedly on the pavement just to get the six dollars in her pocket; Clarence Washington, drug dealer and local hood who decided to play James Cagney and shoot it out with the police; Henry Davis, a fifteen-year-old who was knifed by his classmates because he took a stand to their bullying; Josephine Edwards and her toddler little Jacob, whose father put him in the oven to stop him from crying and whose mother couldn't deal with her child's death so she leaped off West Rock one foggy night. Those were only the ones out front. So many others behind those faces, scores and scores, while some were just too far gone to even make a visual ID.

The little girl led the way, even though Frank tried to aim her in another direction. They gravitated toward the crowd. The more he tried to change direction, the closer they got.

The girl looked up at him and said, "*Daddy, Mommy wouldn't stop staring at me. I called and called for you, but you never came to help me.*"

He looked down and tried to make sense out of her comment.

An accident?

He was certain he'd heard it before but couldn't place it.

And then, all at once, the entire brood in unison noticed them and headed toward Frank and his daughter. It overwhelmed him. He stopped in his tracks and didn't know what to do. He instinctively went for his gun, but it wasn't there, his hand painfully slapping the leather of his empty shoulder holster. He didn't wear his gun under his arm.

Should I apologize for what's happened to them? Or try to reason with them?

Before he could figure out what should be done, they lunged at the little girl, stealing his daughter away from his grip.

"Katy!" he shouted. *Katy*!" It was no use, she disappeared into the crowd. He pushed his way into the mob, past the decaying and the dead, trying to find his little girl. He pushed away Mrs. Martha Evans, who'd been killed on Chapel Street from a hit-and-run his first month on the job, and Dwight Robinson, whose jaw he guessed they never bothered to fix at the funeral home because it still hung off what was left of his head after he'd decide to go out with two barrels of steel and was only found a week later when he began stinking up his sixth-floor walk-up.

Frank stopped dead in his tracks.

It is a dream. Wake up. Wake up. Wake up!

The crowd parted and standing in front of him was Arianna Wallace. Her putrid, rotting carcass bloated from the buildup of gases and body fluids that desperately wanted out of their prison. She stared right into his eyes and the sight horrified him. He staggered back, bumping into the victims behind, shocked speechless. She glared at him with an accusatory look on her face and threw up her finger, pointing. It gutted him to the core.

"I-I...Arianna, I'm so sorry." She raised her hand and put it across his eyes.

When he wiped the hand away, he was alone again.

Katy was gone, and he stood alone in the middle of a snowy field. The peaceful location mixed with the soothing sounds of the blowing winter wind provided a deceptive feeling of serenity, probably the same kind of peace that people felt before they drifted off into a soundless sleep and froze to death. He knew this location well: the wooded base of East Rock. Far off, he heard the instrumental version of *Snowfall* playing somewhere.

Wake up. Wake up. WAKE UP!

His head and body jolted around, searching for where everyone had gone. He was now in the midst of a winter snowfall. It was a late afternoon, the shadows were long, and the sky was turning everything a dusky blue color. Frank whipped his head around to get his bearings, trying to remember *this* place. The falling snow made him feel trapped inside a large snow globe.

He was at the park at the base of East Rock below Farnam Drive. Frantic CB traffic in the distance caught his trained ears. He jerked his head around and caught the bright red flashing lights of emergency vehicles.

Wake up. WAKE. UP. WAKE UP!

First responders arrived on the other side of the park near the batting cage. Frank ran at full speed toward the site, his dress shoes slipping on the wet, snowy grass. He ran as fast as he could, his breathing becoming very heavy, and before he knew it, he slipped and fell onto the frozen ground.

He looked up and realized it was a motor vehicle accident.

The accident…

A crowd of people were gathered around, and one pointed over at him. Among them were Tom McHugh and Chris Wallace. Frank got to his feet as the group turned their attention and started toward him, scared and worried, trying to prevent Frank from getting any further toward… the accident.

NOOOOOOOOOOOO!

The clock in Frank's bedroom read 3:30 a.m. It flipped to 3:31 as he unintentionally let out a sob. Lying in his bed crying hysterically, his fist in his mouth to muffle the noise, Frank tried with all his might not to utter a sound. The occasional moan found its way out of his mouth and he curled up tighter in a ball. His eyes were bloodshot, and he only felt disgust and loathing for himself, to have his feelings betray him like this. He'd left the station house that late afternoon and went straight to a liquor store to get a bottle just to feed the *bug*. He'd blacked out not long after. None of it worked. He'd drunk a whole bottle to go to bed, just so he wouldn't have these dreams. These memories his mind once again betrayed him with, even though he'd fed it the precious drink. Now he questioned if it was the booze bringing these memories back to him after all.

"It's okay, baby. It's okay." he heard his wife Audrey say quietly and calmly to him.

"I'm sorry, baby. I've tried to forget it all. I'm so sorry."

He felt her touch stroke his forehead. "Shhhh. Go to sleep, my darling, it will all be okay," she said soothingly. Feeling her next to him while he was in this state only made him feel worse. That made Frank's sorrow cut that much deeper.

He lay there for probably an hour in the darkness, sobbing uncontrollably. He hated himself.

THURSDAY

October 16, 1976

FRANK WAS ON his way to meet Tom but first wanted to swing over to the Wallaces' house to see how they were holding up, and also see if he could discover any new information. Perhaps they'd thought of something that could be useful to their investigation.

Frank had been up quite early. He had to shower and shave, so he wouldn't smell like a brewery. He also used the time to cook a pan of lasagna to take to the Wallaces so he wouldn't go over empty-handed. He baked his mother's old recipe and took it in a foil-wrapped casserole dish, which was still piping hot when he knocked on their front door.

Rhonda answered and let him into the unusually-quiet house.

The kids were sleeping over at friends' houses, which was probably a good idea to take their minds off everything. Chris was nowhere in sight. They went into the kitchen and Rhonda took the lasagna. Frank could tell she was still shell-shocked, like a zombie out of an old Val Lewton movie. He'd seen it a hundred times before. Trauma occurring this severely was hard for anyone to deal with, to have to bury a child. Parents weren't supposed to outlive their kids.

Rhonda placed the food onto the stove. "Chris and I can have this for lunch," she said pleasantly.

The silence in the room was unbearable. They locked eyes, and through her bloodshot daze, she was distant. He didn't know what to say or how to broach the subject. How many times had she already heard a condolence? Added the fact that *he* was the one who broke the news to her? She seemed to snap out of it, realizing where she was, and rolled her eyes in embarrassment.

"Oh, I'm so sorry," Rhonda started. "Thank you so much for the food. It means a lot. And I want to apologize for how I reacted the other day when you told us about—"

"Rhonda, please. No apology necessary. Forget about that. You did nothing wrong." He wagged his finger playfully. "I want you to have some of this lasagna later. It's Mama's old recipe she got from her mama back from the old country. It'll put some meat on your bones."

Rhonda smiled and went in for a hug. "Thank you, Frank, for all you've done for us. Thank you for being such a good friend…to all of us."

They embraced, and he gave her a firm, tight hug. They stood together there for a long moment, and when the moment was over, Frank held on to her a little longer because she seemed to not want to let go either.

It was then that she broke down in his arms, sobbing uncontrollably and losing all her strength. Frank had to hold her up, so she wouldn't fall. They stood there in the cold and lonely kitchen, Frank doing his best to hold himself together and be strong for her. It took everything inside of him to keep his composure. He felt like that was his job, his duty. To stay strong for them.

Frank found Chris in his bedroom sitting on the bed staring at the wall. Frank knocked on the half-open door and Chris whipped his head around.

"Hey, Frank."

Frank opened the door all the way and cautiously stepped into the room. "Hey, Chris. Just wanted to come over and see if you needed anything."

"Naw," Chris said after a moment. "We're good."

"Would you like help with anything? Anything around the house need doing?"

"No, everything around here can wait."

Frank waited a few seconds, then changed the subject. "Chris, I know this is a very tough time, but I need to ask you some questions I'd rather not speak to Rhonda about, and the quicker we get past them, the quicker we might get a break in finding whoever did this."

Chris didn't reply, only slowly turned his head away back toward where he'd originally been gazing and nodded slowly once.

"Do you have any idea who could have done this to her?"

Chris sluggishly shook his head. "Ari and I ended up g-g-getting into it after her party Monday night. Rhonda found a fake ID before she was going out, and we just…we were worried about her."

"You found a fake ID of hers?"

"Yes. We knew where that would lead and…" Chris broke off, staring again toward the wall. Tears came to his eyes.

"Where is that ID now?"

"Rhonda ripped it up and threw it out Monday night." Tears began to fall, and he looked toward Frank, for the first time making eye contact. Chris looked like he'd aged twenty years in two days. "That was the last time I talked to her. Can you believe that? The last time I-I-I talked with her, we were arguing, and I was yelling at her." He put his hand up to his eyes to wipe his tears. Frank took a step forward.

Chris took the hand away from his eyes and once again looked back at the wall. Frank peeked over to where Chris was looking and saw on the large mirror connected to the nightstand, pushed under the frame, a picture of Arianna and her father, laughing together at Christmas. Chris just stared forward, lost again in his own thoughts.

Edgewood Park was a beautiful place where Frank used to play as a boy, and it always held fond memories for him. He would play down by the pond with his friends, most of whom were now either dead or in jail or, as in Dennis Jakobowski's case, MIA in 'Nam. The park had succumbed to a lot of what the public areas were beginning to endure, a brew of decay and crime (mostly at night, thank God), lightly salted with a fair amount of neglect. Yet it still attracted families during the day, ones like Frank's, who himself had brought his daughter here on occasion. It was a place remembered as being safe and comforting. Kids played on the grass and atop a large, strange-looking cement fountain that had been erected in the middle of the park. One could only guess that it was some modern art sculpture tied into New Haven's new image or possibly even donated by Yale. Benches encircled it, while in the background a huge playground could be seen. Frank thought the swing sets could be as old as him, but add a new art sculpture and the park had been deemed re-envisioned. Mothers pushed strollers and talked, while other families supervised their children playing around the huge lump of concrete.

Frank and Tom finished putting condiments on the hot-dogs they'd gotten from their favorite vendor, Uncle Oz, a legend going back to Oak Street days, who sold dogs for twenty-two years on the same corner until he was forced to move for the sake of "urban progress."

Frank bit into his boiled Hummel frankfurter while Tom started the workday by getting straight to business.

"Coroner concluded that there were no signs of sexual assault, but she wasn't a virgin."

Frank swallowed what was in his mouth. "Her boyfriend told us she was saving herself for the right time." The implication that Arianna was not a virgin really opened the spectrum to everything from abuse or assault, to her actually losing it willingly to another fella she was hanging out with.

"The prints on the zippo don't match Arianna's or Blake's, but we knew that. It does match a partial thumb print on the parking ticket stub." Frank used his free hand to count the points on his fingers. "We got a guy who she seems to be comfortable with, evidenced by the multiple cigarette butts outside on the ground, which brings us to the fact that she was sitting shotgun in her own car."

"This is almost Iceberg Slim-level tactics here. So the perp wanted a place out of the way to talk and—"

"And he wanted control of the car, so she couldn't go anywhere or..."

"Or, they were going someplace?"

"Maybe he wanted something from her and she didn't have it on her person."

"Could be why we think the perp was watching her beforehand. We can rule Albert out 'cause his alibi has been verified. He was at his dad's landscaping garage on Waters Street."

"Did he have access to a vehicle? Could he have left and come back?" Frank thought out loud. "Waters Street is only a two-minute drive from the Chapel Street Garage."

Tom took another bite of his dog, relishing the taste. "I'll look into it. You wanna know what I think?"

"Sock it to me, Charlie Chan," Frank said with a half grin.

"Bottom line, she was seeing somebody else. Had to be. Same guy that she did it with? Maybe the relationship went bad? She was breaking up with him. He's a bit controlling, maybe?"

"All seems plausible. Bottom line, something was wrong with her. I even caught wind of it the night before she passed. She was closed off to everyone and partying more and more. Her dad told me they found a fake ID of hers, which makes you think what?"

"She's going to clubs."

"Yep."

"They still have the fake ID?"

"No," Frank said with disappointment. "I mean, she was contemplating her own mortality in a conversation we'd had together. Hell, you're not supposed to do that until your thirties, not when you're sixteen."

Tom finished his dog, wiped his mouth, and looked over at his partner. "Sounds like she maybe was doing drugs, when you say hanging out with different people and partying, plus the club scene. We should see if a toxicology report was ordered by the M.E. and see what that says. Find out if anything legal or illegal was in her system."

That was definitely something Frank did not want to think about, his goddaughter at sixteen already pushed into a life like that. "Let's chat with her best friend MaryAnn Decan again. She may have some insight into her sudden mood change." Frank glanced toward the children playing over by the fountain. Watching the kids play in their insulated world made his mind wander to happier days. He didn't know it at the time, but a slight smirk came across his mouth, revealing his inner thoughts.

"You drinking again, Frank?"

Tom's candor took him by surprise. He didn't immediately look back, betraying his astonishment, but purposefully stayed focused on the children playing and kept his demeanor the same. "No, not really," he replied. "Just haven't been able to fall asleep these past few nights, so been having a nightcap. Take the edge off, so to speak."

Tom didn't acknowledge his answer, which could go either way. Frank knew the young detective was concerned and knew his history, but the last thing he needed right now was a lecture from his protégé. He was glad Tom did not reply, but it did put a worrying idea in his mind about the issues he'd so long ago been able to compartmentalize and forget, especially if they were now beginning to resurface and become more transparent.

Arianna's body lay in a beautiful pine coffin with accenting brass handles and an elegant lace interior. Her hands were positioned together at the waist and her face still held its beauty, looking as though she was only asleep. The difference was the excessive amount of makeup that was common among morticians' work, betraying the fact she was no longer alive, and looked *too* overdone and made-up.

At the base of the coffin, a large collage of pictures had been collected on a framed board for visitors to be able to view and remember happier times.

Mrs. Scala, the Wallaces' elderly neighbor, knelt by the coffin and said a quiet prayer. The viewing line started by the collage and went around the room into the next, out into the hall, and was so long people had actually started to queue outside in the funeral home's driveway. A pair of old women patiently waited for their turn to pay their respects and used the time to review each photo in the montage, pointing at one or another to show the other and share a memory.

Out in the hallway, Arianna's thirteen-year-old brother Tyrell excused himself through the line of people, so he could make his way into the adjoining smoking room. The area was only accessible from the parlor by three steps that led down into the smoke-filled room. An aging Italian woman put out her cigarette in the two-foot high ashtray and made her way over to Tyrell to give her condolences. After conferring with her, someone caught the boy's eye.

He crossed the room to the corner where Frank sat alone smoking, staring down between his legs at the floor. Even though he'd shaved in the morning, he now looked scruffy. It took a moment before Frank looked up at Tyrell and realized who it was. He snapped out of it and immediately moved over to let the boy sit down. Tyrell took out a pack of cigarettes and removed one. Frank looked at him in surprise but figured this was not the time to lecture the young boy.

"I didn't know you smoked," he said lamely.

"Neither does my dad," Tyrell said, slightly embarrassed. "He'd kill me."

"Well it's no good for you. 'Course, I'm probably not the first one to tell you that."

"You got a light?"

Frank gave him his zippo. The boy lit up and handed the lighter back. Frank looked across the crowded, smoky room and saw Albert Fisher on the other side. The two made eye contact and Frank nodded. Al looked away, took a last drag, put out his cigarette, and exited the room.

Next to where he sat, Frank recognized Arianna's best friend, MaryAnn Decan, who was taking the last drags from her smoke. She looked up at him and he smiled politely.

Frank glanced back to Tyrell, who appeared distant. He'd seen that look before. Hell, part of his job was to deal with people who were suffering a significant loss. He had a thought and started to chuckle.

"What's so funny?" Tyrell asked.

Frank took a drag and leaned in. "I remember when you were real friggin' little," he said, purposely changing the subject. "I showed you this trick one time where I made a quarter disappear and then made it reappear in my hand. You loved it. Then you followed me around the whole day asking for me to make your Tonka dump truck disappear and I couldn't do that. You got so mad at me."

Tyrell laughed. "I don't remember that."

"Yeah, you were mad. You didn't talk to me the rest of the day."

Tom walked into the foggy room and his eyes found MaryAnn. He looked over to his partner and Frank nodded to him. "I don't understand these things," Tyrell said. "Why have all this in the first place? How's this help Arianna?"

Frank was trying to be cautious and choose his words carefully. "In my experience, it's for the relatives and other people to help them deal with the loss of someone."

"By getting people into a room who you either never liked, or you see once a year?"

"Being surrounded by friends helps one to temporarily get their minds off the sadness, gives you support, even if it's for just a few moments at a time. Try looking at it that way.

See the happiness in it all and take in as much as you can, because eventually, everyone leaves and gets on with their lives, and you're alone once again with your own memories, and that hole inside of you that the loss has carved out of you. So try to treasure this time with everyone around while you can, so you can remember it later on."

The priest made an announcement for people to find a seat, so the small ceremony could commence. All at once, the smokers started to get up and leave the foggy room to find a chair in the viewing area.

"Come on, we'll talk more later."

"Okay, Uncle Frank."

While everyone moved into the other room, Tom took the time to introduce himself to MaryAnn and started up a conversation.

The two detectives offered to give MaryAnn a ride home by way of something to eat. This way they could easily fit in the 'questions' they wanted to ask, and at the same time, not give her the feeling she was being taken downtown to be interrogated.

Frank had always had an affinity for Chuck's Steakhouse on the Post Road, not because of the food or environment, but because he'd passed it so many times and it just looked so darn curious over the years. More importantly, he'd heard it had a really good jukebox.

So far, all his expectations were satisfied. It had the seaside catch-of-the-day/mariner feel, and the The Mills Brothers with Count Basie's version of *Sunny* blared out of the restaurant's ceiling speakers, even more bonus points in

Frank's book. He chuckled at the scene of he and Tom seated on one side of the table with MaryAnn on the other, looking very much like an episode of *Dragnet*. All they needed to do was the patented Jack Webb/Harry Morgan nods to each other and they'd be set. MaryAnn sipped on her glass of Coke while waiting for their appetizers to arrive. Frank felt that she wanted something a little stronger but was afraid to ask. Honestly, he could go for the same thing.

Tom broke the uncomfortable silence and started the conversation, which was okay with Frank. Tom usually had a way with the ladies, especially the younger ones, perhaps because he looked young enough to be their peer. It helped to build a confidence with the detective, something he sometimes used for not-the-most-noble of purposes.

"So how have ya been holding up, MaryAnn? You alright?"

MaryAnn did not look up from her glass. "I'm livin'."

Frank didn't like her demeanor. "How are your friends taking it?" he asked.

When she started to reply, the waitress came over delivering chips, salsa, and mozzarella sticks to the table.

"I guess okay. We're just trying not to think about it."

Tom waited until the waitress left the table before diving right into where they wanted the conversation to go. "MaryAnn, was there anyone you can think of that mighta wanted to harm Arianna?"

"No," she replied with an air of underlying sarcasm that made the two wonder about the statement's sincerity.

"You sure?" Frank pressed.

"I don't know." She seemed irritated at this line of questioning, which did not sit right with them. Why would she be uncomfortable?

"Was she may be seeing anyone new?" Tom probed. "Like a new boyfriend or someone? Or made friends with anyone new?"

That struck a chord with MaryAnn. She looked up at Tom. "Well…" As soon as she let the word out, she apparently changed her mind. "No, not really."

"What were you going to say, MaryAnn?" Frank asked.

"Oh, nothing. And no, no new friends that I can think of." She nervously tore at her paper placemat and did not touch any of the appetizers, then unconsciously started gently tapping the table with her nails.

Frank took his eyes off her and had a mozzarella stick. "Where'd you all like to hang out? How was the scene downtown?"

She remained silent. The song had changed and now Frank spotted Paul William's *A Little Bit of Love* quietly filling out the room, accented by the faint clinging of silverware on ceramic plates.

"We know she had a fake ID, MaryAnn, and to be honest, we don't really care about any of that. Our sole purpose here is to get whoever did this." Frank chewed, swallowed, and went on. "If she had a fake ID, five-gets-you-ten that you do as well. Like I said, we don't care about that. We just want to get to the bottom of this," Frank finished.

MaryAnn looked back and forth between the two detectives. She visibly relaxed, as though she no longer felt she was being put on the spot. "We used to go to discos. Studio 71, we hung out there a lot, and The Neuter Rooster on Hamilton Street. We know a lot of people there, made friends with all the waiters. Tons of places around the Green. Toad's Place. Um..."

The waitress was back in no time, excusing herself and setting dinner plates in front of Frank and MaryAnn. She took a bottle of A1 steak sauce out of her apron pocket and set it on the table. "I'll be right back with yours." she politely informed Tom.

"Thank you." Tom folded his hands together on the table, mustered the gentlest voice he could, and asked, "Was Arianna drinking or experimenting with anything heavier?"

MaryAnn reacted to the question but did not immediately answer, cutting her blood-rare steak.

Frank wanted to look at his partner to confirm what they both saw, but also not give anything away. "Honey, you're just talking to us. We aren't gonna tell anyone what you say or get mad at you. Our only concern is finding out who did this to Arianna."

"She wasn't doing any drugs. She was drinking, yeah, but everyone drinks." MaryAnn hesitated, as if she were debating to herself if she should volunteer anything further. "Um, do we have that thing that lawyers have when we talk? I mean, you won't tell my parents or anybody what we talk about?"

This was the breakthrough they'd been looking for. Perhaps she would unravel the whole story right here and give them the clue they need to crack this case wide open. Only Frank didn't want to sound too excited. "Honey, yes, it's just us talking right now, no one else."

"Well, there was this guy. Lamb."

"Lamb?" Frank repeated to make sure he heard correctly.

"Here you go," the waitress said, placing Tom's plate in front of him, completely ruining the moment. They both patiently waited as she handed out steak knives to the detectives, then retreated back to her server station.

Tom attempted to pick up right where she left off. "What were you saying about this guy Lamb?" He took out his little notebook and made a notation in it, something MaryAnn was not at all comfortable with.

"I—nothing. It was nothing."

Frank put his hand across the table and pushed Tom's pad away. "Please, MaryAnn. If there's anything you can tell us, just to point us in the right direction..."

She looked down and played with her food, seeming to debate with herself on how to proceed.

"Please, MaryAnn," Frank pleaded. "Arianna was your best friend."

"How do you know I can help you find them, anyway?"

"*Them*?" Tom echoed, surprised.

MaryAnn's face turned red. "What?"

"You said *them*. What makes you think there was more than one person involved?" Frank asked.

"I-I don't know. You guys are confusing me. I just meant whoever did this, you know."

Frank and Tom glanced at each other, actually pulling a Jack Webb and Harry Morgan, realizing what they both understood.

"MaryAnn," said Tom, "if you think this Lamb has anything to do with Arianna's murder, you need to tell us."

"No, he's just someone Ari introduced me to. Nevermind."

Although frustrated, the detectives didn't want to lean on her too hard, especially under the circumstances, because they were not technically doing an official interrogation.

MaryAnn looked at the two of them. "Well, if I were you guys, I'd check out a kid named Phil Pinckney. Works as a busboy across the way from us in the mall. He was crazy about Arianna. Obsessed. He used to call her all the time from the restaurant. It drove her crazy."

"Phil Pinckney? Thank you, we'll check him out."

MaryAnn stared out the window, drifting away. Frank did not like what that meant. Without looking up from his food, he tried another tactic.

"Let me ask you a question then, if I could?"

She turned to him. "Okay."

"You know anyone who just recently sliced open his right hand or arm?"

MaryAnn's eyes betrayed her, unconsciously widening before immediately composing herself. "Nope, w-why? Should I?"

Frank forced a polite smile. "Just thought I'd ask, is all."

Frank was in deep thought after they dropped MaryAnn off and returned from the Savin Rock area of West Haven where she lived. Savin Rock was a beautiful turn-of-the-century Victorian amusement park with all the newest, cutting-edge rides and attractions. Into the Depression and after the war, it wasn't maintained properly, and as the crime rate soared, people lost interest. It became run down. The surrounding areas where huge mansions were erected on the shores of Long Island Sound by the rich turn-of-the-century aristocrats were now torn down and condominium developments built instead, and 'The Rock' as they called it, went belly up and finally closed some ten years ago. Fragments still littered the West Haven coast, amusement park skeletons that stood as a reminder of a bygone era of innocence.

Frank sat shotgun while Tom drove on I-95, passing the Long Wharf strip area by New Haven harbor. The Delfonics' *Hey Love* filled the car with soothing, heavenly harmony. The moon was full and bright, reflecting shimmers of light off the water of the Sound. Across the harbor, the lighthouse on Morris Cove shined bright into the night sky.

Frank stared across the water for a long time before he finally spoke. "We need to get her to tell us more about that Lamb cat. I was worried to press it there. But she knows more than she wants to let on."

"What about that Phil Pinckney name she gave us?"

"It's definitely worth a check. I recall that name on the list of employees working that day at the restaurant. I gotta check our notes. It's interesting that she fed us that when we probed about Lamb. Let's bypass the pleasantries and get her down to the station tomorrow."

"You notice how MaryAnn didn't reference Albert having a hurt hand?"

"Maybe she doesn't know he had it, or—"

"Or she's covering for him. That little shit told us he didn't smoke, and there he is tonight, puffing away at Triple 5's. We gotta get her downtown asap," Frank huffed.

"Can't go that hard on her, you know. We need to ride that thin line. We don't want her introverting."

Hey Love ended and the DJ seamlessly transitioned to Les Paul and Mary Ford's *It's a Lonesome Old Town*.

"Well, that was the reasoning behind our dinner date. We need to find out who that Lamb is, if he is, in fact, anyone and what she meant by *them*."

Frank was irked. It wasn't a random attack, it was someone Arianna knew. He could feel it in his gut. Someone she knew quite well, he ventured, evidenced by the overkill and the possible sexual implications.

He reached over and turned down Les Paul on the dial on his pocket radio to stress the seriousness of what he was about to say.

"The other day I was approached by that Councilman Theodore Pregosin and probably one of the wealthiest men in New Haven who heads the Urban Coalition, sits on a board at Yale and about a dozen of fucking things, about our investigation into the East Rock homicide," he said.

Tom let this sink in. "Where?" It was more of a statement of astonishment than a formal question.

"At my house, rather early in the morning. They just showed up."

"What did they want?"

"Worried about the exposure the case was getting and the negative attention it was giving East Rock Mountain Park. I guess they don't want the public to hear any of the normal everyday stuff that we have to deal with like robbery or murder affecting the areas where they're trying to have people come spend money."

"They offer you a bribe or something?"

"No, nothing like that. Just politely told me with their fake sneers that it's my ass if this hurts the city's image. They want us to put the case on the backburner so as not to grab too much of the public's attention. And this was before yesterday's new murder case."

Frank watched Tom out of the corner of his eye to see his reaction.

"Assholes. Well, I hope we crack this Temple Street garage case wide open, so we can smear all that yolk over those pretentious bastards' faces."

That made Frank smile. He knew he had a good partner, someone that thought like himself and someone he could trust, but hearing that just reaffirmed everything. Tom caught Frank's smirk and couldn't help but chuckle himself, for the situation seemed instantly comical.

Frank watched the streetlamps fly past in the rearview mirror and then jockeyed the radio to another station he liked. He settled on the Beatles, an acoustic version of *While My Guitar Gently Weeps.* It seemed appropriate, for it suddenly reminded him of the ugly task he had before him tomorrow.

The two said nothing for the rest of their journey back to the station. Little did they know, they were dreading the same thing.

THE FUNERAL

Friday, October 17, 1976

IT WAS A gray day and it had been drizzling on and off all morning. The detectives parked in the horseshoe driveway in front of the entrance to the funeral home. All the businesses on the street inhabited large, lavishly-built, converted single-family homes that were about a century old. After their wealthy aristocratic families died off, the homes were either donated to Yale (who had the income to keep them up, for the most part) or the interior would be cut up like a defeated faraway country after a war and turned into three-family homes or offices, or as in this case, converted into a gigantic funeral home.

They exited the car dressed in matching black suits. Frank glanced around, his eyes concealed by dark sunglasses. It took a moment, but he finally pushed himself to enter the funeral home. Tom stayed outside under the awning, ready to move the car.

Frank was greeted by an employee and led down to the last room where Arianna lay in repose. He approached the doorway hesitantly due to the eerie vibe these places inherently gave off.

He stuck his head into the viewing room and saw the other pallbearers standing near the door. On the far side of the room, the Wallace family was positioned by the casket. They took turns saying a prayer by the coffin, and then it was closed and locked. Rhonda Wallace could barely walk on her own. Chris acted as a crutch, stabilizing his wife. Frank and the other pallbearers got the cue from the funeral director, proceeded to the coffin, and moved it out into the hall, with the family following.

"The lord is my shepherd, I shall not want. He leads me to lie down in green pastures. He leads me beside the still waters..."

The group followed the casket out of the funeral home, where it was carefully placed into the waiting hearse. Everyone took their predetermined places in each limo and the convoy started off. It snaked its way across town at a snail's pace, going through red lights while other cars patiently waited, the occupants eager to catch a glimpse of the mourners inside the procession.

"He restores my soul. He leads me in the paths of the righteousness of His names' sake..."

The convoy finally made it to St. Michael's church next to Wooster Square, about a block east from Frank's brownstone. The pallbearers exited the limo and hurried over to the black Mariah which held the coffin and slowly, but ever so gently, pulled it out. After getting it on their shoulders, the men, followed by the Wallace family and the other mourners, took Arianna's body into the church.

The family sat together in the first row. Rhonda wiped smeared eyeliner and tears from her eyes with a tissue, while Chris sat stone faced and solemn, completely devoid of emotion. Frank and the other pallbearers were seated in the adjoining front row in front of the casket. The church was filled to capacity, with Tom barely able to get a seat in the middle section.

"Yea, though I walk through the valley of the shadow of death, I will fear no evil; for you are with me; your rod and your staff, they comfort me. You prepare a table before me in the presence of my enemies; you anoint my head with oil; my cup runs over..."

It was raining again by the time they arrived at the cemetery. The pallbearers carried the casket up a small slope to a covered area where the plot was located. The coffin was placed on the ropes over the hole. After the others entered, the priest said his final words over the grave.

"*Surely goodness and mercy will follow me all the days of my life; and I will dwell in the house of the Lord forever.*"

Starting with the immediate family, roses were placed on top of the casket.

"*For God so loved the world that He gave His only begotten Son, that whoever believes in Him should not perish but have everlasting life...*"

Frank stood alone thinking for longer than he should have. He regarded the vast garden of stones, mausoleums, and obelisks. He used the moment to reflect. He came here more than he cared to. It brought back memories he didn't want to revisit. Life had become too surreal and fast for him all of a sudden, and he needed to slow it down. Just crawl away and hide from it all.

He followed the last trickle of exiting mourners back to the cemetery road and found Tom, who was waiting by their Dodge Monaco undercover unit.

The detectives crossed back into New Haven. The rain had stopped, and the sun was finally breaking through the clouds. Stevie Wonder and Jeff Beck's *Lookin' for Another*

Pure Love played on Frank's small FM transistor radio, while the CB crackled faintly in the background, giving out information.

They traveled east over the Boulevard, on their way back to the Chapel Square Mall to speak with the busboy MaryAnn had suggested. Entering into the lower Legion Avenue area, they passed the surrounding neighborhoods that had been bulldozed to make room for the city's projects, large blocks of land still empty and barren. Huge, aging billboards every few blocks advertised the slogans "Build America Better," "Action on Slums," and "Better America, Inc.," promises that the construction was to bring to the area. Under the phrases were artist's renditions of what the community buildings and businesses would look like completed, with both white and black couples enjoying the new modern, urban, trendy neighborhoods to come.

Under the erected marquees, Frank watched people going about their business just the same, even though the blocks were leveled. People still had to get from one part of town to another. The biggest affront for most was that these neighborhoods had been bulldozed, then never built upon. People were pushed out, their homes erased, then the land sat unused. The empty lots still stood as a stark reminder, like a forgotten battlefield after a war. They passed a group of children playing in a trash-strewn fenced-in lot, stumbling through the ankle-high grass.

Frank stared out of the window in silence, taking it all in. He'd been getting more distant these past few days and, as much as he tried, he could not stop the feeling inside. The drink didn't help, and he'd once swore to himself and his family he would never touch it again, but now he was aware of a breaking point he thought he'd never come to again.

Boy, he could use a drink.

"MaryAnn didn't attend the funeral," he said to Tom.

Tom didn't look over as he responded, keeping his eyes on the road. "Yeah, saw that. Weird huh, not attending your best friend's funeral?"

Frank was wary. Something felt wrong. Why this hadn't occurred to him prior could be anyone's guess. The drink was starting to cloud his thoughts again maybe, taking his idle mind away from the case. "It don't feel right. We better get a line on her quick."

An announcement came over their radio that sparked their interest.

"*Detective Seventy-One. Detective Seventy-One. Do you copy?*"

Frank picked up the transmitter and responded. "This is Detective Seventy-One, come back."

"*Detective Seventy-One, we've got Detective Eighty-Four with an update for you.*"

"Alright, patch them through."

"*Skipper.*" They both recognized Spinall's voice.

"Yeah, Joe?"

"*Frank we got a tip that our person of interest. Irving Skippermeyer was positively IDed at his address. Me and Randy are heading over there now.*"

"Copy that, Joe. What's the address?"

"*113 Scranton Street.*"

"Roger that. Tom and I are right near there. We'll meet you there, by the market on the corner."

"*Copy that, Skipper. See you there. Over and out.*"

"Detective Seventy-One, over and out."

Frank replaced the transmitter back on the Motorola radio. Spinall and Jurgens had had someone sitting on the house since the East Rock double shooting. They had been unable to locate the victim's ex-boyfriend, like he'd dropped off the radar some time ago. Supposedly, he'd neither returned to the V.A. nor his mother's home, potentially going off his meds in the process. Fingers pointed to him, and now they had an identification sighting at his mother's house. Tom put the turn signal on and headed left toward Scranton Street.

Frank looked at the barren landscape around them, the complete destruction. A feeling of disgust washed over him; an emotion he'd never felt before until now, when he thought about the whole Urban Renewal Project. The thought of New Haven's pretentious 'Model City' image made him sick.

The dark side of urban renewal and what no one liked to discuss was that, to get community organizers in urban areas around the country to go along with all of these proposed programs, growth coalitions agreed for these neighborhoods to be leveled, *only* with the caveat that new public housing was to be included in the planning to relocate the displaced populations. It was agreed that fifty percent of "slum housing" cleared in cities would be returned to "predominantly residential use."

This number was eventually dwindled down significantly as the years went on, which was why it got the name "the federal bulldozer" by detractors, the *"ghettoization of Black America"* and "*the great Negro Removal*" by its critics, sowing the seed for deep-rooted problems within these affected communities that would probably remain well into the twenty-first century. Entire neighborhoods were leveled, and its predominantly black and ethnic populations displaced. Other areas around the downtown that were not yet rundown, but areas that *could* "potentially become slums" in the future if they were not included in the local renewal programs, were erased.

The new housing that was built in place was, in some cases, cheap, substandard units, consolidating everyone into one area or another. Referred to as "the projects" in New Haven, or in huge high-rise buildings that were built in the many boroughs of New York City or Chicago, where thousands were cramped together, and where no work or opportunity for employment could possibly be found for the thousands of prospective workers. Heck, they were writing sitcoms on network television about it, like *Good Times.*

By 1974, it was estimated that between twenty to thirty thousand people of New Haven—one fifth of its population—was displaced due to the revitalization plan that started in 1954. Frank read some scholars already speculating that it was having the opposite effect than intended, because it unintentionally destroyed all the civic and governmental programs put into place to help these newcomers to the big city assimilate into indigenous neighborhoods. According to crime stats, it might even make it *easier* for street gangs to get a better foothold within the newly constructed skyscrapers and housing projects, because it was a lot easier without fences, walls, or gates.

It was all now coming to a head for Frank. All this bullshit bureaucratic malarkey that played with people's very lives was one of the reasons frustrated communities sometimes took their anger out on the closet thing that represented the governmental oppression, on the man present on the street that directly represented all this bullshit to the public, the police officer.

"Frank, I've noticed a change with you the past couple of days. You don't seem to be sleeping..." Tom hesitated, trying to choose the right words and not offend his partner but still properly convey his feelings. "This case is so close and personal for you. Please try not to take this case home with you."

Tom didn't know Frank in the bad part of his life, and he'd hid his drinking at the time the best he could from his coworkers on the force. Spinall and Jurgens who were with him then had never called him out on it either.

"Too late for that, my friend," he replied. "They all end up getting to you over time. If they didn't, I'd think there was something wrong with me upstairs."

Tom wanted to challenge him, try to show him, in fact, that may not always be the case. Before he could figure out the right way to say it, Frank spoke again.

"You know, I remember coming down here with my pop to Legion Avenue here." He smiled to himself. "Galucci's Grocery, Caparossi's Meat Market, and the Jewish delis down here." His smile faded. "Now look. Entire neighborhoods gone, and for what? To make some new luxury skyrise apartments? Already yesterday's news. Or an Interstate Connector that wasn't needed? What they won't tell you either was how they thought this also could work as a convenient barrier, a wall between Yale and the brand-new downtown, between all those new low-income projects and housing developments they were supposedly putting up on the South Side. Just in case we have any more neighborhoods riot like in '67, they'd have a brand-new artery to be able to pipe the National Guard in with if the world exploded again."

Tom took a breath. "I don't look at it like that, Frank. These renewal projects are happening across the country. Trying to update people's living conditions and neighborhoods they're forced to live in. You know as well as I do, some of those neighborhoods had degenerated into dilapidated, rotting shells. Some of those wooden rows of housing were over a hundred years old. Some didn't even have indoor plumbing. I mean, to have someone living in a modern city, in those conditions?"

Frank didn't entirely disagree with Tom.

"I also never heard anything as acting as a wedge between parts of the city. I just think it's for the best, so New Haven doesn't die and rot, like what's happening to Bridgeport or Waterbury." Tom shook his head. "It's got to happen at some point to better the community. Progress. They're delivering much-needed new schools as well, in certain areas. I never heard of anything about a barrier going on."

"Agreed. I just don't think it necessitated wiping an entire section of town off the map, coming in here like it was Robert Moses carving through the Bronx. These were mom-and-pop businesses and people's homes. Yeah, some were outdated, but just as many weren't. It's all that people had. Instead of fixing what elements that needed fixing, they just level everything? Stuff that isn't even a ghetto yet, but just *might* turn into one down the road in who knows how long? I mean, look around you." Frank gestured to the barren land around them covered in high grass, "They tore all this down ten, fifteen years ago and haven't done *anything* with this land past Yale University and the hospital. All they've done is put a parking lot on part of the land purchased to be part of the connector project."

There was a silence for a long moment, then Frank sighed.

"I hope you're right, Tom. I just don't see how demolishing entire neighborhoods, erasing their culture and displacing people, without any plan to where those citizens will relocate, can be a positive contribution to the city and its communities, whatever color they may be."

"They really designed the connector so they can deploy troops quicker in case of more riots?" Tom asked.

Frank cracked a smile and nodded.

"And what about the pale people?"

"Pale people?"

"My people. The Irish."

"Oh, they're especially fucked."

Tom grinned.

They pulled up on Scranton Street in front of a small corner bodega. They exited the car to grab a caffeine fix at Sansone's Market while they waited for the other officers to arrive.

They eyed the address in question across the street from them. It looked to be a once-beautiful three-story Victorian home that long ago had been converted into a multi-family, with a sagging front portico that ran the length of the house. The entire aging residence was covered in a deep two-tone green and yellow, which was in a state of decomposition, the old paint cracking and peeling right off the entire home.

Now that the sun had crept out, it brought with it children who played on a lawn across the street and neighbors were tending to their yardwork. Meanwhile, Frank had piqued Tom's interest.

"Any other urban planning secrets you know about?"

"For New Haven, specifically?"

"Anything."

"Every two miles of an interstate, there is a mile of perfectly-straight highway."

Tom thought of the significance as they walked up to the entrance to Sansone's. Next to the large front window of the store that had been painted over white, stood an ice machine, and leaning against it was a couple with a child in a stroller who were debating where they wanted to end up by the end of the afternoon. They entered the store.

Tom still was wrapping his head around Frank's 'secret knowledge.'

"So where's the secrecy in a mile of perfectly-straight highway?" Tom asked as they both went to the back of the store where the coolers were located. Frank poured some black coffee into a Styrofoam cup while Tom reached into the cooler and retrieved a Foxon Park Soda.

Frank carefully finished pouring out his cup of Joe before he answered. "That's so in case of any kind of disaster they can land aircraft in the area. Cold War stuff."

Tom's eyes widened. Frank thought that was common knowledge, but apparently it wasn't.

"No shit?" Tom said under his breath in wonderment.

When they reached the front counter to pay, a young, very attractive Hispanic mother stood with her young daughter getting cash out to pay the cashier. Frank eyed the two over and a smile came to his face. The child whispered something to the young woman. She nodded and then handed the little girl a dollar. She quickly turned to her mom.

"Mommy, can I please get them?" The mother nodded, and the child quickly grabbed a bag of M&M's and put them on the counter. "Me and my daddy love eating chocolate after supper," she said to the cashier.

Frank smiled at the mother, who looked at him in embarrassment. Tom chuckled at the little girl's innocent comment.

"She loves M&Ms," the woman said.

Tom nodded. "Yeah, my daughter is the same with popcorn."

They finished paying and the mother and daughter exited the store. Frank and Tom paid and headed out as well.

Frank had always loved this little corner market; it had been here ever since he could remember. Luckily, it was spared from demolition, just two blocks from the bulldozing zones.

On the way back toward the car, Frank thought to himself how lovely a day this was starting to be. He listened to the neighborhood ambience of lawnmowers buzzing, children playing, and the overall hum of the world around him. Life really did go on. One person's day of mourning was another's day of bliss.

Spinall and Jurgens rolled up in their undercover unit behind Frank and Tom's Dodge. They exited, and the four detectives convened for a pow wow.

"We rolled a black-and-white over to have uniforms make the initial contact," Randy explained.

"We figure we'll do everything by the book and even have them make contact," Spinall added. "Just to play it safe."

"This guy's supposed to be a loose cannon, right?" Frank asked.

"Yeah," Randy answered. "And the V.A. hasn't seen him for close to a month, so we're working with the idea he may not be on his meds."

"We know what kind?"

"Antipsychotics," Spinall chimed in. "Everyone we spoke to related to the East Rock shooting, and everyone that dabbles in the 'lifestyle,' says he's off his rocker since 'Nam and should be considered dangerous."

"Dangerous?" Tom echoed.

"Hence the radio car support," Randy said as they spied a black-and-white turn the corner and creep up to where they were. Out came their rookie friend McCurdy from East Rock, along with another officer. They walked over to the small group of plainclothes in front of Sansone's.

Frank recognized the young officer. "Good day to you, Officer." He turned to Tom. "You remember McCurdy from the other day on East Rock?" Tom nodded. "How's pounding the arches been since we last saw you? Sick of all these mopes yet?" Frank smirked.

"No sir. Enjoying it, actually."

"Good. Well, we'll be putting you to use today." Frank glanced over at McCurdy's partner. "Alright, Sage. What's your first name?"

"Matthew, sir. We worked together on the Salvatore and Lucci case, when I was just starting out."

"Yes, I thought I recognized you. That was a rough one. Good to see you again. Okay, you both are on point. We're looking for a person of interest, name of Irving Skippermeyer, in connection with our East Rock shooting."

Frank finished briefing the uniformed officers and the group headed across the street. Spinall stayed close to Frank, smoking a Marlboro.

"We got a tipoff from his mother that he was home," Joe said. "She sounded scared, said he was yelling and rambling and wouldn't answer her to where he's been for the past couple weeks."

Frank nodded, his mind half in the game and the other half wrapped up in Arianna's case. "Peachy," he replied.

They strolled up the sidewalk that led to the front porch. Joe and Randy lingered on the front step while Tom, Frank, and the two officers climbed up the creaky steps and walked across the rickety porch. The front door was one of the older, narrow double doors that had a pane of textured glass in each, which was supposed to prevent seeing inside. Both windows had curtains on the inside, which were drawn. The curtains had a yellow tint that might have been from years and years of cigarette smoke.

"Use caution, fellas."

Frank looked the porch up and down, his eyes passing over what used to be the metal skeleton of a love seat and a rain-soaked, mildew-stained carpet that had been rolled up, deposited there and forgotten-about long ago. He put his back to the house, looking out into the street. The Hispanic mother and daughter were still in front of the bodega, the mother on one knee trying to help her child adjust the zipper on her jacket. Tom stepped over to have a closer look at the rotting metal skeleton as McCurdy gave a knock on the door.

"Skipper," Joe said to get Frank's attention. "Skipper..."

Frank looked down to Joe, who stood next to Randy with one foot on the first step of the porch. Spinall flicked his Marlboro to the sidewalk and motioned with his hand to the two officers. McCurdy stood dead center in front of the door. A big no-no as a policeman. Randy rolled his eyes at Joe's littering. Joe picked up on the cue and started to kick the cigarette with his heel toward the yellow grass. McCurdy knocked again, a little louder this time.

"Police."

Frank sighed. "Fellas, I don't know what they're teaching you at the academy these days," he said to the uniformed officers, "but you certainly don't knock on the door of a person of interest of a violent crime with your body center-mass, square in front of their door. Understand?"

They heard movement inside, as if someone was slowly making their way toward the door.

Officer Sage moved toward Frank, away from Officer McCurdy and the doorway. On the other side of the door, the floorboards creaked, indicating someone was on the other side.

"C'mon, police, open up." McCurdy said again.

"Did you hear me, Officer McCurdy?" Frank asked.

An ear-piercing thunder made everyone flinch and jump a foot off the ground.

The close-range buckshot from a twelve-gauge double-barrel shotgun cut right through the wooden door and glass window like they were cardboard, landing a perfect hit on McCurdy's upper body. The impact kicked the young officer clear off the porch, over the heads of Spinall and Jurgens, and onto the sidewalk immediately behind them.

"Ronny!" Sage said, instinctively lunging for his partner. Frank missed grabbing the boy's belt. Just as the officer was in sight of the doorway, the other barrel was discharged, catching him in the back and propelling him down the stairs to where his partner lay.

Frank and Tom threw themselves up against the wooden siding of the house, their bodies like wooden soldiers at attention.

A deafening, jackhammer-like sound pierced the air, a reciprocating noise that was all too familiar to the detectives, a sound that was the last thing Frank thought he would hear today: automatic gunfire.

Tom's Foxon Park soda shattered across the street on the curb from a ricochet. Holes randomly appeared in threes on the front façade of the house as forty-five caliber projectiles exploded out of the residence, sending splinters and chards of wood throughout the portico, turning the front siding into Swiss cheese. Frank and Tom simultaneously leap-frogged over the wooden porch railing, bullets tearing through Tom's Burberry coat that flapped up in the wind. They hit the grassless front yard with a thud. Joe and Randy were dragging the uniformed officers toward the street. Frank and Tom drew their weapons from their holsters and fired toward the front door, laying down cover fire so Joe and Randy could get the wounded off the line. In seconds, they were all across the street. Jurgens and Spinall made it behind their car with the wounded officers, Frank and Tom fired the last rounds out of their weapons, rolled around their Monaco, and squatted as low as they could, reloading their guns. The automatic gunfire had stopped from across the street.

Frank knew that burst of gunfire *anywhere.* This was 1976, and that sound wasn't a new weapon like Eugene Stoner's M-16 or even a fancy high-tech Kalashnikov; it was ancient, primal. Only one gun in the world made that pistol-pounding sound, something that was originally conceived to swipe the trenches clean of soldiers in World War I, nick-named a 'Chicago Typewriter' by the gangsters of the Roaring Twenties. It was a Thompson submachine gun, another of Connecticut's many firearm exports manufactured by the Auto Ordinance Company out of Bridgeport. Oh Jesus.

Frank and Tom immediately determined neither was harmed, but in shock. After what felt like an eternity but was only five seconds since the burst of rounds, they started to hear a banging sound, a cracking of wood and glass. Frank carefully poked his head up over the door of the car and looked through the windows across the street to see where the gunfire had originated.

A black man was kicking the remaining bits of the double doors out of the way and walked out onto the porch wearing a military style trench coat and carrying a stockless Thompson and a sawed-off double-barrel shotgun. The weapons were strapped to either shoulder with what appeared to be clothesline twine. The children playing tag on the lawn next door to this house were frozen with terror like little statues, not processing what they were seeing.

Frank glanced over to the other undercover unit and could tell by the expression on Officer McCurdy's face that he was dead. Blood poured like an open faucet out of his ears and nose, his head arched back, his eyes in appalling shock, staring up to the sky. Parts of his body still even jerked about in convulsed movements due to neurological damage. His fingers clenched the air in tight spasm.

Frank fired off several rounds that hit center-mass on the assailant, emptying his gun.

The gunman raised his Thompson and the exposed side of the Dodge Monaco behind which the detectives were hiding exploded. Shattered glass and debris showered over the two, making them retreat behind the vehicle's wheel wells. The assailant began targeting the pedestrians that were left out in the open. He crossed out into the street and stopped right in the middle, obtaining a vantage point over the entire block in either direction.

The children next door finally dashed toward their backyard, just as their front lawn exploded with impacts of red-hot metal. Tom peered over the trunk of the car and unloaded his automatic at the gunman, hitting him several times in the back with no affect. The militant spun around and unloaded the rest of his clip at the Monaco, sending projectiles tearing through the aluminum body, leaving exit holes the size of apples within inches of both men.

The street grew silent as both the gunman and police reloaded their weapons.

"You've come to take me away! I'm not going back there!" the gunman cried out in a convoluted panic.

Tom knocked the butt of his gun on the side of the car, to get Frank's attention. "We gotta get a Signal 4 out on the air." Frank knew a Signal 4 call, an officer down/needs assistance call, would get the entire force there in minutes. He cautiously poked his head over the driver's side door to look into the cabin of the Monaco. The radio, along with the dashboard and much of the interior, was trashed, and the CB was smoking.

"Radio's had it," Frank announced.

"Fuck," Tom spat. "Rand!" he yelled over. Spinall was desperately trying to stem the bleeding on Officer Sage while Jurgens reloaded. He looked over to Tom, who pointed inside their undercover unit. "Get a Signal 4 out over the air!"

Tom unloaded his second to last clip of his .45 automatic and hit the gunman again in the back. The man jerked and spun around. "I come home from the jungles of Hell just to get spit on and be called a traitor? A faggot, even! I'm the queer?"

Frank fired his revolver twice, again hitting center mass in the chest. He saw no blood, only explosions of cotton, the impacts only making him stumble back. The gunman let the shotgun fall to his side, then reloaded another drum clip, clicked back the Thompson's breach, and began to unload onto their Dodge once more.

"Tom, he's got a vest on!"

Battery acid and antifreeze shot out of the front of the car, making Frank retreat toward the back, closer to Tom. Both front tires popped. Another ten seconds of continuous fire and the Thompson's slide kicked back empty, and then came the delayed echo of the shell casings ejecting and clanging onto the asphalt.

"He's wearing a bulletproof vest."

"I kinda figured that," Tom growled in frustration, "Fucking swell."

The drum clip clanked to the ground and another clip was put in. The Thompson started its terrifying wail in another direction. A scream came from across the street as someone else was hit. They could hear sirens now, marking the distance in their journey toward the havoc. At the top of the street, a black-and-white police car flew around the corner about one hundred yards from the gunman while people ran for cover around the neighborhood. The assailant spotted the cruiser and whirled in that direction. He clicked back the breach to clear a jam, raised the machine gun toward the incoming prowl car, and pulled the trigger, and the barrel lit up like a fireworks display. Simultaneously, the windshield of the black-and-white spidered, and the hood sprayed metal and steam like little volcanoes erupting. The car jumped the curb and screeched to a stop on a front lawn a few houses down.

Other traffic cops arrived on the scene. The gunman's attention was diverted to them, spraying hot lead in all directions. The machine gun again emptied, and the man let it fall to his side, grabbing the double barrel that hung to his left. Buckshot from an officer's shotgun hit part of his face and arm, though it seemed to have little effect. All the while, he continued his rant.

"You can't take away my home from me, goddamn it! I fought for this country!" The gunman took out an army-issue 1911 Colt .45 from his waist and opened fire on whatever moved.

Randy and Joe were empty. Frank crouched by the fender and took aim on the gunman's head but was distracted by loud screaming.

He glanced over to his left and saw the little girl from the store standing motionless over her mother, who'd been struck in the neck. Blood shot out of her jugular like water from a drinking fountain, coinciding with her heartbeat, all over her daughter's feet and the ground. The woman squirmed on the pavement, vainly trying to apply pressure to her own mortal wound.

Frank's eyes widened in horror, his attention now focused on the two.

The gunman was beginning to lose interest in the traffic cops and spotted the little girl. "You crackers already took my world away! Why not take everything?"

"Thomas! Covering fire!"

Frank dashed toward the child as he and Tom opened fire on the man. The assailant returned fire on Frank with his machine gun. Sansone's storefront behind them exploded with a rain of glass, cement, and mortar. The ice machine shattered with a thunderous crash and icy steam from the Freon shot up into the air. Frank snatched up the child and rolled behind an adjacent orange VW bus. The mother was hit again, grazed in the leg. Frank quickly placed the girl behind the front tire of the VW and locked eyes with her. "Don't move, baby. Everything's gonna be alright." He kissed her forehead.

Frank focused his attention on the wounded woman and the gunman. He attempted to leap out and grab her but as soon he tried the area exploded with fire, forcing him back behind the VW's back tire.

He tried again and was still prevented.

Frank let out a barely audible scream of rage and frustration that was muffled by the Thompson's staccato automation.

Frank reloaded his weapon with his last three rounds and realized he couldn't run out and tend to the gravely wounded mother. Tom's gun was out of ammo and he could do nothing. Beyond Tom, behind the next car, Randy was screaming on the radio while Spinall performed CPR on Officer Sage.

Frank focused back on the gunman and edged out to get a peek. The gunman lowered the Thompson in one hand, turned around, and took aim with the .45 at Randy and Joe's car. He shot slowly and methodically, trying to hit the tops of their heads that sometimes rose behind the car. The repeated impacts from the various police projectiles were finally taking a toll on the assailant's stamina, as he bled now from multiple wounds.

This is it. The End, my friend.

"Hey!" Frank exclaimed as loud as his hoarse voice would allow. The man turned. Frank stood up, walked out from behind the VW, and started toward him, his gun raised.

"Frank! Don't!" Tom shrieked at the top of his lungs. The gunman fired the .45 at Frank, the projectiles embedding into the aluminum of the VW behind him with different rhythmic echoes. When the Colt's slide locked back empty, and only then, did Frank aim his .357. The man dropped the 1911 and raised the Thompson in his other hand.

Without breaking his stride, Frank fired his last three shots. The bullets entered the front of the gunman's head and the back of his cranium exploded. It took a minute for his body to realize as he staggered and gasped, then he fell to the ground like a ragdoll. The Thompson still in his hand, let out a final quick burst due to a muscle spasm.

Silence echoed through the afternoon air, like God muted the scene. It was surreal. Frank couldn't hear a thing, not even ambient everyday noise. All sound was gone.

Tom stared in disbelief, horrified at Frank's actions.

Gradually, the sounds of the day came back again: a siren, a child far off crying, then a woman screaming, and finally Joe counting the compressions he was performing on the young officer. Frank lowered his gun and glanced over at the little girl, who he realized had watched what he'd just done. He held eye contact with her. He remembered her mother and rushed over.

Tom was already at the woman's side, applying pressure to her neck. Nearly all of her blood looked to have been pumped out at this point, staining the pavement a dark, almost black color that became a deep red once disturbed. In a matter of seconds, whatever remained was literally all over the two detectives as they attempted to save her. An unsettling gurgling escaped the mother's mouth when she tried to speak, as if she was drowning in her own blood. Frank grabbed her hand to comfort her. "Shhhhhh," he said. He didn't bother to lie and say everything was going to be alright. Frank and the woman locked eyes. Her gorgeous, now ghostly pale, face showed signs of confusion. Her eyes were dilated and glazed, and the spots of dark red blood on her face stood out as if they were freckles on a white wall.

She started to convulse and then exhaled a loud, tired sigh from deep within, and stopped moving. The muscles in her face relaxed and she fell still, her eyes still locked on Frank.

Tom checked her pulse, looked up to Frank, and confirmed the worst.

The little girl ran toward her mother, but Tom caught the child before she reached the body and scooped her into his arms. Frank shut the dead woman's eyelids, took a few seconds, and then stood up, took off his jacket, and placed it over her head.

Bewildered, he took in the carnage around him. An ambulance pulled up and started to tend to the wounded. Joe and Randy carried Officer Sage onto a stretcher and helped load him in as another ambulance arrived. Frank walked back out into the street where the gunman lay dead. Another victim from across the street was put onto a stretcher and stabilized before they attempted to move them. Frank helped Joe and Randy shut the back doors of the ambulance that held Officer Sage.

Its siren turned on and it sped off, leaving Frank covered in blood in a world of confusion and death, the vehicle getting smaller and smaller as the distance increased between him and the ambulance. The sound faded with it, and only an eerie ringing stayed audible in his mind.

Frank made it to Rudy's bar where the funeral reception was being held. It had degenerated into a long drinking session for family and friends, inevitably progressing into the evening. Everyone was still in their suits except Frank, who'd changed because he didn't want to scare anyone and arrive covered in someone else's dried blood. He'd been stuck at the scene all day, trying to get everything under control. He was debriefed by Lieutenant Warner and had a lot of paperwork ahead of him. Upon making entry into the shooter's residence, they found newspaper clippings plastered all over the walls of his small room, about Vietnam, New Haven's Urban Renewal, the recent shooting up at East Rock, a map circling various night spots that were quite popular on the city scene, and pictures of male models and male Hollywood stars in various stages of undress or completely nude. Connecting all these pictures, articles, and the map of downtown were various hand-drawn lines and barely-legible scribbles in what appeared to be hot-red lipstick. Very perplexing to say the least, especially since the suspect supposedly hadn't been at the residence for weeks.

Frank snuck away when the lab and photography guys asked to have the room cleared so they could to get started.

He sat alone in the bar, though at the same long wooden table as the Wallace family. He drank heavily, a beer and a shot with another two on order, and was lost in the bottom of his glass, staring with no real interest at all the names that had been carved into the bar's wood benches and panels by decades of Yalies going back to 1934 when the place was established.

Across the bar, sat a rather drunk elderly man who was trying to get the attention of the small, scattered crowd. "Seamus is gonna play," he slurred. "Everyone, let's hear Seamus play..."

Another older man whose face was flush-red from the drink, Seamus, looked like he'd just walked off an Irish country lane in his red checkered button-down shirt and gray cardigan. Everyone turned to him as he prepared his fiddle. He tested the bow against the strings, then began a passionate, sorrowful version of *Nearer My God to Thee*. The entire bar fell silent, stopping their conversations to listen, taking in every tearful note.

Frank stared off into space, his face blank. Chris Wallace, his arm around his grief-stricken wife, looked over to his friend, and only then realized that Frank was drinking alcohol. He made this observation but decided to say nothing. It wasn't the place or the time.

Frank had only just gotten back from the rear of the bar where he'd collapsed into a booth and phoned his old friend and sponsor, Vincent Channing. The conversation kept replaying over and over in his head, Frank second-guessing every answer he'd made to Vince. He politely tried yet again to make another excuse about why he couldn't meet up at Lime Rock tomorrow as planned and race. He knew by the silence on the line that Vince saw right through the excuses. Vince didn't live under a rock and had certainly seen the reports of Arianna's murder in the Temple Street garage and, without even beating around the bush, flat-out asked if Frank had been drinking, which Frank vehemently denied. He hadn't even thought about his answer before it escaped his mouth and he immediately felt his face getting cherry red. It was the feeling of shame, lying through his teeth to his friend, mentor, and sponsor. He felt despicable. He felt worthless. He was being deceitful and didn't even mean to be. Vince could only do so much without Frank asking for help. But his silence on the other end said volumes of what went unspoken.

"There anything you want to talk about, Frank?" the old man (as he liked to call him) asked on the other end of the line. Everything in Frank told him to speak up and level with Vince. Every inch of his being said to say something before it was too late. That was how they bonded; the old man helping Frank through some of his darkest days. He was possibly the only one, even including Frank's wife, to whom he could speak honestly about his drinking and the job.

Tell him the dreams are back.

The visions. The hauntings. The memories…

Tell him!

"Naw, Vince, I'm okay," he lied. "Sorry to let you down again." He heard the contention on the other end of the line by the old man's exhale of air, as if he were fed up. They said their polite pleasantries and that was the end of it. Frank would get back to him when he was ready. That was the lie Frank used to get himself off the phone. He hung up, devastated. Later, when he walked back to the table, he felt the unnerving suspicion that this might have been his last talk with Vince. His friend had tried all he could, and Frank had boxed him out. So it was on Frank, not Vince. He'd lied to one of his best friends, but most importantly, he'd lied to himself.

The scene replayed over and over in his mind. Better that than having the afternoon's events go round and round in his head, he supposed.

Why didn't you listen to me the first time, McCurdy? Why didn't you get out of the way? That poor woman who looked so much like his sweet Audrey.

Frank found the energy to wander over to the bar and order another drink, then found his way back to where the Wallaces were sitting. He didn't care who saw him drinking at this point. After burying his goddaughter this morning and then being a major player in a shootout on a public street where a civilian *and* one of New Haven's finest were killed, while others were critical? My God.

He sat there, starting to get drowsy. The day, the exhaustion, and now the drink, were catching up to him. He needed to stay awake.

The music faded. He was nodding off.

No, no. Stay awake!

His eyes shot open. Everyone was clapping. Seamus was maybe playing another song on his fiddle? Frank didn't know.

He started to fade again…slowly. He felt himself going… going…

That was it. He was gone, lost inside the world of his head. Held captive in the mansion of his mind, haunted by the demons that hid within.

It was a winter's day as he could remember it. The falling snow masked everything like the inside of a snow globe. He remembered running through the park and not being able to determine what was occurring on the other side, but could feel his distress and could hear it in his hitching breath.

This isn't real. This is your own invention, now.

He heard frantic CB traffic getting increasingly louder as he approached the site. Out of nowhere, he remembered slipping and falling, banging his chin on the frozen ground.

Was that where that scar underneath the chin came from?

He looked up, touched the bottom of his chin, and felt his tightly kept beard to see if he was bleedi—

Wait, I have a beard? When did I last have a…oh no.

A second later, it no longer mattered. The wind shifted behind him, and with it, the heavy snow. It brought with it the drifting noise of his abandoned car, which was still running, driver's door open and its CB radio inside, floating unintelligible chatter on the breeze. Across the field was an accident scene. It looked as though a car had left the road above the park, torn through the woods, down the incline, and wrapped itself around a tree at the far side of the field by the batter's box.

Get out of here. Wake up!

Several police and firemen were already on the scene trying to stabilize the situation. It was their CB radios he heard. Frank felt himself get to his feet, realizing he had no hand in affecting what was happening, only that he was a passive observer within himself. He desperately stumbled toward the commotion.

Several rescuers were now alerted to his presence and ran toward him in an attempt to cut him off, stop him from getting any closer.

WAKE UP!

Young patrolmen Tom McHugh dressed in his uniform and Christopher Wallace in his firefighter gear led the pack to stop him.

"*FRANK!*" Tom shouted.

"*WAIT! DON'T!*" Chris screamed.

Frank awoke lying on his stoop, soaked from a bottle of booze which must have spilled all over him when he passed out.

How had he even gotten home? He had no memory of leaving Rudy's. Had he just walked across town? The blue of the morning sky was approaching. His shoulder and neck hurt terribly from lying on the cement stoop of his brownstone. He picked himself up into a sitting position and found the energy through his mind-numbing headache to stand.

It looked like it might rain, actually, he supposed through the foggy static that was forming inside his head.

SATURDAY

October 18, 1976

9:30 a.m.

IT RAINED ALL day without letting up. Quite a cold rain, bringing along with it a chill in the air that seemed to permeate right into the bones. The sky was as gray as he'd ever seen it, which was fine, because Frank couldn't imagine nursing a hangover like this on a bright, sunny day.

As soon as he'd gotten into work he was ambushed by Mike, his boss. The lieutenant was concerned about the shooting his team was involved in, along with the other high-profile Arianna Wallace case. Mike floated the idea that maybe Frank should remove himself from the Wallace case, particularly in light of the events that occurred yesterday on Scranton Street, resulting in one officer and one civilian killed, another officer clinging to life in the hospital, and several others in various degrees of jury. It perhaps was a good idea for Frank to voluntarily assign himself to desk duty, at least until the full scope of any kind of oversight investigation that would result from yesterday's shooting and death of Officer James T. McCurdy could be fully realized. Frank's immediate reaction was to patently refuse and hammer home the notion that he and his team did everything by the book yesterday, even having a radio car come and make the initial contact, and that his team was very close to breaking the

Wallace case wide open, especially with the lead Arianna's friend MaryAnn Decan had given to him. Instead, Frank said he needed the lieutenant's help within the department to find MaryAnn, and also to get the media and maybe hold a press conference. Frank knew the latter was a losing battle before he even brought up the notion of getting the media to help, but at least it moved the conversation away from Frank withdrawing from the case.

They'd had Graham swing over to speak with the busboy at the Chapel Square Mall, something Frank and Tom originally intended to do before their encounter with Irving Skippermeyer on Scranton Street. The busboy, Phil Pinckney, turned out to be fifteen years old, with the mind of a ten-year-old, who his mother brought everywhere and was literally his constant companion. He was hardly the person, in their opinion, who could be the mastermind behind a murder like this when you added up all the factors like the perceived intimacy between Ari and the perpetrator. Besides, he was actually busing tables at the exact time of the murder and had no injury on either hand.

Frank now found himself standing by his small office window, staring out at New Haven Harbor and East Haven beyond. The colors blended within the same palette, various shades of gray and black. A flash of lightning caught his eye in the clouds above Long Island Sound, accompanied by a crack of thunder. Frank's glare focused down to across the street at the railyard that sat behind Union Station. The massive yard was filled with idling train cars and equipment. A worker in a yellow hard hat carrying a bright orange lantern caught Frank's eye. The man sluggishly walked over the tracks and then pulled a switch to change a signal.

Behind Frank, in the dimly lit office, was the annoying buzz of the fluorescent tubes overhead that didn't actually do anything in the way of providing light, instead only just adding to the pounding in Frank's head. The mobile bulletin board loomed against the wall with the evidence photos and various notes and reports they had compiled to date about the Arianna Wallace case. Tom sat at his old, worn-out desk, which was closest to the door, just finishing up on the phone with his wife. She was distraught about yesterday, and from Frank's end, it sounded like she was at her breaking point with Tom and his job. All policeman had this talk with their significant others, and poor Tom was having his today. Frank tried not to listen, but it sounded like she was crying on the other end of the line and Tom was doing his best to calm her down and reassure her. This kind of life was impossibly hard for a young couple. Hopefully they'd be able to cope, and their marriage would survive.

A uniformed officer walked in and handed Tom a piece of paper. The noise of the receiver being placed back into the cradle snapped Frank out of his deep thoughts. Tom read the memo and glanced over his shoulder to address his partner.

"MaryAnn's parents haven't seen her since two nights ago, and can you believe are only *now* reporting her missing this morning?" Tom rubbed the bridge of his nose to fight off an oncoming headache. "This case is getting very cold, very fast."

Frank leaned against the window, still half-daydreaming about the dreary day, which mirrored his disposition. The fact that he was *just* asking for departmental help with perhaps putting out a BOLO on MaryAnn Decan right before her parents filed a missing persons report, solidified to him that his head was still in the game, and at the moment, that he was still moving in the right direction with this investigation.

"Are we gonna talk about what you did yesterday, almost getting yourself killed by that nut?" Tom asked. "That's not cool at all, Frank."

Frank was glad that none of his team had mentioned that stunt to Mike, or he probably would be relegated to mandatory desk duty by the upper brass, or worse. He turned away from the train yard below, back to his partner.

"This whole thing reminds me of this short story I read as a kid once: *The Signalman*, by Charles Dickens. A writer goes back to his hometown and interviews an old man who is a signalman stationed in this sorta canal."

Tom settled into his creaky wooden chair.

"This canal connects three tunnels. His little shack is between the three and this guy watches over the signals at the mouth of the tunnels. The guy's been doing this all his life and spent his entire existence in this tiny shack, pulling the switches to switch the tracks. The Signalman's got hundreds of books in this little place, 'cause all you could really do for entertainment back then was read, so the guy's pretty well-educated." Frank turned completely around to face Tom, silhouetted against the window. "Well, he tells the reporter that, every night for a week now, at the mouth of the south tunnel, he sees this specter by the signal light, waving its hands and calling to him, like it's attempting to warn about something.

"The reporter tries to justify it by saying it's the wind or the glare caused by passing trains. But the Signalman still stands by what he believes he has seen. So the reporter takes the old man outside to prove it can't be a ghost. The skeptic states that the seven-foot-high signal at the mouth of the South tunnel is so bright you wouldn't be able to see anyone at the base of the light, even if there was someone below it. He then proceeds to walk down to show—"

"Who?"

"The reporter. The reporter proceeds to walk down the fifty yards or so and stand under the signal while the old man watched. The reporter called to the man and waved his hands. The Signalman walked away from the shack onto the tracks to try to see him better. And the reporter was right, the Signalman couldn't see him under the huge signal light."

The room was silent as Frank let the pause in the story breathe a little bit.

Tom was completely engaged. "Well, what happened next?"

Frank turned back toward the window and looked down at the rail yard as he answered, tracking a slow-moving freight passing through the yard. "Out of the northbound side of the tunnel behind the Signalman came the express train, speeding toward him. The reporter saw and tried to warn him, but the Signalman couldn't hear or see him..."

The two were silent for a moment and then Tom said, "Frank, does that story remind you of our case, or of the path you've put yourself on?"

A knock at the door interrupted them, and a young rookie popped his head in. "Got someone who wants to talk to you out here."

Mrs. McGuire still questioned if she was making the right decision to come forward and tell the police what she saw, but since she had only read the article about the murder in the *New Haven Register* earlier in the week and hadn't heard anything about it in the news since, she figured she had to say something. Mrs. McGuire could only dream of the horror the Wallace family must be experiencing with the loss of their daughter. She only wished she could control her two young children a little better as she waited on the police bench, because their acting up was the last thing she needed today.

Frank and Tom were brought over to the mother and she gave her two children one last poke to shut them up.

"Mrs. McGuire? Hi, I'm Lieutenant Detective Sergeant Frank Suchy and this is my partner, Detective Tom McHugh. We heard you had something that could possibly help us?"

She shifted uneasily and shot a final glare at her two children that instantly made them stop fidgeting. "Well, detectives, I was at Macy's the day that poor girl was murdered, and I think I saw the man chasing her." Frank and Tom looked at each other, both trying to contain their excitement before looking back at their potential witness.

"Right this way please, Mrs. McGuire."

They had a sketch artist with her within the hour and retained the services of a young female officer to play the role of babysitter, so Mrs. McGuire could have her complete attention devoted to helping with the composite. Frank waited outside and watched through the open blinds that hung on the inside of the safety-glass-wired window. Tom finished jotting down notes in his little pad and politely excused himself. He exited the office and looked down and read it verbatim to his older partner.

"Our perp was real thin, lanky, and had black hair, kinda pale, mid-to-late twenties. He looked either Italian, Arab, or, quote, 'foreign.'"

"Hmm...could be our Lamb character," Frank replied. "Thoughts?"

Tom nodded. "I think she sounds legit. Shopping at Macy's, comes out with the kids on the exposed upper level of the garage on her way to her station wagon, hears a girl screaming, and sees the chase into the staircase. Most importantly, she confirms Arianna was coming from the passenger side, while the perp was coming from the driver's side."

"Something we didn't release to the general public."

Tom studied his notes and added, "So where does that comment MaryAnn made about '*them*' come into play?" Tom flipped back several pages to go over his notes from Chuck's Steak House and their conversation with Arianna's friend. "Damn, where is that girl? You think she could have given us the slip and is on a train to New York City or something?"

"I can't see why she'd up and leave. Doesn't seem right. Where'd she rabbit to?"

A uniformed officer broke in before Frank could reply. "Detectives, East Haven P.D. called." He handed Frank a teletype.

Frank scanned it and then handed it to Tom with a look of dread.

Just Before Noon

Lighthouse Park at Morris Cove had been around since the city's inception, with its large lighthouse shining the way for ships sailing through Long Island Sound entering New Haven Harbor. Located on the East side of the harbor, it bordered East Haven by Lighthouse Park. New Haven had used Morris Cove as a beach and a public swimming ground for years and called it the East Shore, which Frank always thought sounded too much like something from Long Island.

A couple of hundred yards from the shore was a decaying wooden structure that housed a once-beautiful carousel, which now sat in an almost complete state of disrepair. Only the diligent work of three elderly men who volunteered their time, sweat, and toil kept the glorious carousel operational. But the building that housed it sat rotting, with peeling paint and decaying wooden paneling. Frank did not know how those men could keep that machine running, but they did, and sadly, with the crime rate in the park and lack of public funds, he worried how much longer the city would keep the ride open and not scrap it like so many other great attractions from a forgotten era.

Inside the large wooden hall, a dozen children rode the huge, sixty-one-year-old carousel. A mechanical carnival organ played, as an eerie accompaniment to the three-minute-and-twenty-second ride. Along with an inch of dust coating every inch of the large space, with the exception of those items that retained a dull shine because of daily use, the whole scene appeared somewhat detached from the world. But the kids still came to ride and tried to grab the gold ring as they blissfully rode by it.

Ahead of the ancient carousel within the hall lay an immense abandoned wooden dance floor as wide as the building that enclosed it. It once hosted lavish swing parties and community dances, now forgotten under inches of dirt, dust, and grime. Time could be cruel to outdated things. Around three sides of this dance floor were long plate-glass windows which illuminated the whole hall. Past them outside, the park and beach area beyond were visible with the huge Morris Cove lighthouse in the foreground, overlooking the bay.

It was a beautiful, brisk day, with a strong wind blowing in from the harbor. Flashing lights and people moving to and from the rocky area next to the lighthouse distracted some beachgoers from what was happening by the shoreline. Beyond the lighthouse, several policemen were in the process of closing off the beach area by the rocks, putting up large tarps to shield the area from curious eyes.

Frank and Tom walked over to the roped-off area and were greeted by a uniformed officer. He pointed them in the direction of a waiting East Haven detective. The detective escorted them down to the point.

"We got the call about an hour ago. Some kids playing on the rocks found the body. Thought it was a mannequin when they first saw it. When uniforms arrived, they discovered it was still in your jurisdiction. Amazingly, it had ID on it and a BOLO out as well, which said to contact the investigating detectives."

When they hit the rocks, a female lab technician examining a body came into view. Frank knelt down, and she handed an ID to him. It read, "MaryAnn Decan."

Frank looked down at the face. Though it was difficult to see, due to the bloated, pruned appearance and a very large wound on the head, it was her. Her lips and eyelids were gone; common for a body fished out of the water, after being food for the various ocean scavengers. It just made the confirmation of her identity all the more unsettling.

Frank handed the ID to Tom.

"Fucking shit," Tom uttered.

Frank stared at the body, trying not to let it affect him, but it was becoming too much. He rubbed his forehead to knock out the last of his hangover. "How long would you say she was dead?" he asked the technician.

The technician looked up for the first time and made eye contact with Frank. "Might be too early to tell, but by the liver temp, post-rigor, and how the marine life have had at her, I'd guess the body's been in the Sound for at least forty-eight to seventy-two hours. I'd place the T.O.D. around Wednesday night, or possibly early Thursday morning."

Tom shot Frank a look and leaned in to whisper, "After we spoke with her?"

Frank did not consciously acknowledge the comment. "Too early to speculate on the cause of death?" he questioned the young technician.

She looked down at the body. "Uh, I'd guess massive head trauma."

"If she was strangled or stabbed, *then* dumped into the river and a barge or tanker leaving or coming struck her," Tom said, "could that have caused the same head trauma?"

She looked up at Tom, squinted, and raised a hand to block the sun's glare. "Not unless she was alive at the time. Look at her eyes, telltale signs of eight-ball hemorrhages, massive head trauma." She pointed with her pen to MaryAnn's eyes, which were purple and fogged, her pupils huge, taking up most of each eye. "The eyes cloud like that because the capillaries explode, which also can be caused by strangulation, but no marks here on the neck, see? This wouldn't be present if she'd already been dead when the head injury occurred. Blood was still pumping when the head trauma was inflicted, meaning this was most likely the cause of death, in or out of the water."

Frank nodded. "Yeah. Thank you."

He slowly stood up and walked about thirty feet away along the coast. He breathed out and tried to relax. He couldn't understand why he was feeling the way he did; his nerves felt as if it was his first day in homicide. He hadn't felt like that in ages. He peered down at his hand and it was again twitching. That frightened him. He tried to jiggle it out. His breathing was also more elevated than normal. He took another long breath to calm himself. Boy, he already felt the bug. He wanted a drink.

What sounded like Roy Orbison drifted to his ears from a far distance, barely intelligible, perhaps carried on the salt water breeze. Frank noted it but didn't spend a thought beyond that on where the faint melodies originated or to clarify and confirm to himself if it was even Roy Orbison. His mind needed to focus on other matters.

Tom walked over to him. "Well, we can deduce that she was killed within a few hours of the wake and talking to us. Either she told someone she was with us or someone saw her leave with us. Either way, I think our conversation together might have put this action in motion."

Frank shot Tom a look. It disgusted him to even think that, but he knew his young partner could be right. He adjusted his glare and looked back at the Sound, watching the high waves. "I hope to God we didn't play a part in her killing."

They stood there in silence for a long moment.

"We're confident she knew more than she divulged," he said then, "and she could have become another loose end to someone. Alright, get anyone who is free tonight and can help. We need to make a move fast before this ship sails once and for all. Let's meet in one hour in the conference room."

"Okay. What are you going to do?"

"I'm gonna check some things out, try that Lamb lead she gave us again. You go talk to the witnesses and see if you can learn anything East Haven PD or our blue suits might have missed. I'll be right back."

Frank walked up from the beach while Tom ventured back to the Point and found the two young boys who'd discovered the body standing with an officer. Frank reached a payphone by the bathrooms, placed a dime in, and made a call. "Leroy, Frank Suchy. I gotta call in that favor."

He spoke on the phone for about a minute, hung up, and made his way to Tom, who was finishing up querying the boys.

"Better make it about two hours from now. We'll reconvene with the others," he said. "And, uh, I'm gonna need to borrow the car."

1 p.m.

Frank drove the motor pool's 1971 AMC Matador that he borrowed, which was incredibly difficult to acquire after losing the Monaco only a day ago. Motor pool was so strapped that he practically had to swear on a Gideon Bible and promise to return it by the end of their shift just to secure his own transport.

He surfed the radio waves for something to listen to, stopping on Big Maybelle's *That's a Pretty Good Love,* before shutting off the radio entirely and throwing it on the seat next to him. Frank needed to focus.

He couldn't get McCurdy's face out of his mind.

He drove toward the center of New Haven to the Dixwell Avenue area to meet his informant. Now that he was alone, Frank let everything go. His eyes were erratic and his face frantic, his white-knuckle grip on the steering wheel intensified. He was starting to lose it, no question about it. He teared up but held it in, then let out a moan. Regaining control, his breath deepened in an attempt to relax himself.

He snickered at how silly it all was. A grown man acting like this.

He drove down Whitney Avenue and stopped at a red light. He looked over to his right at the Peabody Museum, where a line of first graders were queued up next to their teacher waiting to enter. He saw Tom's daughter, Grace, standing near the front of the line. Two boys behind her pulled as hard as they both could on a Stretch Armstrong figure, trying in vain to break off his arms.

Frank smiled, watching the children wrapped up with childhood innocence, detached from the world, the real horrible, hard world that awaited those bright, innocent souls. His smile faded away when a horn behind beeped because the signal light had changed. His mind was brought back to focus on the thoughts that haunted him.

That poor woman. Her daughter watched her die.

He drove away. A minute later, he savagely beat his steering wheel in a fit of rage. He violently punched the dashboard and then the ceiling. He pulled over on a side street before he hit the Grove Street cemetery block. He double-parked, exited the car, popped the trunk, went into his bag, and found what he was looking for. He took the pint of no-name whiskey and nearly drank the entire thing in one gulp. It felt good, feeding the bug. His nerves started to settle, his mind numbing, and the remnants of his hangover now gone. What he detested most was how it relaxed him. He hated himself because of it. Frank let the juice take effect, then threw the entirely empty bottle back in the bag, jumped back into the car, and went for the gum in his pocket before setting off.

♦ ♦ ♦

Leroy walked ahead of Frank, leading him toward the large boxing ring that was positioned in the center of the decaying gymnasium, surrounded by rows of old, creaky wooden folding chairs in the cavernous YMCA. Even though the enormous antique space was filled with men exercising and training, the air was consumed by a thick, smoky haze from cigarettes and cheap stogies. The decades-old nicotine fog that permeated every inch of places like this was as standard as the weights, boxing gloves, and punching bags that were used to train.

Leroy was an ex-Black Panther with affiliations to the Black Liberation Army, among probably a half dozen others. Ex, as in: he hadn't been arrested lately; not someone Frank would normally pal around with. They'd gotten close while Frank guarded him back when he was a witness, sequestered during the notorious Alex Rackley murder trial against Black Panther Party New Haven chapter founder Elizabeth Huggins and Panther Party cofounder Bobby Seale. The consequential Mayday rallies in support for the 'New Haven Nine' as they were called almost plunged the city into riots.

The FEDs, under their dubious classified program COINTELLPRO, had basically caused so much paranoia within the BPP in the late '60s that the organization started to cannibalize itself, with everyone suddenly thinking the other was an informant. In a lot of cases, they were right.

Poor Alex Rackley was called a traitor, and since the unfortunate, slow-minded young man was not affluent enough to competently defend himself against the outlandish accusations, he was tied to a bed, tortured with boiling water, beat about the body with a blunt object for days, a metal coat hanger was put around his head and used as a noose, and all the while, the whole affair was audiotaped for posterity. Near dead, he was then taken a half hour upstate and murdered by a small group of the New Haven chapter.

Since, coincidentally, the cofounder of the Panthers, Bobby Seale, was in town that very night giving a speech at Yale and was IDed entering the Huggins residence, he too was deemed culpable.

Alas, the trial of the century did not end up focusing on the death of a poor man murdered by these individuals who took advantage of Rackley due to of their own fears and paranoia. It instead became a case against the government, the 'establishment', represented by New Haven against the left, 'the radicals', the latter using this case as a springboard to go after the sometimes-admittedly illegal tactics by J. Edgar's FBI and the whole broader system itself, which in their eyes just wanted to keep the 'man' down, more specifically the Black Panthers, who just wanted to fight the power, and kill some pigs and maybe whitey in the process. Nothing wrong with that, according to all the young Yalies who stopped going to classes and rallied against the city, its bureaucracy, and its police. Poor Alex Rackley fell through the cracks, like so many other victims in the past and probably others in the future.

But Leroy was cool in Frank's book. They discovered they'd grown up in the same area and, oddly enough, became pretty tight while holed up together in the Yale Motor Inn off the Wilbur Cross Parkway. Best of all for Frank, Leroy learned an invaluable lesson that not every police officer was a baton-carrying, pistol-packing racist dressed in a blue suit, despite how that narrative was painted with a very broad brush. Nowadays, they helped each other out whenever it was needed.

Leroy's goatee wasn't really kempt, and his salt-and-pepper afro looked like it hadn't been taken care of in days. He wore thick black-rimmed glasses, which looked like a throwback to the '50s, particularly in the style Brother Malcolm and the ones popular with the Nation of Islam.

They sat down in the old wooden fold-out chairs and faced the ring. Inside the small expedition area, two gigantic wrestlers rehearsed tonight's routine, while two managers and the promoter watched and gave pointers. Wrestling was popular in the region and gaining in popularity, nationally.

Leroy lit a cigarette and exhaled through his nose. "Haven't heard from you in a long time, Frank. Must be something really big to call me up and use your last favor."

"It may actually be, Leroy. That's not to say that I don't enjoy your company."

Leroy smirked. "Well, from what you gave me to go on, only a few girls I talked with had any input. I think his full name is Lombardo Poe. White boy about twenty-five years old."

"Got anything on what he looks like?"

Leroy exhaled the harsh smoke from his filter-less cigarette and watched the two performers throw each other around the ring. "About five-ten, blond hair, thin. Supposedly has a big, bushy handlebar mustache. Rents a house out in Westville, so one would think he gots to come from money."

Frank leaned forward in interest. "Blond hair?" MaryAnn's admission was right, then, about there being more than one person, because the eyewitnesses, Mrs. McGuire with her two kids, described seeing a dark-haired man. "You spoke to girls who have met him?" Leroy nodded. For the first time in as long as he could remember, Frank could hear excitement in his own voice. "Do you have an address?"

Leroy took the last drag of his butt. "No, I think they were too drunk to remember. Only the area. Westville."

"You think any of them would talk to me?"

Leroy glanced at him over his glasses and gave him the 'you-got-to-be-kidding' look. Frank knew not to press the issue, at least not yet.

"Is he alone?"

Leroy smiled. "I was just getting to that. This guy hangs out with two others."

"Did you get descriptions?"

"A black guy, don't know about the third, all the same age, mid-to-late twenties. The third motha might match the cat you were telling me about over the phone."

"What did these women tell you specifically?"

"All white girls. The cats hang out at the big discos—Studio 71, Top of the Park, Neuter Rooster—trying to pick up women. The few I talked to don't remember the rest of the night with them."

"Like they were drugged?" Frank speculated.

"Maybe, or just too drunk to remember. These girls could put the booze away. Girls who like to party."

"You think these guys are slinging to the local addicts?"

Leroy was already lighting cigarette number two when he replied, "Don't know. Pushing drugs never came up with who I talked to. Though that is always a great way to sustain an income."

"Anything else?"

Leroy let loose what could only be described as a loud cackle. "That's a whole lot of info for only an hour and a half. Yeah, that's it. I'm spent."

Frank relaxed and leaned back in his chair. "Thanks, man. How's the war going for you?"

Leroy shrugged. "Just trying to get all these youngbloods out here now to understand, is all. They gotta stop thinking about themselves and start thinking about what they doing to the community. Dig?" He dropped his finished smoke and shook his head. "They don't even give a fuck 'bout their own mothas. Guys coming up out here now don't even care about being black. Niggas like that? How they gonna care about the neighborhood? Fools just worried 'bout hustlin' their sistas, killin their brothers, gettin' high, and countin' dead presidents. Things done changed since the revolution."

Frank nodded. "I hear you, brother. World's gone to shit." A growing pile of butts was collecting between Leroy's feet. "They say the urban renewal will help spark life in the city."

Leroy gave a dry half smile that was mocking in its tone. "Yeah, well, out here, we like to call it the Great Negro Removal." He snickered. "Can't wait for the day when they want to bulldoze some Italian neighborhoods on Arch Street up in Hamden for a fancy sports coliseum or interstate."

Frank couldn't argue with that. "Yeah, I hear ya. I hear ya. Take it slow, my brotha."

3 p.m.

Frank returned the '71 AMC Matador to the motor pool and hurried up to the third floor to meet with his team. When he walked into the room, he spotted his partner waiting with the other officers, poring over data and paperwork.

"Sergeant Suchy," a young officer said when he spotted him, "Chief Stratton wants to see you."

"Can you give us a minute?"

The young officer shrugged, indicating it really wasn't his decision to make. "Sorry, Sergeant, but from the look of who's with him, I don't think it will wait."

Assistant Chief of Detectives James Stratton, whose title was the equivalent of a captain's position in the New Haven Department, had the biggest office on the floor, though it was clearly not designed to make a statement. It was large enough to allow conferences to take place comfortably, but still echoed the cold concrete exterior that reminded any visitors that this was not, in any way, luxurious. He loomed in his doorway, and from across the room, made eye contact with Frank.

"Join me, Detective Suchy," he said, and headed back into the office, not giving Frank a choice to respond. Assistant Chief Stratton was seated at his desk while Councilman Theodore Pregosin looked out of the window at the view of New Haven Harbor and Long Island Sound. The elevated Oak Street connector was predominant in the foreground running to the left, and between them and Long Island Sound, was the I-95 highway and the railroad yard to the right.

Chief of Police Joseph Kearns paced the length of the office with his hands clasped behind him, while the councilman's wealthy friend, Urban Coalition leader Edward Gladstone, stood on the other side of the desk, patiently waiting. The councilman's aide was seated on the couch, looking through an itinerary. Lieutenant Michael W. Warner stood, leaning against the back wall near the office door with his hands folded in front of his chest.

The door opened, and Frank and Tom entered.

"Just you, Sergeant Suchy," Chief Kearns said.

Frank was taken aback, and with a quick scan of the faces in the room, it became apparent that the decision had been made without his consent. Tom politely nodded and exited the room.

Stratton extended his hand and pointed at an empty chair in front of the desk in the center of the room. "Sit down, Frank." By his tone and the frown on Stratton's face, he did not care for this situation.

Frank looked behind him back to Mike, who stood stone-faced against the back wall, also making it very clear that he was not comfortable with this meet-and-greet.

Frank felt uneasy and out of his element. "I'd rather stand if that's alright," he replied politely.

"We insist, Sergeant," Chief Kearns pressed.

After a moment of hesitation, Frank gave in to the big boss and took a seat.

"Frank," Stratton started, "I don't know if you've ever been formally introduced to Councilman Theodore Pregosin and Urban Coalition President Edward Gladstone?"

"Not formally," Frank replied.

The councilman crossed to the front of the desk and stuck out his hand. "Please, call me Ted." Frank did not offer his hand in return, only nodded a greeting.

The councilman started off in a familiar way, "Well, I've heard a lot about you. Your reputation precedes you, Frank."

"Thank you, Ted," Frank answered with a dry smile.

The councilman displayed a puzzled look, unable to determine how to take the tone of the remark. Chief Kearns, who was a no-nonsense kind of guy going back to the "golden age" of the department, appeared indifferent to the whole affair and more concerned about the clock than anything else. He adjusted his round wire-framed glasses and immediately jumped right into the business at hand.

"Detective Sergeant, the councilman has shown a concern in the investigation your team is heading up and asked to meet with you for a personal report. You can understand this can be a *very* delicate situation, due to the potential exposure."

"The East Rock shooting and homicide, sir?" Frank said. "We're all still in shock about what happened yesterday to Officer McCurdy. We did everything by the book, even having the uniforms make the initial contact along with us. The assailant appeared to have a complete psychotic break and—"

"No, no. We mean the murder at the Temple Street garage, Detective," Gladstone replied without bothering to make eye contact.

"Oh, really?" Frank said, topped with a slight touch of sarcasm.

The councilman planted himself on the edge of the desk and leaned in. "What can you tell us about the incident, Frank?"

"Well," Frank clasped his hands together between his knees, "we think the perp knew her, so we're checking—"

"What makes you think that?" Chief Kearns interrupted.

"From witness reports and what evidence we have gathered thus far, it seems they had some sort of relationship. They were talking prior to the assault in her car. She got to work and suddenly received a phone call from a payphone directly across from her department, an area that had a direct line of sight on her location, a call which then lured her away from work and to the garage."

Gladstone stopped battling a cuticle and finally made eye contact with Frank. "You don't think he could have been a random vagrant or mugger confronting her? Or worse yet, gang-related?"

Frank had had it with this guy, who, in his view, had no authority or business being involved in this meeting to begin with, let alone actively engaging in questioning.

"We don't think so," he said, strained.

"Why?" asked the aide who'd been sitting in silence consulting his paperwork.

Frank glanced over at the aide, and after an extended pause, made eye contact with Lieutenant Warner, who nodded to continue. "Well, like it says in our initial report, for whatever reason, the phone call lured her away from her job, at which time she claimed to be ill and asked to take her break," Frank said, addressing Stratton, "so it appears at that moment that she was covering for someone. Um, nothing was stolen from her person. She was originally seated in the passenger's seat of her own car prior to the chase. There were also several cigarette butts that had her saliva and lipstick on the filters on the ground outside that window, indicating she was, to some degree, comfortable with the situation, at least initially. We found a note we believe came from the assailant in the car that asked for a meeting that she may have initially ignored before the escalation to the call."

"So you're confident with all this evidence that they were acquainted?" Gladstone loudly interjected.

"Yes."

"And this could *not,* in any case, be random then?"

"That's what I just said," Frank replied politely with a tad more sarcasm in his tone.

"Sergeant, you know we're just trying to evaluate how we should pursue this investigation," Chief Kearns said.

"Are you asking me what I think should be done, sir?"

Stratton thoughtfully interlaced his fingers together on his desk and sat back. "Well, what do you have in mind, Suchy? Your professional opinion."

This could be the only chance Frank had at getting the resources he needed to get this case solved and bring these bastards to justice. So he took a breath, cleared his throat.

"For starters, I'd like a few more detectives cleared for OT to help my partners and me. Also, I think it's imperative that we get the media involved and see if we can get any leads. This was the middle of the damn day. Someone had to have seen something. The longer we wait, the less likely we are to find a reliable source that actually might have witnessed the crime, or the exact car that was used in the getaway. Maybe we hold a press conference with her parents and contact Channel 8 or—"

"Absolutely not," the councilman said. "Going on TV would do nothing but bring negative attention on the Chapel Street Mall and the downtown area, completely stigmatizing the entire situation and the entire area, which is exactly what we don't want." Pregosin looked at the other faces in the room as if it was taken for granted that this was a synonymous idea. "Christ, we don't want to be fucking scaring people away!"

"Bring negative attention? A sixteen-year-old girl was murdered outside a mall in broad daylight. Her best friend who went missing after we spoke to her just washed up on Morris Cove with her head bashed in. Right now, we need all the help we can get to figure out who the hell is doing this. And the clock is ticking, gentlemen. Christ, we just got a lead that it could be more than one perp and you—"

"More than one perp?!" the chief shouted.

"That's right, sir," Frank confirmed without skipping a beat.

"Jesus. Like a gang thing?" Gladstone asked no one in particular, placing a hand on his forehead.

"That could be a false lead, of course," the councilman added into the mix.

"I think I'm in the best position to determine that," Frank retorted dismissively.

Chief Kearns glared at Frank. "Suchy, this is Councilman Theodore Pregosin you're talking to here. Have—"

Stratton stood up in protest. "Sergeant Suchy and his team are doing the best they can with what resources they have at their disposal."

"Everyone, just settle down," Pregosin stated politely. "We're just here to evaluate the situation."

"Yes, it may be hard for the councilman and Mr. Gladstone if we have the detective overreacting," the aide added without even looking up from his papers.

"*Overreacting*?" Frank said with disgust. "Listen, when the grownups are talking, butt out and read your little book there."

"Frank!" Assistant Chief Stratton snapped.

"Hey," Mike finally chimed in. "Detective Sergeant Suchy is working day and night on this and has virtually been on the clock since this all started, so we all need to cut him some slack and stop—"

The councilman put his hand up as if to say calm down. "We understand, of course." There was a long pause before he continued. "Sergeant, try to follow me here. It's a bit long-winded but there's a point." He left his perch on the corner of the desk and walked toward the window, looked out, and gestured.

"In the early part of this century, something like one in seventeen thousand owned a car. When Dwight D.

Eisenhower became president twenty years ago, he knew this country desperately needed a highway road system that would connect the country, and at the same time, make it easier and more efficient for folks to travel in their jalopies. That was the future. So he put the interstate system in place, revolutionizing this great country."

Pregosin turned to face the group but still spoke directly to Frank. "But, and a very big but, the one problem that no one could have foreseen, what backfired and would then affect every major metropolis in the United States, was the mass exodus from the inner cities that this new highway system afforded people after the war. Citizens didn't have to live cooped up in congested urban centers anymore. They instead could move out to the suburbs in their big new cars, buy cheap, and have a house with lots of land *and* still have the convenience if they felt the urge to commute back into the city." He paused for dramatic effect like a born politician. "But that *wasn't* happening. Before long, city leaders feared our urban meccas would decay and die a slow, suffocating death. Most left now in these affected areas were minorities or poor families, who were unemployed, maybe uneducated, or the elderly. So how do we reinvigorate the downtown areas? Give the people who moved away a reason to come back and spend their money where it is most needed, so to pump the funds into the stagnant local economy and fund these necessary programs that the inner-city residents needed so badly?"

Frank felt like a kid in a classroom. "Yes. Urban Renewal," he said wanting to roll his eyes.

"Yes! That's why in 1965 the Department of Housing and Urban Development mandated that cities use a large portion of federal grants to build low-income housing in stable neighborhoods. Scatter-site housing, they called it, which the white middle class embraced. You turn the old rotten ghettos of yesterday into sparkling new spaces designed for businesses, commerce, and recreation to rebound the failing local economies. Racial and economic integration. Do you know New Haven receives more urban renewal funding per capita than any other city in the United States? That's a fact. We were on the cover on *Time Magazine* for our downtown development of the old Oak Street ghettos into that," he pointed outside toward the elevated connector. "New Haven, the model city. The ultimate success of the urban renewal initiative to offset and, possibly, financially correct the economic and social devastation the national interstate plan unknowingly inflicted on America's cities. We, my friends, proved it can be replicated in any American city."

Frank stared with his hands folded in front of him.

"Sergeant, you have something to say? By all means, we're all friends here."

"Are you asking me my opinion, then, sir?"

"By all means, say your piece, Sergeant."

"Well, okay, since we're all friends here and since we're speaking freely..." It just was another example of the ledge Frank was now putting himself on, which only had one way off—to jump. "You must excuse my immediacy, but what about turning that record over and discussing the direct impact to our minority communities? Where's the low-income housing for them? The ghettoes of downtown New Haven weren't broken up, complete blocks were leveled, and only in the Wooster Section, where the Italian community had the means of taking any kind of meaningful stand, was a scalpel used. The residents of Oak Street, on the other hand, were relocated, consolidated, and forced into the projects.

Ever been inside one of them leaky shoeboxes? You destroy, pave over, and displace entire *neighborhoods,* and replace it with that," Frank stabbed a finger outside toward the connector and the coliseum, "what some consider a wedge between the haves and the have-nots. Nothing out there in view will help house these communities you've plowed and rebuilt over. They weren't invited back to live. None of that was conceived with *their* welfare in mind."

The councilman looked agitated but kept his cool. Chief Kearns was red in the face.

"I did ask our sergeant for his frank opinion," Pregosin said, "and he is free to solicit it. Don't worry. We're by no means finished, Detective Sergeant. Soon there will be downtown apartments and condominiums for purchase or rent, just like the complex going up right behind this very station house. We're making community programs that help keep kids off the streets after school. Sergeant, I do care about these people and I want to get them employed and off the drugs, get them educated. All over America, we are being called America's City, moving towards a bright new future."

He crossed back around the desk to stand in front of Frank. "This brutal and appalling act occurred in downtown, the center of New Haven, right in the middle of the day, where families and children congregate, discouraging the exact demographic we are trying to attract back downtown, the citizens from the suburbs. If we can avoid any unwanted coverage—I mean, look at this in the full scope, Detective. We don't want to lose the twenty years of ground work we've gained and run the risk of going backwards. My sole question to you, Sergeant, is what are we facing here? Gang violence or worse, occultists even?"

Fatigued, Frank felt himself snap. He tried to stop it, but the words were already exiting his mouth. "We're facing a goddamn murder investigation here, that's all I'm worried about. And solving the murder of one of New Haven's citizens should be the city's top priority too!"

"Suchy!" Chief Kearns broke in. "Now listen, you little—"

"Well, what do you expect here?" Lieutenant Mike Warner snapped. "He's doing the best he can."

Gladstone decided then to add his two cents into the fray. "Well, yeah, but that isn't the point we're—"

"Alright, alright everyone." Stratton stood with his arms in the air, trying to inject some calm back into his office.

Frank was done. "So just to clarify, am I hearing this right? You bring me in here for a history lesson, all of which I already knew, by the way, then suggest we curtail our investigation to your parameters because of public perception?" Everyone was struck speechless by that. "And what of that poor kid who got his head taken off by a shotgun on East Rock? We shouldn't need to worry about that either, because he was a homosexual and the city doesn't want to draw more people like *that* here, eh?"

Completely confused by this last remark, Chief Kearns adjusted his pants which were around his belly button. "Homosexual? What the hell are you going on about?"

Frank pointed at Gladstone and the councilman. "Why don't you ask the two of them why they approached me earlier this week?"

"Now hold the fuck up!" Gladstone roared. "I don't think you understand what we're trying to—"

Frank stood up. "No, I understand perfectly. You've got us stretched as thin as tissue paper all over this city and instead of funding programs that need it, like police, fire, and education, and go to bat for us when *we* need it, you instead build and build, building stuff that makes our city look like some modern art sculpture." Frank couldn't stop himself now. "And you *really* wanna know what I think? What about Yale? They own something like sixty percent of the land downtown. They even help you get this urban renewal deal through Congress, yet they are tax-exempt on their properties? You think that's smart when the rest who are left there have the burden of keeping the entire city afloat on their shoulders? Then you *ignore* the issues these communities really face and how the inhabitants are affected. And you wonder why the city is in the shape it's in? Frankly, you're more concerned about its image than its people. Sadly, this meeting only provides more evidence of that."

Frank turned to walk out but stopped and looked back at them. "I have nothin' to say to any of you, except I'm investigating a murder and time is a luxury we do not have. Good day, gentlemen."

"Hey now," the councilman protested. "Wait. I—"

Frank turned around again and headed toward the door. Standing in his way was the councilman's aide with a confused expression on his face. Frank's teeth clenched together as he addressed the pretentious young hanger-on. "Screw!" Spittle flew out of Frank's mouth along with his command.

The aide leapt out of Frank's way and he stormed out of the office, slamming the door behind him. There was a long period of silence while the room processed what had just occurred. Chief Kearns opened his mouth to speak but nothing came out.

"Let him go," Stratton said. Kearns shot a furious look over to Stratton, for he was now the only one in the room he could properly yell at.

"What the hell was that?" He looked over to the councilman. "You've met him before? What East Rock matter was he referring to?"

Pregosin and Gladstone exchanged a glance, wondering where to start and what to say.

The entire floor was quiet, trying to listen in on the shouting and yelling, but the instant Frank threw the assistant chief's office door open, the fifty men and women on the floor suddenly went back to work, the whole office once again sounded like a crowded bus station.

Frank gestured at Tom, who was seated outside, and they walked briskly back toward their office. Tom had to take long strides to keep up with his enraged partner.

"Anything worth talking about?" he asked.

"Nope."

The two reached the small group of cops who'd been waiting for them outside their office. "Follow me," Frank said to the team.

They entered a small room and quickly found seats. An officer handed a stack of papers to Tom. Frank paced to clear his mind and calm himself enough to give the briefing. After glancing over the first pages of the Xeroxed case info, Tom handed two to Frank, then passed them out to the other officers.

Frank stopped moving and stood behind the lectern. "Alright, this is what we've got. We're looking for three males, mid-twenties, running around the New Haven area, picking up girls at discotheques. They're after young ones, probably fifteen to twenty-two. We don't know what they want yet—to get their ya-ya's out or some sort of shakedown—we don't know." Frank took a breath. "I know this sounds vague and could be the M.O. of most males that age, but we do have a name. Lombardo Poe, going by the nickname Lamb. Graham, get someone to check the files for that nickname. Informant says he rents a home in the Westville section of town."

One of the officers whistled aloud and looked around with a half smirk.

"I know," Frank continued. "He's got to be bankrolled to afford something around that area, so it could be drug-related. Basically, this is all we have. We know that more than one woman has been picked up by them and they don't remember anything after the club. Unfortunately, none of them will talk to us officially. We think Arianna Wallace, and most recently MaryAnn Decan, who washed ashore this morning on the Annex/East Shore at Morris Cove, were victims and linked to them. The pages Tom's handing out right now are what we believe to be the perps' descriptions.

"Time is something we do not have. We need to keep all of these leads quiet, so the press doesn't get wind and alert the suspects that we have a vague description and places of interest. Tonight, we're going to be checking out some of these local discos we think they could be operating at, and since its Saturday, maybe we can spot them. Of course, it becomes more difficult if they're not operating in a group, but if we're, by chance, able to grab one, we can squeeze him to give up the other two. It may be a needle in a haystack, but if they are hanging out together, this could be to our advantage in identifying them."

Joe Spinall, still wearing his yellow-tinted glasses, took a toothpick out of his mouth and looked up from the handout. "Real pioneers of the asphalt frontier, huh? Is there any indication at all from your CI that they're slinging and using the girls to push junk?"

"That was my first impression too, Joe, but it's unclear at the moment," Frank replied. "I know we don't have a lot to work with, but we've done our job with a lot less. Okay?" Everyone appeared to be on-board and up-to-date, which satisfied Frank. "So let's go get educated."

The men filed out of the office. Frank walked out next to Spinall. He pulled Joe's cuff to get his attention and spoke low, so only Spinall could hear.

"How are you and Rand holding up after yesterday?"

"We're okay. Trying not to think about it and focus on the work. Skipper, I gotta tell ya, I think the initial ballistics report from yesterday's shooting is gonna come back that the sawed off double-barreled shotgun is our murder weapon from that East Rock shooting. Looking at that guy's house with all the stuff he had on the wall—pictures of the discos, social clubs and bars, and all the insane rambling he had scribbled on his walls—I really think he was gonna take that Chicago Typewriter into a disco and light the place up."

"Really?"

"Yes. So as horrible as yesterday was, we might have prevented a *bigger* tragedy."

Frank nodded thoughtfully. "Okay, Joe. Thanks."

Mike Warner came storming out of the assistant chief's office, right for Frank. As the lieutenant passed the various desks on the floor, officers slyly followed him with their eyes. Frank patted Spinall on the back to hurry him along and moved into a corner with Mike.

"Hi," Frank said like he hadn't seen his boss in a couple of days.

"Was what you said in there true about Pregosin and Gladstone secretly meeting with you?" Mike asked, all business.

"Absolutely."

"What exactly was said?"

"They wanted me to curtail our East Rock investigation. Handle it discreetly and away from the public eye, having no negative impact on the locale."

"Well, right now, that is the only thing keeping you on this case and not sitting behind a desk for the rest of the year. So you better tread lightly from here on out. I don't know if you're looking to shit your career down the toilet, but that blowout in there and that shootout yesterday has you teetering on a very precarious ledge, and you ain't fucking Spiderman. Dig?"

Just then, with a clang of the blinds whacking against the glass door, the rest of the group exited the assistant chief's office led by Chief Kearns, who seemed to be trying very hard to keep Pregosin and Gladstone happy as they left the floor with their young aide trailing behind. Assistant Stratton was the last to walk out of conference and as soon as he set foot on the floor, the overall buzz from the fellow officers ceased as Stratton searched for Frank. He'd taken his jacket off, showcasing his short-sleeved white dress shirt. His eyes met Frank's, and he headed toward him. Mike moved to the side and Stratton came face to face with Frank. A subconscious hush continued across the floor as everyone waited to see the dust-up.

Frank stared at his boss, defeated and waiting to be berated. Assistant Chief Stratton looked in his eyes and said nothing. He was close enough for Frank to smell his Pinaud Clubman aftershave. Although Frank would never admit it to anyone, the smell of that old-fashioned cologne was one of the most comforting smells in the world for him because his grandfather used to wear it. That smell harkened him back to his childhood and happy memories. Assistant Chief Stratton was the only other person Frank knew apart from his Papa that wore that scent.

"You have a timetable in place?" Stratton finally asked.

Frank glanced at his partner Tom and then back to Stratton. "We do. Stakeout tonight at some local spots, with intel that is less than an hour old. We feel very good about it. We have to jump on this before our suspects get wind that we're onto them."

A few moments passed. The downward lighting made Stratton's graying flattop shine in a very unnatural way. Finally, the large man motioned with his head and flashed an exhausted half-smile for Frank and Tom to carry on.

"I can probably stall until tomorrow. After Sunday, we're gonna have problems."

Frank nodded thanks to his boss, and immediately left his sight. Stratton motioned to Lieutenant Warner and Mike replied with a nod and followed the assistant chief back to his office.

The floor went back to its normal bustling once again.

Frank finished making the various calls to the departments he needed to coordinate tonight's stakeout while Tom mulled over a report.

"We're on for tonight," Frank said, sitting down.

"Kool and the gang," Tom replied.

Frank was thinking about the case and becoming even more frustrated. Something was being missed, but he could not place it. Was it right in front of their faces? He stood up and walked over to the bulletin board that displayed the photos and evidence tacked up for the Arianna Wallace case, partly to clear his head, though, also to go over everything they had for the hundredth time. For minutes, he stood there staring intently, taking everything in and trying to come up with something. *Something* was there.

And then he saw it. In a close-up photo of the bruises on Arianna's neck, the necklace she wore was visible. On it, was the skate key she wore, along with a regular key.

Was that there before?

Frank looked more closely at the photo before having a huge realization. "Graham!" he yelled at the top of his lungs, ripping the photo off the board. "I can't believe I missed this!"

Graham came over from his desk. "Yeah, Frank?"

"Where are the belongings that were on the Wallace body?" Frank pointed at the photo he held in his hand and to the key on the necklace.

Graham went over to the other side of the office and retrieved a small evidence box that he'd signed out. Tom hurried over as several detectives crowded around Frank.

"What's up?" Tom asked.

"That key wasn't on her necklace at dinner the night before," Frank said, taking the box from Graham and looking for the necklace. "I'm feeling lucky." He picked up the key and held it toward the light.

He recognized it as a locker key. It had something written on it, which Tom quickly read so all could hear. "Roller Haven, locker number eighty-four."

"Sock. It. To. Me." Frank declared with the first smile that had graced his face since he could remember.

The roller rink, or as the kids called it nowadays, the disco rink, was loud and crowded. The party hadn't looked to have stopped since Frank was there at the beginning of the week. Two birthday parties were going on simultaneously, twenty to thirty children skating along to flashing disco balls, strobe lights, and ABBA's *Money, Money, Money*. Flanked by Tom, he walked past the flashing lights of the arcade room, past the 1776-1976 Bicentennial posters that still adorned the hallway, and came to an area where walls of lockers were positioned, creating a kind of partition, shielding a hallway that led to the restrooms. They quickly found number eighty-four and used the key to open the locker. Tom stood behind Frank, eager to see what would be revealed. Inside, was a pair of skates, a journal, and a videocassette tape. Frank took out a handkerchief from his breast pocket and used it to pick up the videocassette. He peered at the tape with an odd fascination because it was the first one he'd seen in person. He'd seen commercials for them, of course, but had never held one until now. It was heavier than he'd have expected. He carefully handed it off to Tom, who dropped it into an evidence bag.

"Is that what I think it is?" Tom asked.

"One of those new video recorder tapes." Frank thumbed through the journal. "Bingo." He handed it to Tom and looked at the skates and the identification tag on them. He read it aloud. "Arianna Wallace."

"I can't believe we only saw this now," Tom said.

"Tell me about it."

They hurried out to the awaiting radio car that had brought them. They jumped in the back seat and Frank carefully perused the journal. "Something has to be in here..."

The uniformed officer driving turned around, holding a piece of paper. "Here you go, detectives. Just came over the radio." Frank and Tom looked up at the note. It was a homicide call. "Sorry, but they're short-handed today, and there was already a triple homicide on the Fair Haven Heights line, so you're up." He waited a beat, then said, "It's in the Hill."

It was something they could not avoid. If they were up, they were up. They'd have to dump everything else.

Tom could only think of one thing to say. "Shiitt."

Frank and Tom pulled up to the crime scene, an older two-family home in the Hill section of New Haven. It looked, at one time, to have been a beautifully elegant home, four stories tall, with graceful exterior woodwork, probably a grand example of architecture from the turn of the century. It had since been gutted and converted into a multi-family dwelling, with the gradual procession of time not being kind to the old structure. Gorgeous woodworking and luxurious Victorian architectural design now turned into unkempt eyesores with more layers of paint filling in the intricate detail than on Rip Taylor. A long-forgotten widow's walk atop the roof was visible, now boarded-up and falling apart like some antiquated business long-since deemed obsolete. Frank wondered if it were still possible to see the Sound from that vantage point.

The Hill was the area that, in '67, exploded in race riots, the place that he and Chris Wallace had reconnected and almost gotten killed, and was one of the areas in the city that, if you were a cop, you'd have a fifty/fifty chance of getting shot or stabbed. There were no fans of New Haven's finest here.

Only two squad cars were in front, and, already, a small crowd had started to gather to see what happened.

"Jeez, there's no bus here yet?" Tom remarked with a growing level of frustration usually only reserved for a seasoned veteran of the force like Frank. The two exited the black-and-white and walked up the sidewalk toward the house. With the arrival of the two plain-clothed officers, the crowd gradually became more belligerent and hostile. Whispered words started to become verbal taunts to the police.

"What took you so long, pig?" a dark-skinned man who looked either deathly drunk or like he'd just woken up, and in a voice that wasn't quite a yell but wasn't a conversational tone either.

"Maybe if ya crackers' been 'round before, this shit wouldn'ta happened!" a frustrated woman in her early thirties shouted toward Frank and Tom.

"Pigs is always coming to clean up the mess, never to prevent it," another man chimed in.

Frank attempted to ignore the hecklers but glanced down at his hand and saw it was trembling again like before. His heartbeat was elevated now that he thought about it. He tried to control his breathing and accelerated pulse, trying to shake off his hand tic by putting an arm on Tom's shoulder to keep him moving up the path toward the front porch. He scanned the crowd, taking in every possible detail, and his eyes landed on Leroy, his informant, standing with the other onlookers. They held eye contact for a brief second and then looked away.

On the porch, they were greeted by an older uniformed sergeant, a veteran by the name of John Copela who, despite his age, would never leave uniform duty. He'd been taking it on the arches since the late '40s. Another officer outside, a real green rookie blue suit, stood at the end of the porch, visibly shaken and queasy.

"What do you have tonight, John?" Frank asked as he climbed the four creaky stairs of the long semi-porticoed porch.

"Wit escapes me tonight, fellas."

They glanced over to the younger officer at the end of the porch who held the back of his hand to his mouth, so he wouldn't throw up over the side.

"You boys up?" John queried.

"Yep, it's me." Tom ascended the stairs. "No bus here yet?"

"Yep. Ambulance already came, pronounced it, and is on the way to the next carnival show. We're waiting on the M.E. now. My partner is taking care of a baby we found. She's fine, just shook up." John sighed before he continued. "I gotta tell ya, I've been on the beat for over thirty years in this town and I haven't seen something like this for at least a decade. Maybe two."

The rookie at the other end of the porch straightened up finally and walked over.

"We got a suspect?" Frank asked, expecting the worst.

"Boyfriend, we think," John answered.

"Who the fuck knows with these crazies?" the rookie broke in. "Nobody wants to talk to us, even though everybody was home when it fucking happened."

Sergeant Copela glanced over at him briefly, then back to the detectives. "We've determined the boyfriend's M.I.A. at the moment. As soon as the wagon gets here, we're gonna start trying to push the over-friendly crowd down there to speak up."

"Good luck with that," Tom replied, looking back at the increasingly rowdy onlookers.

"C'mon." John led the way, Frank and Tom following, and they made entry.

The left front door led into a sizable living room which had a maroon shag rug. Curtis Mayfield's *Billy Jack* was stuck on repeat on the turntable, but no one turned it off, as if it were unlucky to touch. An officer stood by the coffee table holding a naked toddler that was covered in dried blood, jostling her gently to try to comfort and entertain her.

John indicated toward his partner who held the child. "We found that child in the bedroom with the deceased mother."

"Jesus," Tom said.

"Child okay?" Frank asked.

"No physical injuries immediately noticeable, and paramedics gave the thumbs up as well."

Frank stepped over and turned the record player off.

John continued down the hallway past the kitchen. Frank and Tom peered in and saw an open drawer with knives spilled out all over the floor. They also saw a trail of blood, of which the droplets were in an elliptical shape, meaning the body was in motion as it bled, knowing that if a body was in a static position the droplets would be in the shape of a circle. That meant the person bleeding was on the run during the altercation.

"We think the argument began here and a knife got involved. Notice the blood trail indications?"

John kept moving down the hall, and they pressed on. The trail of blood from the kitchen continued down toward the bedroom. They passed a bathroom, where a bath had been drawn with bloodied water and toys scattered about a dark blue tiled floor.

"The fight moved into the bathroom, indicated by the blood on the floor—maybe the child was gonna be bathed—then continued down the hall into the master bedroom."

An officer exited the bedroom with a pencil and pad in one hand and a handkerchief in the other with something hanging from it. It was a bloody butcher knife. Sergeant Copela said, "Detectives are here. What ya got there, Wes?"

Wes was a burly uniformed officer in his mid-forties and looked like he had a penchant for drinking, bad food, and not shaving. He wore a shirt that Frank thought to be a size too small and because of that, you could see glimpses of his hairy chest through the areas where the buttons were holding on for dear life. That said, along with Copela, Wes Kramerton was one of the best beat cops working the streets of New Haven.

"Murder weapon, I presume," Wes answered. "Must have tossed it behind the dresser on the way out." When Frank and Tom moved toward the bedroom, Wes put his hand up to stop them. "Watch yourselves in there, lads. It's pretty gruesome, and at the moment, it's hard to tell what's evidence, and what is...I don't know what."

They cautiously stepped into the bedroom. Officer Copela waited outside in the hall. Blood was everywhere, even splatters on the ceiling. Most of it had coagulated but there were still some dark, wet pools scattered about. A woman's body was behind a large brass-framed bed positioned in the center of the room. She was a large, heavyset woman in her late twenties with a very pretty face. Multiple slashes could be seen on her arms, which the two detectives immediately recognized as defensive wounds. As her torso came into view, deep stab wounds were present in her stomach and shoulder area. That was when Frank and Tom focused on her upper body, which was completely split open. The entire chest was exposed, and her ribcage was broken and split apart, showing access to the cavity. Her heart had been cut out and was placed on a pillow just beyond her body near the back corner of the room.

The veteran officers were taken aback by this sight, struck mute. They stood in the room for an indefinite amount of time, everything else forgotten. It took Copela to grab them both by the arm to get them to snap out of it.

They stepped out onto the porch to get some much-needed fresh air. Frank's hand was shaking but he concealed it from view. For the first time, Tom seemed shaken up himself. For Frank, it may have been the straw that broke the camel's back.

The uniformed rookie approached him with the latest updates on what they knew. "Looks like her twelve-year-old boy is M.I.A., so we may have a hostage situation. We're putting a BOLO out on him and the boyfriend now."

"Jesus," was the only thing Tom was able to squeeze out. Frank stared out into space. The rookie cleared this throat, put his hat on, and walked back into the crime scene.

Frank turned to Tom in a clean, fluid motion. "Thomas, get someone to get that goddamn baby out of there, cleaned up, and in some new clothes. See if we can find a relative to take it in, okay?"

Tom flagged down an officer.

A new officer, escorting two medical examiners, came walking up the sidewalk.

"I'll start on the people outside here," Tom said to Frank. "See if anyone talks to white cops."

"John," Frank said, "you guys check the backyard?"

"Only when we first got here," Sergeant Copela responded. "Rookie didn't see anything."

Frank looked over to Tom. "I'm gonna take a look 'round back just to double-check, see what I can find."

"Roger that." Tom headed toward the restless crowd, calling out, "Anyone see or hear anything tonight?"

"Fuckin' honkie," an anonymous woman muttered. The crowd hooted and howled with joy.

Flashlight in hand, Frank did another thorough sweep of the backyard. It was much quieter back here, as if it were a world away from what was happening inside the house and out front. He found nothing in the deep yard, which looked to have been, at one time, a garden, something all the old-timers had, complete with a long-since decayed trellis for grapevines by old-world Italians. The unkempt yard had long-since grown into the property line, weaving in with the thick bushes that swallowed the defunct trellis, and the unpruned trees that skirted the fence filled it all in and gave the yard quite a bit of cover and privacy.

Frank turned toward the house, slowing when he approached the concrete back steps. He glanced around, saw no one within eyeshot, and sat on the top step. He sat in silence for a long time, taking in the night air and the serenity of the quiet, dark area.

He laid his head in his hands and began to rock. He wept silently for a couple minutes, at last getting out everything he'd had bottled up for so long.

I can't. I can't. I can't. I can't. I can't do it anymore.

He unconsciously let out a sob and shot his head around to make sure it wasn't loud enough to attract attention. He tried to calm himself but started again. He felt pity, disgust, and anger for allowing this outburst to happen, out of all times, here on a call. But that last scene broke him. Frank closed his eyes, took a breath, and held it to try to clear his thoughts. He should call the old man. That was what Vince, the Old Man, was for, what friends were for. It would save Frank's sanity, which was at stake at this point.

Would Vince say what he himself feared? That he was *too* close? He needed to back away, to step back and recuse himself. Or could this really be the end of him? He didn't need that now, to hear that, but he needed to speak to someone. He should call Channing, the Old Man, he could help.

After losing track of time, he slowly opened his eyes. What he saw surprised him. A lone deer stood in the yard looking for a place to graze. Frank moved his leg, scraping his Sears and Roebuck leather dress shoe on the cement step, giving away his position to the animal. They made eye contact and stared at each other for what felt like an eternity.

How peaceful and amazing, Frank thought. Even though they were in the Hill, with practically a riot about to break out sixty feet behind him, a deer could still find its way into an isolated backyard and completely contrast the night's scene.

The animal seemed to understand that he posed no threat and went back to grazing in the tall grass. Frank couldn't believe it. Everyone lived and they all died, every day. No one cared, and if they sincerely did, that feeling would eventually fade with time, just as every memory does. The pain didn't go away; time just gave you a way of dealing with it by fading and clouding your memories. Frank did not find comfort in that thought, but more of a grounding. It sparked a realization in his head about how little everything really mattered in the big picture of life. No one cared, least of all, maybe even God above.

He knew now what he had to do.

His thoughts were disrupted by a commotion out front. A boy screamed, which spooked the deer. It leapt the fence, vanishing in a blink of an eye into the blackness of night.

Frank rounded the corner and hurried up to Tom, who was jockeying a position next to the growing crowd. The murdered woman's twelve-year-old boy stood screaming and struggling to get past two uniformed officers and into the house.

This was like blood in the water for the crowd, which started yelling and becoming increasingly belligerent to the on-scene officers.

"Hey! Let him go!" screamed an angry onlooker.

"Where's my mom?" the boy screamed, while the officers tried to hold the child from entering the house. "What happened to my moms!?"

Tom leaned over to Frank and whispered, "I just heard from Graham that our victim, Lucinda Davis, called the police on her boyfriend three times claiming domestic battery. The third time was tonight. The black-and-white didn't arrive until fifty-two minutes after the call."

Frank shook his head in disgust. How could you blame the neighbors for their anger? He felt the rage inside of him growing.

Tom observed Frank's hand trembling. "Frank?"

"Sir!" called a young officer who shot over from one of the nearby police cars.

"Yes, talk to me."

"We've got 'im, sir. We got the killer," the young officer said proudly.

This statement thoroughly confused Frank and Tom. The officer pointed over to the house. "Henry Dwight Howard. He was the boyfriend. He just walked into headquarters about ten minutes ago and gave himself up."

The two detectives looked back at the young officer with blank stares. What could be said? This was how it happened sometimes.

"We need to get going, Tom. Give Copela command and let's get to our stakeout." Frank needed to shut his eyes to try and clear his head.

A chant began in the crowd, getting louder, and more people sang along. The chant was set to the Wilson Pickett's version of *Land of 1000 Dances.*

> *"Pick up the guns!*
>
> *Pick up the guns, put the pigs on the run!*
>
> *Pick up the guns!*
>
> *ONE MORE TIME!*
>
> *Pick up the guns!*
>
> *Pick up the guns, put them pigs on the run!*
>
> *Pick up the guns!"*

Frank saw Leroy in the crowd, proudly chanting away with men, women, and some children. Tom had an expression on his face as if he'd been sucker punched in the gut. It might have been his first time having stuff like this hurled at him. Frank put his hand on Tom's shoulder and urged him to get moving.

"Forget it, Jake," Frank said. "It's Chinatown."

He and Tom jumped into the back of their radio car and sped off with his partner giving directions. Frank closed his eyes and desperately tried to relax. Sleep hit him like a brick over the head.

AUGUST 30, 1970

1:47 a.m.

THE ISLE OF Wight Music Festival was a large outdoor event meant to be the British version of Woodstock, located on an island of the same name off the South coast of Britain. The gathering was hoped to reignite the hippie 'peace and love' movement, and usher in a bright and glorious future in the 1970s. But along with what transpired at the Rolling Stones concert at Altamont, and the 1969 Manson murders that were associated and supposedly reflected the 'dark side' of the flower power culture, the Isle of Wight Festival basically spelled the end of the hippie movement in the mainstream altogether. Some concertgoers, angry over the ticket prices, led to some fans revolting and mini-riots erupted. Fences and barriers were broken down to make numerous entry points into the massive event and mini-clashes with the local constables ensued. An ominous forecast of what was to come in the 1970s.

Cut to the early-morning hours of day four of the festival. Frank Suchy and a bearded Jim Morrison walked out of a tarp-like door and exited an enclosed makeshift greenroom that connected to a larger tented area, located in back of the gigantic stage. The singer waved goodbye to John Entwistle, closed the tarp door, and turned to his companion. Frank instinctively kept one foot ahead of his friend and employer to act as a barrier between any potential unwanted attention that could come running up without any regard to setting, respect, or personal space. Morrison was in the midst of a serious court battle back in the States, and it severely weighed on him. There was even a radio ban and his albums were being taken off the shelves. This was causing him to become quite introverted, Frank noticed. Morrison even needed to get special permission from the court to be allowed to leave the country and fulfill this contractual obligation, so he really wanted to keep a low profile and hopefully avoid any journalists.

They walked over toward an outdoor covered bar and sat on stools. Frank recognized Miles Davis walking by accompanied by Jimi Hendrix, discussing something to do with syncopation.

Frank couldn't believe the excitement he felt, all the while still be being paid to do a job. If he could sustain this and earn an income from doing security, he'd quit his job on the force and make a career out of it. Frank still felt the ramifications of breaking up that fight with Morrison three years later. But a new generation was coming onto the force, slowly eradicating any of that sort of remaining sentiment, as the old guard began to retire. Frank was trying to make detective, and if that didn't pan out, he figured this could be as good a job as any. Plus, look at all the fun he'd been having and the celebrities he'd been meeting.

At the moment, his attention focused on Morrison, who was supposed to be going on stage in ten minutes.

"You're piss-drunk, Jim, and you gotta go out there and perform." Frank smiled.

Morrison looked at him through half-closed eyes and threw back a grin. "Do I look piss-drunk to you?" He smirked, and with one eye closed, pointed a finger and declared, "*You* better not be drunk. I don't want a bottle over my head because you're not doing your job!" Frank grinned back at him, feeling quite tipsy as he grounded his spinning head. His eyes met two girls across the bar who were eyeing the singer seated next to him, giggling and whispering to each other. Frank laughed and shook his head in astonishment. "I can't believe what it's like being you. Every girl wants you, guys envy you. You make great music, great art.... What else could you want?" He looked down at his freshly poured glass and suddenly felt self-reflective and more serious than a moment before. "I sit in an RMP all day, helping a very unthankful public, hoping that the next Signal 4 I go to—"

"RMP?"

"Oh, sorry, Radio Motor Patrol. Police cars."

"And Signal 4?"

"Signal 4. Means officer needs assistance, officer down. Um, you made me lose my train of thought."

"You said you worry about the next Signal 4 you go to."

"Yes, thank you, my good man. Yeah, I sit around hoping that the next Signal 4 I respond to isn't a false call to get a cop in a certain area so he, or I, can be killed."

"What do you mean?"

Frank wet his lips. "It's happening all over the country. Up in Harlem, cops are afraid to go north of 110th street 'cause they're targets to be assassinated by the Panthers or the BLA who—"

"Black Liberation Army?"

"Correct! See? You're learning. Our department is starting to get Signal 4's falsely called in, so they can get cops somewhere to murder them."

The smile vanished from Morrison's face and he glanced up at the two girls across the bar and then to Frank. "Jeez, I'm feeling this way and you've actually got *real* problems." He was silent for a minute and looked back down at his own glass.

"Sorry," Frank said, "I didn't mean to upset you. I was just trying to tell you how much I envy what you do, compared to a guy like me, that's all. What's going on? You wanna talk about something?" Frank felt the buzz going away as the conversation became more serious.

Morrison stood, took a few steps, like he was stretching and sizing up what was on his mind. "I always felt like I could talk to you, man." The singer looked over Frank's head and took in the scene around them.

"Of course, you can," Frank replied.

It took Morrison a minute before he let out what was troubling him. "I…I don't feel it anymore. Lately, I've been disconnected from everything and everyone. The whole world, man. I don't know. This isn't what I wanted, to be this huge rock god. I mean, when we started out, I just wanted to make movies. Huge philanthropic sonatas in Cinemascope. Now…" Morrison looked down at his drink, snatched it up, and finished it. "Dig it, *here's* a perfect example of the world we're in; the climate of the times, 1970, here at the Isle of Wight. This is supposed to be a peace festival and there's people breaking down the gates and fences trying to get in. Destroying, fighting, and hating. Peace and love is over, man, dig? That went out with the '60s. This is a new decade full of realizations and uncertainties...death and the decay of society, only concerned about ourselves. It's all going downhill."

"Yeah, I hear ya. The world ain't what it used to be when we were younger."

"Exactly," Morrison agreed. "It's all getting out of control and we can't stop it. *The falcon cannot see the falconer,* man. You wanna know something? All this, this whole thing, whatever it is, whatever you wanna call it, I'd trade it in a minute for your life. What you got," Morrison said to Frank. "I know you have a dangerous and hard and stressful job, but you also got a wife, a beautiful child, but most of all, you've got peace of mind. You help society, the community. You're a good guy. You proudly serve your fellow man. And you're happy where you're at. You may have a thankless job, but it betters the world. Makes us all safe. Me? Society has a queer fascination with destroying idols they've propped up. Do they care about the artist's real passion or thoughts? They give them fame and wealth, learn to idolize, and then eventually, cannibalize and consume those same idols they've preciously put on enormous pedestals to worship. Do you know what the secret to life is? What is the most craved fantasy? Not sex, not money, or a car or anything. It's happiness. Peace of mind, man. All this I have could be gone tomorrow. You have peace of mind that you're out there doing good. You use it to help people, and that is truly beautiful. So cherish what you got, 'cause it might not be there tomorrow."

Frank was speechless. Morrison was opening his heart to him. People like him had to live through masks, facades they hid themselves behind to deal with the full spectrum of a celebrity-obsessed society. But here, Frank saw the real man, not the 'front' he had to put on to shield himself from the prying eyes of the public.

"Thank you, man."

"For what?"

"Opening up and confiding in me. Making me think."

"Men like you come far and few between, Officer Frank Suchy." Morrison looked around him, lost in his thoughts, then back down at Frank and continued with tears in his eyes. "Whatever you do, never lose sight of that. The crazy rock star world I live in, it ain't real. It will be gone tomorrow. Yours…a wife, a family…that's happiness men kill and steal for. Don't ever lose sight of it."

The two stood silent as the sounds of bass from the concert echoed around them.

Morrison motioned to the barmaid and two shots of Jameson were poured. Frank and the singer picked up their glasses and saluted.

"Here's to you, Frank Suchy, and to the '*Blood in the streets in the town of New Haven.*'"

"*It's up to my ankles,*" Frank answered with a wink.

That made Morrison's smile bigger through his thick beard.

"Cheers," Frank replied, and they shot their heads back and swallowed the alcohol. He savored the harsh liquid fire that warmed his gullet. He looked down at his watch and then over to the stairs that led to the stage. "You're about to be on."

As if on cue, the festival's announcer got on the microphone onstage and his East End accent boomed from the loudspeakers and reverberated across the outlying trees. *"It has been officially reported that over a half of a million people have come to the Isle of Wight for this festival…"*

With that, Morrison laughed. "This may be it," he whispered, only loud enough for Frank to hear.

"And one of the reasons is on stage right now. Please welcome…The Doors!"

Morrison threw back one last shot, cracked his neck, and winked at Frank. He put his sunglasses on and calmly walked forward, patting Frank on the back. He continued up the stairs that led to the stage as the opening guitar riffs to *Backdoor Man* commenced, his body silhouetting against the blinding stage lights.

Frank looked away from the glare and massaged his eyes. When he opened them again, only then did he see himself for the first time. No longer was it the younger image, but instead the older, present day, weathered, nearly broken detective sergeant. He sat there, alone and silent, covered from head to toe in splattered, coagulated blood.

Morrison was right.

EVENING

FRANK OPENED HIS tired, bloodshot eyes and rubbed them with his fingertips to get rid of a very old memory. It only took them a matter of minutes to get dropped off at Frank's garage, and he couldn't believe he'd dreamt that much in such a short period of time. Still, even the short respite gave him no relief, no feeling of restfulness, rejuvenation, or anything. It just spooked him. More bad memories that he could not deal with at the present.

He cleared his thoughts and concentrated on driving. He and Tom arrived outside the Neuter Rooster Nightclub on Hamilton in Frank's '67 Ford GT40 Mark 3 Coupe. He stopped in a no-parking zone and they exited the car.

Tom adjusted his three-quarter length Burberry trench coat and shut the passenger door, only then noticing a bullet hole in the bottom back vent area.

It was already becoming busy out on the streets, with people looking to have fun this brisk Saturday night, and could only be expected to get crazier as the evening went on. Two Pachucos in a flashy modified 1960 Ford Galaxie Starliner slowly cruised by with the windows down blasting some Hector Lavoe—perhaps his *El Todo Poderoso*—but Frank was rusty on his Puerto Rican salsa knowledge. Either way, there was an electricity in the air this evening. It was lining up to be a wild one tonight.

Tom stepped off the curb and evaluated the parking spot Frank chose. "You sure this'll be safe here? I mean, what with it being a collector's item now and everything."

"Carpool is out of vehicles at the moment and I refuse to let a black-and-white cart us around when they could be doing something more productive for us, so yeah. I hope it's okay here."

Tom was right, it was completely unlike him to leave the Mark 3 in such a vulnerable and public area, but that, he couldn't think about right now.

A uniformed officer approached them and broke in with an authoritative tone, "Hey you can't park—oh, Detectives. Uh, nice car."

Tom pointed from the officer to the car, squinted, and said, "Don't lose sight of that, Patrolman."

A large Saturday night crowd had already built up and were waiting to be let into the Rooster, one of the most popular clubs downtown, if not the entire region. The autumn night was particularly chilly, with dark clouds moving in, but you couldn't tell that from what the girls queuing by the front door, hoping to be let in, were wearing. Though the Rooster was not as close to Yale and the New Haven Green, which were the city's epicenter, but the 'downtown' area overall had a very lively nightlife, thanks to the surrounding colleges, swarming with young people, whose sole goal when not at school was to drink, do drugs, have sex, and repeat.

They felt the low-end bass even before they set foot into the sweaty discotheque. Frank recognized it to be Donna Summer's erotic journey, *Love to Love You Baby*. He and Tom cut through the outside crowd amid shrieks and angry comments, whispered to the doorman, and were immediately let in.

The Neuter Rooster had a very colorful past, beginning back when it first opened in 1972 as The Snow Chicken, a twelve hundred-capacity dance club, the largest in New Haven at the time. Originally, it was intended to only cater to the gay male crowd, but that gradually changed with overwhelming popularity. Yes, there were other similar clubs, both in New Haven and the surrounding counties, but the Rooster was the first to have that early-era disco look and feel that was being pioneered in Manhattan, Paris, and London. Disco had burst onto the scene, pushing the door completely open to the other side of culture who still wanted to party. This was the post-liberated era, after civil rights and the free love movements. It was the feminists, the gay culture, and affluent Black Americans, some of whom hadn't felt completely at home with the previous cultural trends, now wanting to party just like the hippies had done eight years prior. It was the Roaring Twenties all over again, except cocaine had replaced booze as the go-to drug and the pill and other contraceptives helped further 'free love,' which added another level of self-pleasure to this new era of lavish decadence.

The Rooster was the perfect example. As soon as you walked in, you were greeted by birds chirping, and some felt even overwhelmed because of the club's three-level layout with the dance floor below. The bar ran the entire length of the club on the left, while on the right side there were segregated areas nicknamed 'mini-orgy booths,' horseshoe shaped couches that were hidden and set back that offered some privacy from the masses on the dance floor, which were very popular, to say the least.

In 1975, the Snow Chicken reopened as the Neuter Rooster, with the new logo featuring a rather well-endowed rooster for all to see. With a new name, came a new look for its employees. The male waiters now wore white midriff sleeveless tops and short-shorts, which really harkened back to the club's original intentions to be a gay discotheque, but alas, you can't keep everyone out of a great party. Before long, patrons were not only traveling from out of town to sweat the night away in a coke-and-poppers-fueled night of debauchery, but out of state as well, coming from as far as Massachusetts and Rhode Island. Even celebrities like Grace Jones and Vicki Sue Robinson performed there, while patrons got down in long pseudo-choreographed dance lines while drinking mimosas, wearing glow necklaces, waving glow sticks, and grooving to funk and Euro disco.

Tonight, the Rooster was packed wall-to-wall with party-goers. *Love to Love You Baby* bellowed from the speakers, fueling the undulating dancers on the dance floor. The irony of children roller skating to the same song a week before at Arianna's party wasn't lost on Frank. Club-goers grinded pelvises, legs, and crotches while Donna's moaning reached fevered orgasm on vinyl.

Tom and Frank slithered their way through the sweaty congestion, scanning the nameless faces trying to find a match. They slowly squeezed forward toward the back end of the club, to where a catwalk obscured the front of the DJ booth. The assigned stakeout duo stood there, because this location had better eyes on the dance floor than the actual booth.

The Bee Gees' *You Should Be Dancing* came on next, blending perfectly without skipping a beat, and the dance floor hit an even stronger frenzied pitch. Through the smoke machine-generated fog, Tom approached Joe Spinall, who was still wearing the huge yellow oversized sunglasses, his black hair soaked from the humidity in the club. Next to him was his tall, lanky partner, Randy Jurgens.

Tom leaned in close to Spinall's ear to be heard over the music. "JOE! What's up?"

Spinall moved his soggy toothpick to the other side of his mouth to speak. "YO!"

"Any updates?"

"The names you got for us, Lombardo Poe and Lamb, aren't coming up in our files. Might be an alias."

Frank sighed and took his eyes off the crowd to look at Spinall, then at Jurgens, who scanned the party revelers like a synchronized metronome. Frank felt uncomfortable in the situation tonight, which was a first. He'd always loved the club scene, no matter what music was being played, be it disco or Lawrence Welk. C'mon, who didn't love the bubbles? But this feeling of anxiety and uneasiness he had tonight didn't sit well with him. It wasn't normal.

"Anything else?" he asked Joe.

"Nah, a lot of drunk kids and barely-clothed girls oblivious to the weather. My kind of O.T.!"

"My sentiments, exactly," Frank responded on autopilot.

Frank stepped away to walk around and survey the crowd. There appeared to be a few hundred people below. The Bee Gees ended, and War's *Cisco Kid* began, reducing the fast-paced grooving to a slow, funky grind, which became like a hypnotic meditation in funk. The crowd entered into a subconscious collective level of synchronized meditation right before his eyes. Frank sensed his breathing getting faster and faster, out of his control. The room was beginning to spin.

Shit.

He made his way over to the bathrooms and entered the large men's room, passing the line of kids in the large, dimly-lit hallway waiting to urinate and touch up their David Cassidy-style haircuts. He sidestepped a twenty-something throwing up onto the floor by the stalls and made it over to the sink. His anxiety was getting away from him. He'd never felt this way before and couldn't control the head rush.

Do I need a drink? What the hell?

He realized then he was having a panic attack. He'd never had one that he knew of, but he was having one now.

Not here, he thought. *Not now.*

He closed his eyes, tried to center himself and slow his breathing. He splashed cold water on his face to help stop the feeling. What ended up calming him, funny enough, was his keen ear distinguishing over the water, flushing toilets, and small talk, the snorting of noses from people huddled together in stalls blowing lines. Frank made a decision. With all he was feeling right now, he couldn't deal with *this*. His needed to be clear for this last run. He had to find these guys before it was too late.

He splashed more water onto his face and looked at himself in the mirror. He looked so tired and worn out. If only get could get some sleep.

He took a deep breath and patted his face dry with some paper towels.

Frank walked back to the dance floor and scanned the crowd as Stevie Wonder's *Maybe Your Baby* entered its last verse. He was back in the game, and his body and mind needed to keep up. He continued his search with the skill of a hawk, his eyes jumping between every face in sight. It was a couple of minutes later that Tom impatiently made his way over to his partner.

"Frank!" Tom motioned to him and they started toward the vantage point they had by the DJ booth. When they got there, Spinall was on a walkie-talkie the size of a heavy mason's brick. Tom gave Frank the 'wait-a-second' sign with his finger and tried to confirm with Jurgens. Spinall heard his answer from the radio and then gave the thumbs-up to his partner Randy and the detectives.

"Frank, we might have something over at Studio 71."

It took Frank a moment to register.

"Let's roll."

The GT40 screeched up outside the club and came to a halt halfway on the sidewalk, quickly followed by the unmarked '71 AMC Matador, the last car in the motor pool. As if on cue, two sets of car doors opened simultaneously and everyone inside jumped out. The thundering and overpowering bass emanating from inside Studio 71 (named after its street address and the club on 54th street in Manhattan) wasn't as dampened as the Rooster and made it sound like they were already inside the disco. Loud music equaled a good time to young club-goers, and apparently it worked, because the line to get in went around the block. It was Patti LaBelle's *Lady Marmalade,* a tune Frank usually loved, but tonight, he wasn't paying it any attention.

The group of undercover men descended on the front door, passing through the line of anxious and excited people. It was a bit of a struggle to get through the crowd, but they finally forced themselves into the club.

Just as the men disappeared into the abyss, a young Arab man with a cigarette in his mouth pushed his way out of the same door the detectives had disappeared into. He stopped to take care in removing a lighter from his pocket without disturbing the bandage on the top of his right hand or upset his bruised knuckles and lit his smoke. He carefully replaced the lighter and went on his way.

There was a slight foggy mist lingering throughout most of the club which clouded the view, but also accentuated the colors that shone down from the lighting grid above. Stevie Wonder's *Another Star* echoed through Studio 71 at an insane volume level, which made it hard to think or do anything else. Frank led the way through the sweaty mass. Small in size, Studio 71 was probably able to accommodate about four hundred and was another hugely popular club that sprang up overnight. One day, it was a Greek nightclub named Lakonia, the next day it, opened as a discotheque with such events as 'Tranny Thursdays,' catering to local Yalies, gays, straights, blacks, and whites, and was perfectly located mere blocks from the Yale campus and literally feet away from the Skull and Bones secret society's rumored meeting place.

Tonight, the club was packed to capacity. It felt like they had been transported an hour and a half south to New York City's Studio 54. The place had the look of a black box theatre and did not concentrate so much on the aesthetics as did the Rooster, but more on the never-ending party. Everyone seemed to be in a coke-and-booze-fueled trance while they danced in the haze of a multicolored strobe light, which seemed to be the club's only light source.

Tom leaned in as close as he could to Frank's ear and yelled, "Stevie Wonder again?"

"He *is* playing the Coliseum tonight!" Frank shouted back. "I'd bought Arianna tickets to tonight's late show," he said to almost himself.

Graham and another detective approached Frank's party from the DJ booth, meeting them at the base of the spiral stairs that led up into the crow's nest.

Frank leaned in. "Talk to me..."

"We got two guys hanging out together who match our suspects. Blond guy and a black kid. I think it could be them."

"What's their twenty?"

Graham subtly pointed them out to Frank on the dance floor. Sure enough, a blond man and a black man who matched the descriptions chatted away in a corner to three girls at the far end of the dance floor near the bathrooms. The blond had a thick, sleazy looking handlebar mustache. Frank sized them up.

"Even the mustache," Graham said. "We didn't want to approach them until you guys got here."

"Where's the third?" Frank asked. "Spinall said it came over that there were three?"

"We lost the third about ten minutes ago. Thought he went to the bathroom but he never came back. I went looking for him and he's not in the head or by the bar. He must have left."

"Description?"

"Just like the memo, Skipper. I couldn't tell in this light if either of his hands were bandaged or bruised."

Frank didn't want to seem like the New Haven Police Department was going after random blond and black twenty-somethings hanging out together, but these two did match the working descriptions, along with a third who not only matched their last perp's description, but also was seen by Graham and his team hanging out with their suspects. Frank's gut told him these were the two they were looking for, and it would be only a matter of time to find out the name of the third stooge.

Another Star ended and Wonder's song *As* started, which received a thundering applause, because the DJ inverted the sequential order on the just-released album, which the crowd immediately realized.

Frank weighed his options. "Alright, we don't wanna lose the ones we still have. Let's flank them and take them," he said over the blaring music. "Detective McHugh and I are on point. The rest of you, follow our lead. We will do the take-down. Graham, you're behind Tom. Joe, on my six. Let's be as quick and quiet as possible so we don't freak everyone out. We wanna calmly get them outside, detain them, and we can go from there. Everybody copy?"

"All around," replied Spinall. The other detectives nodded and relayed the instructions over the radio.

The plain-clothed group spread out about fifteen feet apart in the club, weaving through the crowd and gradually fishtailing back in toward the suspects. They covered the dance floor and converged on their targets from every angle. Like a pack of lions crawling through tall grass, Frank and the others slithered their way through the packed dance crowd, moving past the oblivious club-goers.

The blond man was in his mid-twenties and gave the air of having money to spend by the look of his flashy jewelry and loud wardrobe. He was still speaking to the three girls, unaware of the trap that was being hatched. The Black suspect, who looked to be in his early twenties, wore a colorful open-collared shirt that exposed a slew of gold necklaces, chest hair, and to top everything off, had on a camel-colored three-quarter length leather jacket.

Herbie Hancock's solo in Wonder's song began as they drew closer. Frank clocked the men with cool, half-closed eyes. He suddenly realized how perfectly calm he now was. The thought brought him back to why he'd become a police officer. It was the primal side of this life that was so obtuse to the majority of society. He determined years before that he was a rare breed. When his adrenaline was released in a situation, it had more of an adverse effect on him than it did on the average person. He instead mellowed, everything becoming slow motion around him. He saw every detail. From the people he'd encountered through life and by way of his profession, he knew only professional killers and trained soldiers possessed this trait. This was what kept him in the job. In the ten seconds it took for his brain to have this tangent of thought, he realized it was *these moments* that he lived for, what kept him going, and it was ultimately going to be his downfall. His pulse was slow, he was relaxed, and in this moment, he felt the best he'd felt all week.

Perhaps it was the adrenaline coursing through his veins, but the music appeared to be scored for the moment, as if it had been deliberately queued up.

Blondie glanced away from one of the girls and made eye contact with one of the undercover officers, who quickly looked away.

Shit!

Blondie looked around as if he realized what was happening. Frank saw things disintegrate right in front of his eyes in the span of five seconds. Blondie started to disregard his conversation, looked around again, and made eye contact with Spinall. They'd been made. If Frank could, he would have called off the operation, but they had no radios linking them together and because of the loud music, they probably wouldn't be able to hear a command to abort anyway. It was all happening too fast.

Blondie said something to his friend, whose facial expression changed as if a light was turned on. Even the girls noticed something was wrong with the boys and looked at each other in that awkward way that only young, uncomfortable teens could exude. One of the girls said something to the blond man but he didn't respond.

Spinall was the closest to the two perps. He slowed to a halt, so Tom and Frank could overtake him and make the initial contact. Blondie peered over toward Spinall and after a moment, Joe raised his eyes and the two made eye contact.

"Shhhhittt," Frank blurted in the heat of the moment.

Blondie swung around and in one deliberate and fluid motion, grabbed a small snub-nose revolver from the black man's back waist under the camel-colored jacket. He came around, leveled it at Spinall, and without hesitation, fired.

The bullet hit center mass in Joe's chest. Spinall screamed and grabbed for the wound as his legs fell out from under him. Blondie aimed the weapon at Frank just as a young girl dancing got between the two. Frank impulsively grabbed her and dropped. Blondie let off another round, and the discharge sounded ten times louder than the first—the muzzle blast lighting up the darkened dance floor like a flashbulb—with the projectile barely missing Frank and the girl by millimeters. It whizzed past and imbedded itself in the arm of a woman at the bar, spraying blood over a man's white leisure suit.

And then, pandemonium.

If people had missed the first gunshot, the second had them panicking and screaming in terror. A stampede started in every direction to get off the dance floor and make for an exit. Blondie threw the girl he was chatting with at Jurgens, knocking them to the floor, and then ran into the crowd.

The black suspect was gone, disappearing into the group heading toward the front entrance, passing through the gap that was made by Randy and Joe. Blondie headed toward the bathroom hallway. Frank leapt after Blondie. Within inches of being able to grab him, another crowd cut in, coming down from the overhead V.I.P. balcony area, creating a wedge between the two.

Stevie Wonder's *As* hit its coda.

The back door of the club flew open and Blondie sprinted at full speed down the alley. Frank was out the back exit seconds later, giving chase, whipping the metal door open with such force that it smashed back against the brick wall and cracked the mortar. Tom, Graham, and a few other detectives made it out the door within moments and joined the pursuit. Blondie hit the dead end of the alley and without missing a beat, jumped the five-foot-high fence in one quick, slick motion by swinging his legs over his head, followed by Frank, who did it with the same precision, using his hands as a pivot over the top bar. Frank was three feet behind the suspect when they hit the mouth of the alley.

They darted out onto the sidewalk of Temple Street in tandem, hitting the steady stream of people out strolling on a Saturday night. Tom made the sidewalk seconds later, almost catching up with Frank and their suspect.

Without breaking his stride, Blondie swung his arm around and fired off a round, which Frank dodged. The deafening sound and the projectile whizzing just inches from Frank's face and other bystanders' startled people. Onlookers screamed and ducked for cover. Frank did not flinch, because he knew if he did, he would lose the lead he had. "DOWN! Everyone, get down!" he screamed, racing after his perp.

"POLICE!" Tom, inches behind, shouted, pulling out his weapon. "Get down!"

Blondie ran toward the large New Haven Green, blindly crossing out into the four lanes of Elm Street at full speed with Frank following, the two running like Olympic athletes going for the gold. Cars screeched to a halt with horns blaring. Just as Tom crossed out, he was clipped by a large early '60s four-door Impala sedan, rolling up on the hood. The window spidered and he violently fell onto the asphalt. Tom got to his feet and continued on, acknowledging the shooting pain in his hip, elbows, and palms. "Fuck!" he blurted out in frustration at the lead now gained by Frank and the suspect, who had entered the downtown Green.

Blondie and Frank were gazelles at full speed, flying down the middle sidewalk of the Green past onlookers out on the town. Blondie swung around again and let another round off at Frank, the sound reverberating against the trees and outlining buildings. The bullet screamed by, embedding itself in a large elm tree with a loud crack from the exploding bark. Tom was back in the chase, at the lead of the other cops but still a good distance behind Frank and their perp. The foot pursuit turned and headed northeast toward the Yale campus and dorms. A litany of sirens echoed in the far-off distance, closing in from what sounded like every direction of the city.

Blondie made it out of the Green and headed blindly across College Street without yielding to traffic, which screeched to a halt. A forest green transit bus hit its brakes and the driver cut the wheel hard to avoid hitting the runner, making it skid perpendicular to the sidewalk. Frank ran out into the street and actually used his hand to bounce off the skidding bus to get around it and then bounded off a parked Ford Econoline delivery van. The city bus slid like it were on a sheet of ice. Behind it, cars skidded into each other, bottlenecking the avenue, with the transit bus coming to rest lodged between parked cars on either side of the street.

Frank and his suspect made it across, but the pileup caused a delay for Tom, Graham, and the other officers who had to start hopping over hoods and trunks to get across to the east side of College Street.

Frank followed Blondie into the Yale area, racing through the historic dorm courtyards past the old Gothic structures. The two now had some distance between them and the other pursuing officers. Frank was getting winded, his body losing the adrenaline it had coursing through its veins and his breathing became heavy. He had ten plus years on his perp, at least, and after running flat out for probably over a mile and a half, his body was feeling it. His muscles ached; his legs starting to fail, his muscles seizing.

He thought about his partner Joe, shot, lying on a booze-soaked and cigarette butt-strewn dance floor. And officer McCurdy, killed yesterday in the line of duty. And then his subconscious began flashing all the murder victims he'd investigated, the same ones that now haunted his dreams. He saw them all again, like Polaroid snapshots taken by the police photographer, all in the horrible, humiliating, and terrible ways in which the poor souls were discovered. The final insult to each of their lives. He couldn't let this mope get away. With each one that flashed by his eyes, his body found the strength to keep up with Blondie at full pace. The mother from the shootout a day before came into his mind, her eyes locked in with his as she passed. That had never happened to him before. He felt a resurgence in energy.

The perp wasn't going to outrun Frank; not after him making it this far and being *this* close.

Blondie made it back out onto the street and past the Yale Opera Hall, then crossed the avenue and entered the famous Grove Street Cemetery, full circle from the Green. The younger man fired once again at Frank, but the bullet ricocheted off a column of the Opera House, the loud echo continuing on into perpetuity. Blondie disappeared into the darkness of the graveyard, Frank hot on his trail.

The further into the cemetery they ventured, the darker it became as they raced past the huge mausoleums and towering obelisks. For the first time, Frank unsheathed his revolver; no bystanders to fret over now. He started to lose Blondie in the darkness and shadows. The ambient light from the streetlamps from the surrounding streets was completely gone. Frank tried to adjust his eyes to the darkness.

Within twenty to thirty seconds, the other policemen crossed the street into the graveyard, two radio cars skidding up to the gates. A sergeant got out of one and yelled over at Tom as he crossed the street, "Detective! What's the status?"

Soaked with sweat, Tom slowed to brief the sergeant while he unconsciously rubbed his throbbing right knee. "Signal 4, shots fired inside the Studio 71 on Whitney! Code three! Sergeant Suchy chased our perp in here. We got a copter en route. Get some rollers to seal this motha off now!" he yelled, waving his hands at the large cemetery before he disappeared inside.

Blondie slowed and looked over his shoulder. He heard the helicopter in the distance, coming out of dark clouds. He attempted to fire again but the gun's hammer clicked down on an empty chamber. He put it back in his waistband. The helicopter got increasingly louder as it approached. Feeling fatigued, he looked for a place to hide.

He came upon a mausoleum and saw two two-by-fours laying on the grass behind it.

Frank slowed, scanning the shadowed tombstones, obelisks, and mausoleums. This was the first chartered burial ground in the United States, and Frank thanked the gods above that it was one of the first to have a planned layout and paved streets and avenues that were named, so it would be very easy to clear this place once they had completely cordoned it off. The helicopter was on Grove Street and the reflections from its spotlight bounced off the polished garden of marble like thousands of unmined diamonds. Frank raised his revolver and pressed on. In the background he faintly heard the other police calling out to him. He ignored them so as not to give up his position to his target. He passed a few mausoleums and jumped around a corner. Nothing was there.

On the ground was a single two-by-four, next to a dark imprint on yellowed grass, where another had laid.

Out of the darkness, a two-by-four swung out and smacked Frank in the back of the head. He yelped and dropped to the ground. He was kicked in the gut and chest and hit again across his back. Blondie threw away the wooden board, grabbed Frank by his belt and collar, and ran him into the mausoleum wall, nearly knocking Frank unconscious. After the splash of stars, he fell to the ground, dazed and incoherent, realizing he no longer held his gun. He didn't remember dropping it or even what had just leveled him. He had to find it. He grappled for the suspect's leg, trying and get a hold of him.

Blondie saw Frank's gun on the grass. The helicopter's engine was practically deafening at this point as it was right over them, searching with its spotlight for Frank and the perp.

The young man raised the police issued revolver and took aim at the back of Frank's head. Through blurred vision, Frank saw the shadows on the grass of Blondie behind him, with a gun pointed at him.

Is this how it's gonna end? On my knees in a graveyard, with a slug or two into the back of the head?

Suddenly, a flashlight's beam shined across Blondie's face, then another, blinding him. A gunshot rang out but missed, echoing off a nearby marble headstone. Blondie dropped the gun, which hit Frank on the back, and he darted through some tall hedges into the night. Tom ran up to Frank and unloaded the rest of his automatic into the night toward where Blondie had fled, the thunderous booms reverberating off each successive row of stone. The slide kicked back on Tom's gun, indicating it was empty.

The helicopter searchlight finally found the two detectives, and within seconds, so did Graham and the other officers. From the helicopter, all that could be seen on the ground was Frank and Tom encased within a circular spotlight that was roughly twenty feet in diameter, the two resembling performers on the stage of some strange, macabre theatre. Sporadically, figures in uniform and plain clothes leapt through the circle of light that lay on the cemetery ground, continuing after the suspect. Tom knelt down, holstered his empty gun, and rolled his partner onto his back. Frank was conscious but dazed and bleeding from his nose and left ear. Others ran up to Tom and helped attend to his injured partner.

The helicopter pressed on to find the fleeing suspect, leaving the group of police officers in a shroud of darkness, much like the graveyard was accustomed to on any other night. Frank tried to calm his breathing, trying to keep conscious.

That had almost been it. His life almost ended tonight. He felt himself going, falling asleep. Everyone held him; his brothers in blue. He felt Tom's arms tightly around him and others. Now instead of seeing the faces of the victims he'd investigated through his career, his eyes closed, and he saw the two most important people in his life. Audrey and Katy.

His family.

This was why he fought the eternal battle of trying to forget. He *wanted* to forget. Because if he remembered, it would do more harm to him than a bullet fired out of a perp's gun. His wife and his little girl. He saw them.

Now he was reminded of that night so long ago, of *why* he wanted to forget. His eyes closed. Then...

Darkness.

It was snowing hard as he made his way home that late afternoon so long ago, back in 1972. He was younger then and had not a care in the world. He even remembered the well-kept beard he had at the time.

In the background, he heard his CB under the AM radio. Al Green's cover of *The Letter* was playing, and Frank had it blasting.

It was dusk, and the sky was a rich blue with enough light to illuminate the neighborhood houses and the forest surrounding East Rock Mountain. He hit traffic near East Rock Park, adjacent to the mountain. In the distance through the snowfall, Frank saw flashing lights across the park, which attracted his attention but, initially, only for the aesthetic purposes. There seemed to be an accident that was causing the delay, but Frank was in bliss as he daydreamed and listened to Al blaring out from the radio. He couldn't wait to get home to his family.

At that moment in 1972, every other noise faded away as his attention was brought to a bulletin.

"1L-19, go ahead."

"This is 1L-19, you better get in contact with Detective Frank Suchy. We have positively identified the two occupants in the accident on East Rock Ave at the park. His wife and daughter..."

His heart skipped a beat as he took his car on an off-road trek, hopping the curb, skidding between some bushes, and flying toward the scene of the accident right through the park.

"Say again 1L-19. We have confirmation that Detective Frank Suchy's wife and child are the occupants in this traffic accident on—"

The vehicle slid on the snow and grass before finally hitting a lateral ditch which disabled the car's front wheels and suspension.

You need to concentrate on what you're doing and forget this now, some part of his mind told him, trying to regain consciousness.

Frank recalled leaping out of the vehicle, leaving the door open and the engine running, and darting toward the other side of the park. He galloped toward the accident, his hectic breathing the only thing he could hear. The snow masked his visibility and the whole vista looked like the world inside a snow globe. The frantic CB traffic was getting increasingly loud as he crossed the park and approached the site. Across the field, it became apparent that a car had left the road above the park, torn through the trees, headed down the incline, and wrapped itself around a tree at the far side of the field by the batter's box.

Frank remembered slipping and falling to the ground. Through the snowfall behind him, his abandoned car's headlights were faintly visible. Frank was utterly terrified, then and now, reliving it all. He got to his feet and stumbled forward in the snow. People pointed in his direction, noticing him running across the park toward them.

Tom McHugh, who was dressed in a patrolman's uniform, saw the young detective running over first and recognized him.

"*Jesus*!" Tom exclaimed when Frank grew closer across the baseball diamond. He got closer toward the scene and collided with several people, including his best friend, fireman Chris Wallace, who tried to intervene.

"Frank, wait! Wait!"

He stared wide-eyed in abject horror as he grasped the immensity of the situation. They tried to restrain him, but it was no use. He broke free from the group of uniformed men and advanced towards the wrecked vehicle. Audrey's '72 LTD Coupe was completely totaled, with half of the front grill and hood wrapped around a large old tree. The huge elm completely obscured the driver's side of the vehicle.

Chris stepped in front of Frank and was only able to stop him by forcing eye contact. "Frank. FRANK!" His eyes darted to Chris' face. "Worry about your daughter. There's nothing that can be done for Audrey now."

His mouth opened, and he broke away from his Chris.

Overcome by sadness, he staggered toward the paramedics who were treating his daughter on the snow. Frank glanced toward the wrecked car, and once he made it around the elm, the entire accident was in view. He saw a body sprawled out through the windshield on the driver's side, covered with a white sheet lying across the hood. It was his Audrey.

He reached his daughter, who was bloody, bruised, and bleeding from the ears and nose. Her forehead was swelling. She must have smashed it on the dashboard.

Frank tried to be as reassuring and bright as he could but inside his heart was crumbling. "Hey. Hey, little one..."

His daughter looked up at him with confused, bloodshot eyes. "Daddy..." She started to cry. "Daddy, my head hurts really bad, and I can't see very well."

"You're gonna be alright now, baby," he said, his voice cracking. "Daddy's here."

"I...I kept trying to call to Mommy for help, but she just kept staring at me."

It flashed in Frank's mind what his daughter had seen in the aftermath of the crash: her mother, his wife Audrey, awkwardly positioned up on the dashboard, half through the windshield from not wearing her seatbelt, her head bent back and eyes open, staring blankly back at the little girl with blood probably flowing from every opening. The child did not understand that Mommy had died on impact.

This image he conjured up was seared in his memory for eternity.

Frank's eyes welled up with tears as he realized what the girl did not understand.

"It's gonna be okay, baby, it's gonna be okay."

"Daddy, I'm scared."

"You're gonna be okay. Daddy is gonna take care of you, okay, sweetheart?"

She did not reply.

"Baby? Katy!" There was no response. She stared blankly up at him, her face starting to relax. The paramedics quickly intervened, but after a few long moments, they could do no more.

Insane with emotion, Frank grabbed Katy and picked her up in a crushing embrace. He uttered inaudible words, stood up with her still in his arms, and started to walk away in the snowy afternoon twilight. No one tried to stop him from having this moment with his daughter. He staggered around, traveling further into the snowy white mist of the park, muttering incoherently.

It all started falling away from him again as fast as it came, like memories do. He felt the sensation of being sucked back up the rabbit hole and suddenly, he was pulled off of that world, that plane.

He started to hear sirens again, noises, and he opened his eyes to people standing over him inside the cemetery.

He said his wife's and daughter's names to no one in particular, and when he realized he'd said them out loud, he saw that no one was listening, and were instead barking out orders about sealing the area off.

10 p.m.

Back at Studio 71, sobering overhead house lights illuminated the floor of the now-empty club. Police swarmed, interviewing employees and shaken witnesses. Only empty glasses and beer cans littered the sticky dance floor, along with Spinall's blood that had pooled where he fell. The bartenders quickly counted out their tills to close out for the night. One stopped on a still-open tab while closing out the credit card machine. The manager opened the waitress's thin black book that held a table receipt, and inside, a license that had been left with the bill. It took a minute to put two and two together and realize who it belonged to. Smiling, he flagged down an officer.

Frank sat in the back doorway of an ambulance, smoking a cigarette, his feet on the bumper, while a medic tended to his wounds.

Tom and Graham walked over.

"How you doing?" Tom asked.

Frank glanced up at him only with his eyes, careful not to move his head while the attendant stitched a gash on the back of his scalp. "How's Joe? He went down in the club."

Tom turned questioningly to Graham, who had just gotten off the phone with the hospital.

"Missed his heart by inches," Graham answered. "But punctured his left lung. He's going into surgery anytime now."

Frank tried to quickly cover up his disgust by clearing his throat. This was not the time to celebrate; anything could happen while Joe was in surgery. This was his own fault, and now Joe could die because of it.

"Randy is at the hospital, waiting for Joe's girl, Paula," Tom said.

No one said what was on everyone's mind, their overwhelming worry for their partner. They did what any police officer would in this very situation, concentrate on their job. Still, the officers were shaken to the core.

"How are you feeling?" Tom asked again.

"Like a guy who got a two-by-four cracked over the back of his head after sprinting across town."

Tom shook his head in disbelief. "Where the hell did the gun come from? Why the hell would a kid like that be strapped?"

"'Cause they wanna be big-time. They've murdered two girls this week. They're primetime now, and primetime guys carry heaters. One guess is as good as any."

Frank looked up at Tom. "How are you? I saw you go up on the hood of a car."

Tom forced a half smile, "I'll live. Why are you getting stitches here on scene on the back of a bus, and not at the hospital?"

"I told him that," the medic griped, "but he insisted he remain on scene."

Surprisingly, in all the commotion, no one had noticed Frank lose consciousness in the darkness of the Grove Street Cemetery. He was the last one who wanted to volunteer something as dangerous as that. He'd be forced to go off to the hospital, and with all the red tape and mess, he'd never set foot out of the office until the New Year.

Across the street on the other side of the perimeter tape, WTNH, the local ABC TV affiliate, powered up their lights and started to grab 'b-roll' just as an NBC field anchor taped a 'stand-up' with their on-scene reporter. CBS' satellite truck was also looking for a place to set up along the street. A crowd of onlookers, who appeared to be Yalies due to their sleep-wear, awoken and trudging out from the neighboring dorms, filled the area over by the reporters, vying for a spot to sneak a peek at what was happening in their backyard.

A jet-black Lincoln Continental sped up the street and an officer moved the sawhorses so the car could enter into the scene. The Lincoln came to a halt by the press and the driver exited and opened the back door. Councilman Pregosin and

Edward Gladstone stepped out of suicide doors and made their way over to Chief Kearns, who himself had just arrived on the scene via a black-and-white. The press saw the councilman and Gladstone and hurried over for a comment, but both men skirted around the reporters, so they could first be briefed on the situation by the chief.

Tom witnessed their arrival and motioned to his sergeant to get his attention. Frank rolled his eyes, sighing. Tom conferred with a nearby lieutenant about the night's events.

A uniformed officer walked up to the back of the ambulance and addressed Frank. "Sir, somehow the Negro perp from the bar escaped our dragnet. We lost him in the crowds on Whitney Avenue with the others."

Frank glared at him. "*Negro*, officer?"

The officer turned red, trying not to look flushed. "Um, Afro-American, sir."

Frank's left cheek barely indicated a sarcastic smile. The medic finished his stitching and started to apply a gauze bandage to the back of Frank's throbbing head, matching the bandages on his nose and cheek from where he made contact with the mausoleum's rough stone. Frank focused on the councilman who, after quietly being briefed by Chief Kearns, walked over to the press with a huge smile and made a statement. When he finished, the councilman handed it over to Kearns to take questions. He and Gladstone headed over toward the ambulance.

"I think you should go to the hospital," the medic said. "You might have a concussion."

Frank grimaced. If he only knew the half of it.

Pregosin pushed through Tom and Graham and put his left foot up on the ambulance bumper so he could lean in and not be heard by the onlookers. In a furious but subdued voice, he ripped into Frank.

"What the *hell* do you think you're doing?" He paused, his expression indicating bewilderment. "Are you out of your goddamn mind?! This isn't *The Streets of* fucking *San Francisco.*"

"Sir," Graham broke in in an and tried to defend his partner and boss, "we were in pursuit of a suspect who rabbited after opening fire and—"

"You shut the fuck up right now!" Gladstone cut in.

Frank raised his hand toward Graham, signaling to him it was okay to be silent.

"People shot!" Pregosin hissed. "You create a stampede inside a packed disco and then chase after a man right through the downtown area and Yale campus, *then* cause a multiple car pile-up involving a city bus and completely disregard the safety of this city's citizens by exchanging gunfire?"

"With all due respect, *sir*," Tom weight in coldly, "fire was not returned until inside the cemetery. Sir."

Frank cut in before they could cut Tom off and further disrespect his team. "Honestly, I really don't think the sonofabitch had an escape route planned, Ted."

"Are you trying to crack a joke, Sergeant?" the councilman snapped. "Even now, are you that inept? I have to cover for *your* stupidity. Do you realize the harm you might have caused tonight with your recklessness? What we've achieved in this city, the progress we've made, all destroyed in a matter of two hours." He paused briefly to check the growing crowd before continuing, "Do you have anything to say for yourself?"

That was it. Frank's head throbbed, his body ached, and he desperately needed a drink. He was so tired of all this. The last thing he needed was to be lectured. "Boy, you really like to hear your own fucking voice, huh, Ted?"

"Ex*cuse* me?" the councilman said with rage in his eyes.

Frank had opened the proverbial door and Tom and Graham stood wide-eyed.

Frank pointed to Edward Gladstone, "And you. You think you're such a big man and boss New Haven's finest around just 'cause you hang out with this guy and head some coalitions? You realize we have an officer in surgery right now? Wanna show any concern about him or his family?" He paused for effect. "I think you might be the most useless, uncouth, moronic, sad little man I've ever met. I feel sorry for you."

"Listen to me, you little shit!" Pregosin spat. "Your career is out the fucking window with the stunt you pulled tonight. I'll have your shield pulled from you before the night's out, and I'll personally hold you responsible for this. I'm sure I can find negligence on your part, at the very least."

That made Gladstone smile.

Tom was waved over to a police radio in a parked black and white Dodge Polara and stepped away.

Frank was done speaking. He knew his career was over and wanted to be done with the conversation as well. "Well, I guess you win then, Ted."

Gladstone leaned in like he was going to plant a kiss on Frank's cheek and said with a satisfied sneer, "You've just fucked yourself tonight, Detective Sergeant. It's going to be an early Christmas after all. I'm sure the chief's gonna want to start right where Mr. Pregosin left off."

With that, both the councilman and Gladstone walked away.

Frank knew they both were right, and it was only a matter of time before he was taken off the case, as well as probably losing his shield. He hadn't even been able to brief his superior Lieutenant Warner yet. He'd seen Cleveland parked by the other black-and-whites, but Mike Warner could have been at the first crime scene at the club, or in the cemetery where they'd exchanged gunfire with their suspect. Frank tried to think what needed to be done before he was removed. "Graham, I want you to grab that journal we got from her locker and go through it with a fine-tooth comb. Where'd Tom go?"

Someone tapped Frank on his shoulder and glanced over, surprised to see his best friend Chris Wallace there on scene. He rose up off the back of the bumper as fast as his head would allow, which wasn't very quick at all.

Graham shot over, worried about his partner, "What'ya doin?"

The medic also broke in, showing concern. "Wwwaait a minute, Detective!"

Frank waved all their concerns away. "I'm alright, I'm alright." He took Chris by the arm and crossed to the side of the ambulance. "Chris, what the hell are you doing here?"

Chris' eyes were still bloodshot and from the bags underneath, it appeared he hadn't been sleeping a whole lot more than Frank.

"I heard the signal 13 call over the radio and heard you were involved. I got worried. Thought I could help. I know you're close to this fucker that, um, took Arianna's, um..." Chris found it hard even now to actually say the words that his daughter had been taken and was no longer with them.

"You're listening to the airwaves even while you're off?" Frank replied, treading lightly.

"Well, word is you're very close to something. I wanna be there when you get this bastard."

Frank placed his hand gently on his friend's shoulder. "Listen, Chris, Rhonda needs you now, and until you think you're well enough to get back to work, you shouldn't be killing yourself running out to calls, hoping it could be the one who…" He trailed off as he realized he'd probably be doing the exact same thing had Katy been taken the way Arianna had.

"Why not?" Chris replied with anger and tears in his eyes. "It's all I have!" His voice got louder with every word, and heads turned. By this time, many had recognized Christopher Wallace and people started to come over.

"Chris," Frank tried with all the humility he could muster, "please go home. Try and rest. Please." Two firefighters came up and put their hands on Chris' shoulders and his battalion brothers led him away while Frank watched silently, feeling like it was his fault everything was coming apart.

The perps could already be in the wind, and it could all be on him.

Tom hurried over to his partners. "Frank! I think might have an ID on our perp."

"How?"

"Mr. Lombardo Poe didn't get a chance to close out his tab before we caught up to him. He left his license with a barman in lieu of a credit card. The manager saw the shooting and recognized Mr. Poe as a high roller who's come in before, charging everything on his plastic." Tom grimed. "We're getting an address now."

"His license?" Frank said in disbelief. "Lamb-Lombardo?" Frank looked over at the councilman and Edward Gladstone, who were having a conference with the police chief and the recently-arrived Lieutenant Warner.

"This might be our real last chance at this thing." Frank let that resonate with his colleagues for a moment. "It's now or never. We got this one shot before our suspects scatter like roaches when the light goes on. Now, are you boys with me, or am I going at this alone tonight?"

The men made eye contact with each other, contemplating what to do. They nodded and looked back at Frank in agreement.

Frank felt proud of his team. "Good. Let's go make Spinall proud. Graham, Call Judge Coppolino. Let's get a warrant."

The three scattered just as the chief, closely followed by Lieutenant Warner, made his way over to the ambulance looking for Detective Sergeant Frank Suchy.

The Westville section of town bordered the Yale Bowl and the Yale athletic fields to the South, and West Rock Mountain (the twin to East Rock) to the north. Situated in the extreme west part of the city, hence the name, many of New Haven's doctors, politicians, professors, and the well-to-do called it home. Leroy's tip about where Lombardo Poe lived was correct, and because of the boy's clumsiness, they had the address. This brought more questions as to how a young man like Lombardo Poe was able to afford a crib in this neighborhood, because it wasn't a place where one could just rent the upstairs floor of a multi-family dwelling.

Frank's team got a warrant sworn out and, within an hour, descended on the suspect's address. The house was a large porticoed Georgian center hall colonial that could have a quarter-acre for a backyard. The sky was overcast with a dark metallic blue tint. The air was eerily still. They no longer had the chill wind from the harbor, and not a sound emanated from Mother Nature. Something was on its way.

Half a dozen cars sped up to the residence, whose neighbors had decorated their homes with pumpkins, spider webs, and Halloween decorations on a road canopied by New Haven's famous elm trees. The ideal upper middle-class neighborhood. The team turned their headlights off before they hit the block to keep from tipping off the occupants. Frank's crew now consisted of his two partners, Tom and Graham, the others that remained from the original stakeout team, and some blue suit backups they'd corralled under the radar to keep the brass unaware of what they were up to. Randy Jurgens stayed at the hospital with Joe's girlfriend while he went under the knife. Above all, he didn't want his team beating themselves up over their friend and colleague getting shot. It was a tough one, but sadly came with the job.

Frank's mind was foggy, but he kept focused despite the pain, and the bug that still lingered in the background, waiting to be fed. He kept going over everything in his head, hoping he'd crossed all his Ts and dotted all his Is.

The large group came to a halt, exited the vehicles, and rushed the house. The two leads carried shotguns as they approached the front door, pointed high and low, aiming for the door's hinges.

Frank gave the high sign to Graham, who shouted, "POLICE! SEARCH WARRANT!"

Frank waited two Mississippis then nodded to the leads. They discharged their shotguns, taking out the front door hinges. Graham put his shoulder into the door and brought it down. They entered the home with Frank on point.

There was virtually no furniture on the first floor, only large, echoing rooms adorned with rich mahogany crown molding and baseboards, empty built-in bookshelves, and freshly refinished hardwood flooring. Officers ran upstairs to the second level and, after a minute, the third floor and attic were also cleared.

Frank and Tom found the door to the basement and switched on their bulky silver flashlights, cautiously venturing down the steep wooden stairs that hugged a cold, moist, cement wall. They found a switch and turned on the overhead lights, to their surprise revealing a completely furnished basement, much to the contrast to the rest of the house, with modern audio/video conveniences, couches, plants, bar, and mood lighting. Large, powerful photography lights sat on large stands facing a long red leather couch. A portable AKAI video camera recorder was on a tripod facing the settee and adjacent loveseat with long, pig-tailed wires connecting to the fifteen-inch cabinet model Admiral Television console.

"You think he won Bob Barker's showcase?" Tom cracked to lighten the mood.

Frank walked around the back of the couch toward a door that led to a back area of the basement. He motioned over to Tom, and they covered each other, making entry and clearing the back room. This side of the basement was unfinished and, against the far wall, was an old wooden-planked workbench with some forgotten tools, an ancient vise grip bolted to the bench, and on the wall above, repurposed wooden shelves stored long-forgotten half-full paint cans shrouded in spider webs and years of dust.

Contrasting that, next to the wooden basement doors providing access to the backyard, padlocked from the inside, was a Steenbeck, a 16mm flatbed film editing table used to splice motion picture film. Next to that were large, empty bins used to hold chemicals for film-developing purposes, cutting out the middleman, and not sending it out to be developed by a third-party processing company. Hung close to the ceiling from one end of the room to the other were several clotheslines with hooks attached to dry the film once it had soaked in the processing chemicals.

On the other side of the stairs, next to an old furnace in the spot where the defunct coal bin shoot was located, was a large foldout table, on top of which sat cutting-edge video editing equipment, a new technology that could now edit the footage from the video camera on VHS tapes. Stacks and stacks of still sealed, blank videotapes wrapped in cellophane and cardboard were stored where bins of coal once resided on the cold cement floor.

Upstairs on the first level, Graham and the others rifled through various cardboard boxes scattered around on the hardwood floor. A half-dozen officers walked about searching the house, while Frank and Tom remained in the basement. Frank opened a closet door on the furnished side and was startled at what he found.

"Tom," he said, motioning with his head for his partner to come take a look.

Inside the closet were hundreds of videotapes, 8 and 16mm film canisters, neatly stacked on the floor, reaching shoulder height with different names written on each container. It took only seconds of rummaging and seeing the video titles before they both stopped short, coming to the same realization.

Tom ran out to the GT40, where he'd left his Burberry jacket. He swung open the passenger door, rifled through his trench coat in the back seat, and came across what he was looking for—the videotape they'd discovered in Arianna's locker.

Tom returned to Frank and inserted the tape into the Video Cassette Recorder. He turned the large cabinet television on and hit the play button. They huddled around the set to see what they had. The screen was snowy, just fuzz. Tom looked over to the player and at the different buttons. "That means it's blank, I think."

Frank frowned. "Can you go backward on this thing?"

"Hold on." Tom hit the 'stop' button, then another, and the tape started to rewind. They waited for a long moment; the tension in the room could be cut with a knife. When the tape stopped rewinding, Tom hit play.

Finally, the screen came to life. It was an amateur recording.

Their black suspect from the club was sitting on a couch talking with a girl. He was wearing a white domino-styled mask that covered a large portion on his upper face. The detectives recognized the background at the same time and looked over their shoulders, realizing it was filmed on that very settee, in this very room, with the equipment on-hand. There didn't seem to be much thought put into disguising themselves enough not to be identified, which screamed amateur hour. The girl seated next to their black suspect was out cold, either drunk or drugged. The camera zoomed in for a moment and, once it focused, they recognized MaryAnn Decan.

Tom gaped at the revelation. The camera quickly panned over to the adjoining couch where their suspect and the owner of the house, Lombardo Poe who, with his big bushy moustache and a poorly-disguised white domino mask, was seated next to another girl. She looked very lethargic but taken aback by the whole situation. It was Arianna.

Frank's jaw dropped.

The camera then panned back to MaryAnn and the black suspect, who now had his penis out and was stroking it with her limp hand. With a huge smile, the boy started to undress the drugged girl. The camera whip-panned over to Arianna.

Lombardo fondled her left breast and kissed her neck while she visibly fought to remain conscious. The camera swung back to the black subject, who removed MaryAnn's pants and then her panties. It whipped back to Arianna, whose eyes filled with a subdued fright, fighting to stay awake. Lombardo had his penis out, using his hand to forcefully push Arianna's head toward his crotch.

"*C'mon, baby,*" he said. *"Put it in your mouth. You know you know how to."* He snickered.

Someone cheered them on from behind the camera, which panned over to the black suspect, who was pushing MaryAnn's limp legs back over her head, so he could have access to her private area. He turned to the camera, winked, and then licked his palm, using the saliva to moisten the head of his penis. The camera quickly panned down to the photographer's body and his genitals were exposed, he was aroused, and rubbing himself with his free hand. The cameraman's body was a tan, olive complexion, indicating perhaps Hispanic or Middle Eastern in complexion. Their third suspect.

The camera moved back to Lombardo, who had Arianna's head down on his erect penis. It was clear she was being forced to perform fellatio, her head literally buried between his thighs. She let out a strangled cry.

Frank's face filled with an uncontrolled fury. He shot up, which made Tom jump, and stomped away and stormed out of the basement, enraged.

Tom stopped the tape.

Frank attempted to catch his breath in what would be the dining room if it were furnished. A uniform walked over and handed him a book.

"Thought you might be interested in this. We found it in an upstairs bedroom, next to a mattress on the floor. I think it's an address book, filled with names and other shit."

"Thank you," Frank said, exhausted. Tom came up and joined them.

"There's also a bunch of high-tech Hi-Fi equipment up there," the officer went on. "Tons of VCRS, stacked up on racks."

"Probably the equipment used to dub the movies once they're done," Frank said to Tom. "Okay, thank you, Officer."

The policeman went back to searching the house, and Frank thumbed through the book. His head was throbbing, and it wasn't only the bug getting to him now, wanting to be let out and fed. It was also the concussion that he was confident he had but didn't want to admit to anyone, let alone himself.

Detective Graham walked in, looking for him and Tom. "Frank!"

"Yeah?"

"Guess what came up when we did a background check on this kid? His father is *Edward Gladstone*!" Graham exclaimed with an unbridled excitement.

It took a moment for Frank to register the information before it clicked. "Edward Gladstone? How do I know that—wait. The councilman's man, *that* Edward Gladstone, the Urban Coalition president?"

Graham grinned from ear to ear. "Yep. Poe is his mother's maiden name."

"Son of a bitch. I guess it makes sense why he wasn't coming up in our files."

"Wonder how long it's going to take for this to get out."

"Probably already has," Frank ventured. "It doesn't change anything. We're gonna get these mothas."

"Wouldn't they be worried about being IDed in these videos if he was this guy's kid?" Tom thought out loud.

"Maybe that's what all the editing equipment is for down there," Frank said. "They cut around—"

A phone rang, and every sound in the house ceased. The officers froze in mid-motion, no one daring to say a word. The landline rang again.

Frank yelled loud enough so the whole house could hear. "Does this guy have an answering machine? It looks like he'd have an answering machine. Find the phones! Did anyone see one connected to a phone?"

The phone rang again.

Everyone called out from each room, but no one could find one.

It rang a fourth time.

Someone in the basement screamed, "I found it!"

Every officer in the house dashed downstairs as the phone rang for a fifth time. They surrounded a post-modern end table as the "Princess" model phone rang a sixth time. They were in luck; Poe had an answering machine the size of an audio receiver. After the last ring, the machine came to life.

"Leave a message," Tom said to no one in particular.

"You've reached the offices of Back Door Productions. No one is available right now, so please leave your name, number, and a brief message after the beep, and someone will get back to you as soon we can. If this is a distribution house, please specify format and quantity. Thanks."

BEEEEEPP!

"Yo, Lamb, it's Drip. I just got home and me and my girl are gonna lay low here. That shit was fucking crazy, brotha! I think

that fool you shot is dead! Ha! That's crazy, jack! Get back to me when you get this and let me know what happened." The caller hung up.

They recognized the voice as that of a black male.

Tom looked at Frank. "Drip?"

"Our black perp maybe?" Frank guessed. A thought came to him and he ran upstairs, grabbed the address book he'd left on the kitchen counter, and scanned through it, quickly realizing it was not in alphabetical order. "Drip, Drip, Drip... Are you that stupid to have him here under his nickname?" Frank found what he was looking for: A name, phone number, and an address. This was it. They now had another location of one of their suspects.

A uniformed officer came in the front door and approached him. "Detective Sergeant, just got word from Assistant Chief Stratton that Chief Kearns and Councilman Pregosin are on their way over. They'll be here any minute to be briefed by your partner. Um, Stratton wants you to meet him back on the floor immediately. It just came over the radio. He said to drop everything, and he wants you in his office ASAP."

"Okay, thanks. Go downstairs and brief Detective McHugh. See if he needs any assistance. I'll call the station right now."

"Okay." Frank watched the officer disappear downstairs. He glanced over to the front door, then back to the basement door.

Should he get Tom and the boys involved, or should he see this through himself?

He pulled something out of his pocket that his hand had been unconsciously playing with the entire night. It was

Arianna's necklace, with the skate and locker key, smeared with dry blood. He focused on it.

Fate intervened and made the decision for him.

Frank exited the house with the address book in hand and walked toward his car. He passed other officers, who nodded as they went inside. Neighbors were out in their robes, some watching from their porches or windows, others huddled together between driveways, speculating.

As he passed an undercover sedan, Frank helped himself to a twelve-gauge shotgun from a dash mount and the portable siren light that was on the dashboard. Inside the car, he could hear the chattering of the CB radio crackling away.

"*Detective Seventy-One, do you copy? Detective Seventy-One, what is your twenty? Over. Sergeant Frank Suchy, do you copy? Assistant Chief Stratton wants you to see the desk a.s.a.p.*"

He jumped into his Ford GT, plugged the siren into the cigarette lighter, positioned it on his dash, and set off. He passed Cleveland on the way down the dark street. There was no way his lieutenant, Mike Warner, would not have seen Frank's Ford drive past. No way.

Frank watched Cleveland's taillights until he was off the block, but the lieutenant never braked or turned around.

Frank turned off the street and reached across the dashboard and clicked the party hat on.

MIDNIGHT

FRANK PULLED UP to the address in the book and turned off his engine. The building was one of those small pre-war structures that was around five or six stories high but slimly built, as if it was designed to fit between two now-nonexistent buildings; the biggest telltale sign being it had no windows on each side. It was located in the Newhallville section, not too far from the Winchester Rifle Factory and the Hamden town border. The once-grand neighborhood had declined significantly in the past fifteen years and was now bordering on dilapidation and straight-out poverty. He double-checked the address book to make sure he got the apartment number right.

Frank tried to shake off the pounding in his head and throbbing face. He tried to focus but was finding it increasingly harder over the course of the night. It wasn't even the bug now; he was feeling sleepy, like he was walking in a dream. He looked at his reflection in the rearview mirror and hardly recognized the person that was staring back at him. He was close to the end. He knew it. He couldn't shake that feeling coming from his gut.

He glanced back to Drip's building and a taxi pulled up out front. Lombardo Poe paid the driver, got out, and entered the apartment complex.

"Motherfucka," Frank spat.

He put the black address book in the glove box and snatched up Tom's Burberry trench coat and his twelve-gauge Mossberg. He put the coat on as he crossed the street and hid the shotgun underneath. The wind was starting to blow, foreshadowing what was to come. The strong breeze lifted the bottom of his jacket up enough to expose the eighteen-inch barrel hidden underneath.

The metallic sky lit up with flashes of lightning in hazy clouds that lingered far off on the horizon. A few seconds went by and then a crackle of thunder whispered in the distance.

In the once-luxurious cracked, two-toned marble foyer and lobby, Lombardo waited for the slow elevator to arrive back down to the ground level, his eyes focused on the crooked arm of the indicator above the elevator entrance that was slowly descending. Frank peered out from around the corner and watched his suspect step in. The elevator doors closed, and Frank raced up the stairs to beat it. He ran up three flights at full speed and made it up before his perp.

Lombardo nervously watched the numbers above the door as the elevator reached his floor. It slowly settled, and the doors opened. That was where he saw Frank waiting.

They made eye contact and the detective politely smiled.

"Hey-up."

Frank hit Lombardo so hard in the face it floored the young man. He shook the pain out of his fist.

He patted the unconscious body down but found no weapons. He dragged Lombardo out of the elevator by the ankles and slapped him several times in the face to wake him.

Lombardo stood in front of apartment 3F and rang the buzzer. He tried to conceal his broken nose in the distorted image of the shiny brass peephole. Bobby Bland's new single *I*

Got the Same Old Blues belted out from inside the apartment. Frank knew the song well because he'd just purchased the forty-five single himself last week. A dragging of feet could be heard as someone slowly made their way to the door. A moment later a female voice came from the other side.

"Who that? Lamb?"

Still dazed, Lombardo glanced over to his left. Frank stood with his back against the hallway wall, the shotgun in his hand pointed at Lombardo's head, just out of view. Lamb looked back toward the door and addressed the woman.

"Janeka, it's Lamb. I need to talk to Drip. Is he home?"

Frank listened intently with all his focus, even as his eyes fixated and subconsciously studied the innocuous detail of layers of paint that framed the trash shoot, back when so many of these buildings used the incinerator in the basement. It was covered with a lava flow of cream paint, dulling any detail to the once-gorgeous trim work, now just looking like a volcanic eruption. Even as his subconscious mind took all these details in, like a predator hiding in tall grass, Frank waited to pounce.

The door slowly unlocked and opened, and Frank rushed in, using Lombardo as a shield. It timed perfectly to the synthesizer's first appearance in the song's solo.

He plowed right past the woman, who appeared to be in her mid-twenties, dressed in pajamas with curlers in her hair and white powder all over her nose, pushing Lombardo into her. She fell to the floor, emitting an ear-piercing scream. Frank hoped the stereo was loud enough to block her yelling.

"Drip! *Drip!*" she shrieked.

A door flew open and out came a wide eyed but half-asleep-looking Drip, brandishing a revolver in his left hand. Before he could react, Frank threw the butt of his shotgun into Drip's gut and he doubled over in pain, dropping his pistol onto the shag carpet. Catching a second wind, Lombardo jumped off from the couch and onto Frank, knocking him off balance. They crashed into a record shelf causing vinyl and wax LPs to rain upon them as they fell to the floor. Frank held onto the shotgun with a vise-like grip, even as Lombardo got on top of him. Before he was able to get a punch in, Frank grabbed him by the throat, and the young man instinctively tried to remove the clenched hand. Drip's girlfriend hadn't stopped screaming; the shrill squealing continued as she got to her feet and ran into another room.

Frank flung his knees up in a frenzy and made contact two or three times with Lamb's back before the boy reacted. Lombardo eased his body to escape the knee kicks, and Frank used the shotgun as a crutch, putting all his weight on it to stand, throwing Lombardo off and onto the nearby glass coffee table, shattering one side. Drip was getting to his feet and going for his revolver on the rug. On one knee, Frank slid his grip on the twelve-gauge up to the barrel and using it like a bat, swung, cracking Drip in the face with the heavy wooden stock, breaking some of the teeth in the man's mouth. Frank got up and kicked Lombardo in the gut to keep him on the floor. The kid fell back onto the thick carpet.

The music was still blaring, now in the song's second to last verse, with Bobby wailing away. Frank grabbed the revolver off the carpet, put it in his waistband, and started in on them.

"You wanna be a tough guy, asshole?" he said to Drip as the man started to get up again and was met by a smash to the face by Frank's dress shoe. Frank kicked Lombardo again in the stomach to keep him on the ground. They lay there, writhing on the floor in pain. Over on the unbroken portion of the glass coffee table was a small mound of cocaine with lines prepared with a straight razor, ready to be snorted.

Drip rolled over onto his back and spat out the blood and bits of teeth, touching the bruising on his face with his fingers. He leered over at Lombardo. "I can't believe you brought this pig up in here, Blood."

Screaming like a banshee, the woman charged from the kitchen with a butcher knife. When she was close enough, Frank stepped back, and rabbit punched her in the chin. She dropped to the floor, out cold. Frank focused back on the two men. He kicked Lombardo in the gut for a second time and turned his attention back to Drip.

"Get up." Drip did not react. "*GET UP!*"

Drip sighed defiantly and started to his feet with his hands in the air, never breaking eye contact with Frank. His pupils were bloodshot, wet, and emotionless. Neither man was bothered about *why* Frank was there, only that he was and had caught them. He was an annoyance and intrusion in their worthless lives. Here, they had one of the wealthiest men in town's son, engaging in sadistic behavior probably only for a petty thrill. It wasn't like he even needed the money.

Frank's blood boiled and his whole body radiated heat like he had a raging fever. He no longer felt he had the mind-set to make rational decisions, and the little voice inside him feared what he was capable of next.

The goddamn bug didn't even matter anymore.

Isn't that something?

"You couldn't pay someone to do this?" he roared. "You had to drug 'em and rape 'em?"

Neither one responded.

"They were only *kids. KIDS!*"

Frank kicked Lombardo for a third time in the stomach and slapped Drip in the face with a stiff, open palm. He was seeing red.

Drip looked up at him with pure hatred in his eyes. "Fuck you, nigga." Spit came out as he spoke, emphasizing his words.

"Fuck me?" Frank slammed Drip in the face with the barrel of the Mossberg pump, breaking his nose like a squeezed banana. "Alright, bright boy, I'm gonna ask you one question and you're—"

Lombardo swore out loud and Frank instinctively kicked him again; it didn't warrant another whack, but Frank was in the thick of it and didn't care.

Lombardo yelped in pain and spit out a dark red mixture of phlegm and blood.

"Listen, *Drip*. I'm gonna ask you one question and I want an honest answer or me and my new friend from Sears and Roebuck here," he lifted the Mossberg in his left hand, "are gonna experiment with your bone structure." He gave them a moment to process his statement before he went on.

"Which one of you killed MaryAnn Decan?"

Lombardo looked up from the floor at Drip. "Don't say nothing."

Frank unsheathed his service revolver and aimed it at the blond boy's head.

Drip looked down at Lombardo. He looked back at Frank and stared at him for about ten seconds before he finally spoke. "I want a motherfucking lawyer."

Frank held the weapons in each hand for a time, contemplating what to do next.

He holstered his service revolver and grabbed the gun from his waist and pointed it at Drip, then swung the twelve-gauge toward Blondie. He'd already told himself he was going rogue. He was alone, committed, and would see this out, no matter what road it led down. These bastards weren't remorseful and didn't even care about the lives lost. The decision had already been made for him by them through their own actions.

In one fluid motion, he lowered the revolver and squeezed the trigger, shooting Drip in the leg. Since it was at point blank range, the bullet went through clean and exited, digging itself into the faded and scratched hardwood floor under the filthy shag area rug. Drip howled and dropped, writhing in pain.

"I asked you a question. Which one of you killed MaryAnn Decan?"

Lombardo's eyes widened like they were about to fall out of their sockets. "Are you crazy? He just told you he wants a law—"

Frank pointed the revolver at Lamb's face. "That time is over."

"Wait, do you know who I am! Who my *father* is! Well, motherfucker, you're soon gonna!"

Frank pulled the hammer back on the next chamber and pressed the barrel into Lombardo's nose. That shut the young man up, his eyes almost crossed looking down the barrel. Frank swung it back at Drip. "Which one of you killed MaryAnn Decan?"

Drip, defeated and wounded, his tough guy persona now gone because of his bleeding leg, could hardly muster up the energy to speak. He was only able to whimper, "Yasmile."

"What? Who? Is he the third guy involved in this?"

Drip nodded, clearly in agony. "Yah-Y-Yasmile Rasheen. I-I need an ambulance. This ain't funny, I'm bleeding."

"Yeah, you both are probably gonna die today. Now you know how it feels. It's a bummer, huh, man? Now, for the sixty-four thousand-dollar question. Who killed Arianna Wallace?"

There was a long beat before Drip answered, "Yasmile."

"Anything wrong with his hand?"

"What?"

"Tell me what happened to his hands."

"They're bruised, and she cut him. She cut him pretty bad."

"Where is he now?" Frank's eyes went cold. "Where is he?" Drip did not answer. "Where is he?"

Silence.

Frank raised his shotgun and pointed the barrel at his face, nudging Drip with the weapon. "Open your mouth."

"What?"

"Open your *fucking* mouth." He racked a cartridge into the chamber. By this time the song was over, and the record's needle was in the middle of the forty-five, scratching and crackling, so the noise created by Frank chambering a round echoed hollowly in the living room.

"Wha…?"

Drip slowly opened his mouth. Frank raised the shotgun, took a step back to gain the room, and raised the twelve-gauge so that the barrel was about two inches from the boy's lips.

Is this where the world is headed?

"Where is he?"

"Don't worry," Lombardo said with a bloody grin to Drip. "None of this is admissible in court. He ignored our requests for a lawyer and didn't read us our rights." He turned to Frank with a sardonic smile. "You didn't Mirandize us, asshole. After you get fired as a cop, my father will make sure half of your soon-to-be shitty security-guard paycheck goes to the lawsuit we win against you!"

"You wanna be tough guys? You wanna brutalize innocent young girls? Huh?"

Frank looked between the two. A rage was in him that he couldn't dissipate. The little voice inside of him, that he couldn't distinguish from the bug or Cliff Edwards playing the role of his conscience, kept telling him he needed to stop before it went too far, before it got *too* out-of-hand. But he couldn't. Rage surged within him. His hand shook. He looked down at Lombardo Poe, the privileged rich white trash who could do anything and be whatever he wanted because of the affluence of his father. He himself chose this path. Frank could not control it anymore.

Game over.

He leaned down to Lombardo and pressed the barrel of the revolver into his forehead. Frothy white spit came out as Frank yelled, "You think 'cause your daddy's a bigshot, he'll be able to get you out of raping and murdering children!"

"Yep," Lamb chuckled, not bothering to make eye contact with the detective.

He aimed the barrel against the blond boy's forehead and stood for a moment. He pressed so hard that the area around it went white from the pressure. Frank then put the gun back in his waistband and hit Lombardo in the head with his fist. Repeatedly.

He struck him again and again about the forehead and face. It all slowed down for Frank, and he thought he was gonna kill this kid. The whole world slowed down around him. Lombardo's eyes glazed over and rolled back into his head, and he lost consciousness.

Frank was getting ahead of himself and stopped after the fifth or sixth blow. He hit him once last time. That was for Joe. His knuckle broke with that last hit.

"Neither of you deserves to live." Frank pressed the shotgun even harder against Drip's head. "Where is he?"

Silence.

Frank brought the shotgun down and leveled his revolver on Drip.

"I'm gonna count to three. Where is he?"

He couldn't believe the narcissism and self-entitlement of these two.

"One..."

They didn't care they'd killed two young girls with their entire lives in front of them. That never even entered their minds. Who knew what else they'd done? These were the types that would torture poor, helpless animals and take joy in it, for Christ's sake.

"Two..."

His finger intently danced on the trigger. His hand shook. This was it.

12:37 A.M.

FRANK CRADLED THE phone receiver close to his ear. "Yeah? Desk Sergeant? It's Detective Sergeant Frank Suchy. Mario?" He listened intently before continuing. "I know he's got a BOLO out on me. Get Detective McHugh on the radio and tell him I've got the two perps, Drip, aka Stanley Carlson, and Lombardo Poe in custody. They resisted and there was a struggle, one shot the other in the melee. No time for that. Listen! Tell Detective Tom McHugh and Detective Graham Birdsall to take a team and meet me at Union Station as soon as possible. Our third perp, who is our murder suspect, was tipped off and is making a run for it right now. He'll probably be on the next train to New York City. I need a wagon and a bus to 412 Henry Street, apartment 3F to take these guys into custody. Right now. We don't want them to bleed out now, do we?"

Frank hit the gas and the GT screamed down the street. Thunder boomed in the distance, rolling into the valley between East and West Rocks. The party-hat flashed like a red lighthouse on his dashboard and with every other second, the light streaked red across Frank's face.

He got out of the neighborhood in no time, passing the corner The Five Satins used to sing on and where they wrote *In the Still of the Night*. He figured the best way to Union Station was to get on one of the major avenues that led right downtown.

His car made air crossing the hill over Prospect Avenue from the speed he was traveling and the street's incline. The GT40 came crashing back down hard on the side street, and Frank was lucky he didn't pop a tire, lose a shock absorber, or anything else. Shit, he'd just passed Prospect Avenue.

He took a hard right onto Whitney, shifted, and dropped the hammer to the floor. The sports car flew down the street, hop-scotching in and out of traffic. Frank drove with a nerveless absorption; it actually relaxed him.

Then the rain began.

He honked his horn, trying to get traffic out of his way. He darted around the slower moving cars and vans, and narrowly missed being T-boned by a complacent Ford C-900 Tilt Cab G.O.D. truck that tried to beat the light, which then had the gall to lay on its own horn in angry protest.

Frank flicked on the radio, then focused ahead and saw the congestion down the road at the upcoming intersections. There was an accident below a signal light that was causing delays, plus the Stevie Wonder crowd at the Coliseum was probably emptying out as well, and everyone in the Tri-State area had come to town to see that. The whole downtown would be a parking lot.

He rolled the radio knob, stopping the dial on Al Green's cover of *The Letter*, a song he hadn't heard in years and purposely avoided...since the afternoon he stumbled onto Audrey and Katy's car accident.

His family.

He downshifted, put his signal on, and careened around the corner in an expertly controlled slide onto Willow Street, putting it into third. It was raining hard now. His windshield wipers battled to keep up.

Not this song, not now.

Frank kept the GT rolling, trying to knock the thoughts out of his head as he jumped on the highway heading south to make up some time. He couldn't listen anymore and tuned to CBS 880 while he continued to confidently dodge in and out of traffic, which was starting to become heavy. Luckily the bulk of it was in the opposite direction, leaving the downtown area.

Audrey…

The damage was done. Those thoughts he tried for so long to forget were now unleashed and bouncing around in his head, and he couldn't stop them. He couldn't distract himself away from them anymore. He had to see them again. And again. And again.

"C'mon, c'mon…" Frank said as he hit gridlock, advancing downtown toward the connector. The traffic report came on. Frank thumbed up the volume to hear over the engine.

"*—in Connecticut at the 95 and I-91 interchange in New Haven we have bumper-to-bumper delays all over the downtown area because of that Stevie Wonder concert letting out. Elsewhere, at the West Haven Tolls...*"

He snorted back the tears and mucus, trying to calm down and stay focused. Getting on the highway was a dodgy gamble tonight, and if he got stuck in this traffic, he'd never get to the train station in time. A fog had set in off Long Island Sound and was cutting off visibility ahead.

Frank turned off the radio, saw an exit for downtown, and gunned the Ford down the right-hand breakdown lane. He sped toward the off-ramp, finding the visibility worse and worse. He looked down at his watch: 12:42 a.m.

Out of nowhere, a Chevy Nova darted out of the congestion and into the breakdown lane, probably having the same idea Frank had, but not checking its rearview. Frank laid on the horn and had only a second to react. He sped up, swerved to the right, and rode into the guardrail, missing the Chevy by only inches, which was the only option that wouldn't result in a rear-end collision. He braked, trying to regain control of the vehicle and get himself off the guardrail before hitting the off-ramp at such a high rate of speed, but as the GT 40 came dislodged, it shot like a rocket off the landing strip, and the car hydroplaned. It did not respond to the compensation Frank made with the wheel.

The Ford crossed the off-ramp and hit the left exit's guardrail hard, sliding against it, then like a pinball, it crossed over and again hit the opposite rail. Though he was belted in, Frank's hands left the wheel and his body mimicked the violent G-force induced motions like a crash-test dummy in a controlled accident.

The car slid down the slick road at incredible speed, hopped the curb sideways, breaking both the right-side axles, took down a few signs, which again righted the car head-on before it finally crashed into and came to a halt against a cement pillar that held up the connector.

The engine began to smoke in the light rain, and a few other vehicles on the side street slowed to a crawl to view the wreck.

♦ ♦ ♦

Audrey. Katy. I'm sorry. I'm so, so sorry.

His eyes stared out blankly into the night. He did not remember opening them. He must have regained consciousness but was still in a daze. He blinked slowly, coming back to the present.

Someone was shaking him, a bystander standing outside his wreck, seeing if he was okay.

Frank fully came around and looked at his rescuer. It dawned on him where he was and what had just happened. He peered out through the windshield.

The car was totaled. Somehow, even seated, he was getting rained on from the outside. The poor girl had had it.

He looked at his watch: 12:45.

With the help of his new friend, he pried the driver's door open and fell out of the car onto the wet street. He was helped to his feet by another bystander in a public works jacket. Frank wiped the blood from his nose and mouth and took a couple of stumbling steps away from them. There was a shooting pain in his right knee, but he ignored it. He jogged away, toward the train station.

"Hey, mister, where you going? You're hurt! You shouldn't run away! Mister?"

With every step, Frank regained more of his strength, and, in seconds, was lost in the fog. On the other side of the Oak Street Connector, barely visible in the distance, the looming lights of the large railway station shone bright.

UNION STATION

12:53 a.m.

THE RAIN HAD slowed to a drizzle. A dozen taxis sat idling in the driveway of the massive Union Station, waiting for potential fares. Other vehicles came and went, their occupants saying hurried goodbyes or meeting newly-arrived loved ones. A good amount of people walked about, entering and exiting.

Built in 1920, the once grand station had fallen into complete disrepair, which ironically made it a microcosm for the city as a whole. It was on the verge of being shut down because of its state of dilapidation, much like the entire railroad industry in the Northeast.

The New Haven Police Department Building was in view, illuminated across the street through the lingering fog which hung low to the ground. Lightning flashed across the horizon, touching down miles away up on East Rock Mountain's peak, on the three-story high illuminated metal WWI monument atop. It made for a haunting snapshot atop the dark mountainous landscape.

Frank appeared out of the darkness and fog, hurrying toward the station, his jog more of a trot as he favored one leg. He crossed Union Avenue, galloped through the driveway and through the circular doors. As he entered, the sky gave way with a huge flash and a crash of thunder, and torrential rain pelted down once again.

Once inside he immediately relaxed, making his disposition calm to avoid attracting any unwanted attention. The rain had pretty much cleaned all the blood from his face, but his cheek was bruised and swollen, and his lip was cut, probably needing stitches. The bandages on his face were wet and made the blood underneath show crimson through the white gauze. He tucked his shirt in and straightened up as best he could. His knee was giving him problems and felt like it was swelling.

The interior of the station was enormous and styled after its sister station, Grand Central Terminal in New York. He glanced up at the large clock. 12:55. He checked the large track board to see what trains were departing. He took a deep breath, exhaled, and walked toward the ticket windows. He glided along the floor of the immense station between the large wooden booths and scanned the crowds like a shark, his eyes never stopping for more than a second over the faces of the various commuters, workers, and homeless who napped on the large pews. He zigzagged around the bouncing antenna of a denim-clothed eleven-year-old's AM/FM radio headphones, which, even though they covered the boy's ears completely, Frank still discerned the muted beat of Iggy Pop's *China Girl.* A loud staccato of dress shoes banging on the floor caught Frank's ear as six men rushed toward him. Tom, Graham, another undercover, one uniformed New Haven policeman, and one Conrail security officer approached Frank.

Tom was shocked by his partner's appearance. "Frank, what the hell happened? You alright?"

"Yeah, I'm cool. I got two of the perps in custody. The third is our killer, Yasmile Rasheen. He's rabbiting."

"We heard, but—"

"Jesus, you look like shit," Graham broke in. "You know Stratton's got a BOLO out on you? He wants you off this case and is threatening to take your shield. Warner's on his way over but is stuck in traffic."

"Thank you, Graham."

"You're out of breath. You okay?"

"Uh…" Frank squinted, trying to make his answer sound as sane and in control as possible, "I TCed on the east end of North Frontage Road by the Coliseum on my way over here."

"You were involved in a traffic collision?" Tom raised a brow and his voice rose an octave in concern.

"Yes, a single vehicle. Just me."

"I think you should go to the hospital."

"No," Frank snapped. He tapped Tom on the arm. "Walk with me." They started to roll ahead of the group, Frank with a noticeable limp. "Our guy's here. Tom, talk to me. What have you got?"

"We have a 1:07 Amtrak leaving for Penn Station. You got a sixty-four-car freight train passing at 1:13 bound for Philly that'll make one more stop in Newark, and you got the 1:10 local bound for Grand Central—the last train out until five in the morning."

"Buses?"

Tom nodded. "One's leaving in about six minutes."

"You got a description being handed out to employees and security?"

"We do have a description being handed out on what you provided over the radio."

Frank looked around, "Okay."

Tom turned to the undercover and Graham. "Prokop, get some more guys over here. I want you to hang in the terminal and keep your eyes open." He spun around to the two uniformed officers. "Go linger up on the two platforms by the local and the Amtrak, see what you can find. Justin," he said to another officer, "go hang in the tunnel between here and the platforms. Alright, get!" The men scattered, and Graham slowed down to watch the terminal. Tom raced to catch up to Frank, who stalked with a fury toward the south-end parking lot. His knee ached, with each step getting harder to make.

"Why the hell did you leave me in Westville, Frank? What the fuck?"

Frank knew there was no explaining what he did. "I didn't want to get you wrapped up in all of this and put your head on the chopping block. You have your family to worry about. My shield's being taken as soon as I see Mike, Stratton, or Kearns, and I can't have that happen right now. It was my only chance to protect you guys. I'm sorry. I was working on a timetable I didn't put in place." He paused. "I owe Arianna this. I owe this to all of them," he mumbled.

They exited the station into the pouring rain and approached the embarking Greyhound. Tom approached the driver, who was at the head of the line holding a black umbrella collecting tickets, and flashed his badge.

Frank boarded the bus and maneuvered toward the back, checking all the faces. He stopped at the middle of the vehicle, did a 180, and walked off before Tom was even able to get on.

"No go," he said as he stepped down.

They went back into the station. Frank glanced at the clock: 12:58. His eyes shot to the departure/arrival board. The departure light for the 1:07 Amtrak to Penn Station flashed. Below that was the New York-bound 1:10 local. Frank checked the track numbers. Turning around, he darted toward the Amtrak ticket window with Tom on his heels. He jumped to the head of the line and flashed his badge to the ticket agent. Tom was stopped by the sight of three other uniformed officers arriving through the main entrance along with Sergeant John Copela.

Tom hurried over and had just about got the group up-to-speed when Frank joined them.

"Frank, the councilman—" the sergeant started in.

Frank ignored Copela and turned to speak to Tom. "No tickets for the 1:07 Amtrak have been sold since about 10:15. He might not have gotten here that early, but don't let it leave until you check it." He glanced over to Copela and another, "You two come with us."

Tom handed them a description of the suspect.

The councilman and Edward Gladstone entered through the revolving doors, trailed by Lieutenant Warner. They immediately had eyes on Frank and Tom.

"Sergeant!" Pregosin shouted.

"That's what I was trying to tell you, lad," Sergeant Copela whispered.

By his anxious expression, word had obviously gotten to Gladstone about his son Lombardo. This was the first time Frank had ever seen Gladstone in this state. The man had lost his stature, all the power and leverage he liked to wield around, and now was just a small, helpless man, a father who needed Frank's help. Behind them, Lieutenant Warner stood silent, sizing up the developing situation.

"Detective," Gladstone started with a smile and put his hand on Frank's shoulder, leading him away from the others. This might have been the first time he gave Frank his full attention.

"Sergeant," Frank corrected him.

"Yes, Sergeant. I am sorry. Sergeant, some information has come to light that implicates my son in this whole nasty affair."

"I'm not at liberty to discuss an ongoing investigation."

"Now wait, Detect—Sergeant. I was wondering if we could talk about this. Maybe we could come to some kind of understanding. He's a good boy and I would like to talk about his future."

Frank looked from Gladstone to the councilman, who focused intently on what Frank's decision might be. "I'm working a case right now. Maybe we can speak tomorrow at some point."

Gladstone took Frank by the shoulder and stepped away from the group, but still within earshot of Councilman Pregosin. "Listen, Sergeant, we both know that certain… indiscretions can be made in youth, and tragically two young adults lost their lives. But that was the act of one individual working on his own and my son had nothing to do with it, which the evidence will bear out."

"So you've spoken to him about it?"

Gladstone took a slight pause and cleared his throat, attempting to tread lightly and not incriminate himself. "He just apprised me of the situation on the way to the hospital."

"Very convenient."

"Sergeant, I am willing to overlook any injury laid upon my son during his arrest."

"That's what happens when you try to shoot and beat-up police and resist arrest: people get hurt."

"Of course, he and I will zealously help you prosecute this Yasmile Rasheen to the fullest extent of the law."

"I don't know what you're quite getting at, because at this point, only the D.A. can do anything for your offspring, so please excuse me." Frank turned to continue with his stakeout. Gladstone grabbed him by the arm. He was grasping at straws and Frank saw the frantic desperation in his eyes.

The zillionaire had realized he was now vulnerable.

"Sergeant, if you were willing to play down my son's role in your report and subsequent investigation," he said under his breath, "the sky could be the limit as to your future. Lieutenant, Assistant Chief of Detectives, maybe even public office. Whatever your heart desires. You would have an endless coffer with my family behind you."

Frank's eyes jumped to Pregosin, who looked more surprised than anything to where the conversation was leading. "Anything I want?" Frank repeated, not taking his eyes off of the councilman.

"Anything your heart may desire."

Frank looked at Lieutenant Mike Warner, who stood stoned-faced. He turned back to Gladstone. "Well, I guess the only thing I'd want, which has been what I've wanted since we met, is to tell you to fuck off. And I hope your son rots in prison," Frank said with a smile. The first smile he felt like he'd had in a week.

Gladstone's face reddened and became enraged. The councilman smirked at Frank, agreeing with his statement, granting Frank the affirmation he had so long denied him.

"Me fuck off? Fuck *you*! I will make it my personal mission to take you down and spend every *cent* I have to ruin you, Sergeant. Enjoy your last night as a policeman, you fuck!"

Frank gestured to the councilman. "I hope you heard all that because he may have just implicated himself in our case."

"Are you going to stand for this, Theo?" Gladstone bellowed.

Councilman Pregosin looked from Gladstone to Frank. "Not only am I supporting him, I wholeheartedly agree with him."

Frank nodded to the councilman, who nodded back and smiled.

"What now, Lieutenant?" Frank asked his boss.

The wheels in Mike Warner's head turned. Then the faintest crack of a smile appeared on the side of his face. "Go play this hand out, Sergeant. Then we'll talk."

Frank nodded and continued on, followed by Tom and his group. The team headed toward the steps leading to the lower tunnel connecting commuters to the above-ground track platforms. They travelled down the old, noisy escalators toward the underground tunnel.

They entered the large, neon-lit metallic tunnel and waltzed through the crowd, then dashed to the left, up the stairs toward track four, where the Amtrak was departing. Frank and Tom exited out onto the platform as the doors of the train were about to close. Tom flagged down the conductor and Frank scanned the people still on the platform. He motioned to the uniforms with him. "You start from the back; you from the head. Shouldn't take you that long."

The occasional streak of lightning illuminated the sky like a flashbulb. Frank glanced over to the next track where an FL-9 diesel engine idled, connected to three spare 'standard' cars. On the next track that shared a platform with the diesel, the 1:10 local was loading its passengers. Frank signaled to Tom and they shot down the stairs and made a right, while the other officers searched the Amtrak.

The two walked onto the platform of track eight, next to the 1:10. Tom approached the officer stationed there, while Frank walked up to the conductor who was by a payphone.

Frank handed him a description of their suspect and turned to Tom, who approached them.

"Conductor said he hasn't seen our guy."

"Yeah, neither has the officer there," Tom replied.

"Let's just feel it out here."

"Groovy."

The two separated. Tom walked along next to the idling FL-9 diesel triplet and headed toward the back area to cover that end of the platform. Frank stood poised and studied the small crowd of commuters. The FL-9 was put into gear and it immediately got very loud as it powered up to move.

It startled Frank. He glanced in the FL-9's direction. Just as he did this, a man walked out onto the platform from one of the open cars of the 1:10. It was Yasmile Rasheen. He started to light a cigarette but froze, realizing that two uniformed cops were searching the crowd about ten feet away from him. His eyes crossed to the platform exit and noticed another beat cop positioned there. He calmly stepped backward, did a 180, and stepped back onto the train.

Frank glanced back, unaware of what had transpired. He checked his watch: 1:08. His back was killing him. His arm felt numb and his knee was swelling, but he couldn't think about all that now. He moved up toward the head end of the 1:10. When he hit the first car, he looked out into the railyard. He turned back toward Tom, who was all the way on the other end of the train, walking back.

Tom's eyes found his partner through the crowd. Frank checked his watch: 1:09. The echo of the train's public-address system started as the conductor made the final announcements.

"*Good evening, ladies and gentlemen. This is your 1:10 local Conrail train to Grand Central Terminal. This train will be making station stops at Milford, Stratford, Bridgeport, Fairfield, Southport...*" Tom lost sight of Frank, as the last-minute crowd of travelers rushed onto the departing train. "*...Stamford, express to Harlem 125th, then on to Grand Central Terminal. This is not an Amtrak train, so Amtrak tickets will not be honored on this train...*"

When the crowd thinned out, Frank was gone as if he'd vanished, no longer on the platform.

"*1:10 to GCT. First stop Milford. Mind the closing doors. All aboard!*"

The bell rang to alert everyone that the doors were closing. Tom hurried down the platform, looking for his partner. He rushed over to the beat cop by the stairs. "Garrison, where's Suchy?"

The doors on the train closed and it began to pull away just as Tom realized what had happened. He threw his hands in the air and ran toward the stairwell that led to the tunnel below.

♦ ♦ ♦

The train cleared the platform and Yasmile breathed a sigh of relief.

Frank was at the head end of the train and made his way through the cars toward the back, searching the faces one by one.

Yasmile felt at peace. He stood up, had a good stretch, and went to the nearby bathroom and locked the door. Seconds later, Frank walked past, unaware that only a door separated him from his suspect. He continued into the next car. The toilet flushed and Yasmile exited and returned to his seat. He leaned back and closed his eyes.

Frank made it to the last car. He reached the back door and saw nothing but darkness and the faint lights from the railyard.

Had this gamble backfired?

He turned around and headed back up toward the head end of the train.

Yasmile opened his eyes and saw the conductor come out of his small cab and start walking toward him, making eye contact as he passed. The conductor stopped dead in his tracks; he recognized Yasmile. Spinning around, he casually made his way back toward the cab from which he came out of. Yasmile noticed and took interest, and the conductor made the mistake of looking back. The man looked away, but it was too late. The highly paranoid boy realized something was up.

The conductor made it to his cabin, but saw Frank in the next car at the far end walking toward him. The conductor hurried into the next car and headed toward the policeman. Yasmile, who'd been watching intently, stood up and leaned into the isle, keeping the conductor in sight. The little man raced over and exchanged words with the detective, pointing back toward the other car, and Frank followed with his eyes.

Yasmile Rasheen locked gazes with Frank Suchy. Neither looked away.

Yasmile bolted in the opposite direction toward the head end. Frank promptly followed, and the chase was on. The conductor raced back to his cab to radio the engineer.

Frank was about a car-length away from Yasmile, who was weaving his way through the passengers who were still trying to acquire a seat. The suspect raced down the aisle, knocking people over, his only focus now on evading Frank.

With a sharp squeal from a microphone, the conductor's voice came over the P.A., "*Uh, Patsy, We've got a problem. Alert the New Haven P.D. and let's pull it back onto the platform immediately.*"

Yasmile's eyes bulged after hearing the announcement. He drew a shiny new .45 automatic from under his jacket. People screamed, collapsed to the floor, and ducked into the already-crowded seats. Frank saw and pressed on at an even faster pace.

"Police. Everybody, down! Get down!"

"*Roger that there, Jimmy, taking her back into the yard,*" the engineer responded to the conductor over the announcement system.

The train began to slow.

Frank was now half a car-length away from Yasmile and closing in. "Get down! Everybody, down!"

The train came to a complete stop with a gradual jerk.

Yasmile hit the next door and realized he had nowhere to go; he was in the last car. Wild-eyed, he frantically spun and fired a round at Frank.

The bullet whizzed by behind a deafening noise that exploded through the enclosed car. Passengers screamed and ducked for cover. Frank dived into the vestibule, slamming with a bang against the train door.

"New Haven PD, Everyone, stay down!"

Yasmile began to pull the locks back on the front door of the head car. After a quick scan to see if anyone had been hit, Frank poked his head out to get eyes on Yasmile.

He was gone, and the heavy door at the front of the train took its time swinging closed. Frank got to his feet, favoring his swelling knee, and hurried after him.

The engineer's cab door opened unexpectedly, and the man stuck his head out. "What the hell's going on? Someone just jumped off the front end!"

"New Haven P.D.! Take this train back up to the platform! Now!" Frank opened the heavy metal front door. Temporally using it as a shield, he looked outside to see if the suspect was taking aim.

The train started to lumber backward toward the station. Frank unsheathed his gun and jumped off into the railyard.

It was drizzling now, but foggier than before, visibility only fifteen or twenty yards. Frank situated himself on the gravel and realized he was on the outskirts of the yard and could barely make out the inbound lights that led back to the train station. Out in front of him through the fog, he could see the two faint lights of an approaching train coming in, about five hundred yards away. It let out a squeal of its air horn that echoed out into the valley. Frank's right arm hurt and now felt like pins and needles. His back ached between his shoulder blades; he was probably developing whiplash from the car accident.

He took a chance on which direction Yasmile would have gone and started to head back toward the station. He caught up and ran along the left side of the slow-moving 1:10. The train's catenaries occasionally sparked as they glided against the overhead power lines, casting a haunting flash of neon blue light on Frank and the surrounding area as the power arced above.

A gunshot sounded in the distance and Frank dropped to the ground. He looked in the direction of where the sound came from as another shot rang out. This time he saw the muzzle blast from the weapon as the bullet hissed by his head.

When the 1:10's final car passed, Frank jumped up and ran across the tracks to the other side of the train and shadowed alongside, using it as cover. He stayed low, looking through the undercarriage by the wheels, trying to see the suspect on the other side. He dropped to his good knee on the gravel, situating himself to fire, exhaled, and cracked his neck.

The local train finally passed and there was silence; no suspect.

Frank heard a faint noise…running on gravel. He cocked his head to determine what direction the sound was coming from.

Yasmile's sneakers smacked into the ground with a pained fury. His mind was frantic; a caged animal looking for an escape.

Frank took off after the fading sounds.

Yasmile headed toward the platforms, figuring with the fog being so heavy, if he ran in any other direction, he could easily get boxed-in and become lost in the railyard.

The lights of the platforms were getting brighter, so he knew he was going the right way. He spotted two brakemen with some large rail equipment in the yard. Their lantern-style flashlights were illuminating a junction box, and one threw a large switch that moved one track toward another. The other then lazily waved his flashlight at an idling FL-9, letting it know it could now pass. The train's bell rang rhythmically, and the massive machine crawled toward them and the intersection of track.

The two workers noticed Yasmile at the same time, instantly realizing by his demeanor that he didn't belong in the yard. Within seconds he was on them. He flew by as if they weren't even there.

"Hey! Where in the hell do you think you're going?"

Yasmile jumped the tracks and narrowly missed being hit by the passing FL-9. In response, the massive engine laid on its loud air horn.

Frank came out of the fog and sized up the situation. He reached the two brakemen as the FL-9 crossed the tracks, pulling two standard cars.

"Who the hell are you?" one shouted at him.

"Police! Where'd he go?"

"He just almost got fuckin' run over, jumping in front of that diesel!" the other yelled.

"He went that way?" Franked slowed to let the final car pass. It cleared, and his eyes searched desperately to find his suspect.

Another shot rang out and one of the brakemens' thighs exploded, the force of the projectile impact pushing that leg back into the air, causing the man to fall forward and crash down onto the jagged gravel. He screamed in pain. Frank dragged the other man to the ground. The detective saw Yasmile for only a second before he disappeared into the darkness.

Frank looked over to the man next to him. "You guys got a radio?"

"Yeah," the older mustached man answered back. Frank took off Tom's Burberry trench coat and wrapped it around the injured brakeman's leg.

"Apply pressure to that and call somebody now to get him an ambulance!" Frank shouted back over the rumble of the FL-9. He jumped up and ran in the suspect's direction.

From the end of the platforms, the visibility was down to about twenty yards. Yasmile emerged out of the darkness, sprinting toward them. He ran up onto the one that paralleled the 1:10, which was now letting its passengers off, unintentionally shielding him from the eyes of the police on track eight who were on the other side, scanning the disembarking crowd.

Frank appeared in hot pursuit, with a severe limp, barely able to bend his knee. He ran on it anyway. His arm was getting worse, becoming even more numb with every impact of his shoes on the uneven gravel. He was increasingly feeling pins and needles and a shooting pain in his upper back.

Yasmile ran across the long platform and down the stairs into the tunnel.

Frank hit the same platform at full speed with grunts and visible expressions of pain.

He got into the crowded hallway at the bottom of the stairs that led to the station, and his eyes darted for the lanky, dark-haired suspect. Frank kept his firearm low against his hip, so no one would see it in his hand. His eyes bounced off a dozen people of various sexes, ages, colors, and sizes before he finally zeroed in on Yasmile, who was trying to blend in to those upset commuters coming off the 1:10. He was thirty feet ahead of Frank. The detective quickly looked down and changed his path, zigzagging to the right, concealing his presence, even any police officer recognition. If someone spotted him now and ran over, it could blow everything. Yasmile looked back and amazingly, did not see the Frank.

Yasmile turned back around and saw a uniformed officer running toward him. He panicked, thinking he'd been made and raised his gun. The passing officer did not notice Yasmile or his automatic until it was too late to draw his weapon.

"YASMILE RASHEEN!" Frank yelled before he realized he was reacting. He raised his .357 and pushed a black woman out of the line of fire.

Yasmile swung around toward Frank and fired.

People screamed and dropped to the cold cement floor.

He let off another shot and Frank returned fire. His two projectiles grazed one shoulder and, hitting the same arm, spun Yasmile around. The uniformed officer leaped onto the suspect and tackled him. He punched Yasmile and knocked the gun out of his hand, causing it to slide away on the floor.

Tom jumped onto the scene and aided the officer. Putting a knee into his back, Tom handcuffed the dazed and injured Yasmile.

Silence echoed eerily through the air, followed by whispers and moans.

"They shot that kid!" someone shouted.

"The cops killed a kid!"

Frank lowered his weapon, exhaled and swayed. He looked down at his chest. His dress shirt began to turn a dark, wet, red color.

He took two shaky steps and partly collapsed, catching himself on his knee, using his revolver as a crutch. Frank remained in that position for a moment, exhaling, his batteries finally out of juice. He was done. He tried to rise but again fell to his knees, feeling the hot liquid dripping down his body under his clothes, wetting his stomach and legs. His injured leg finally gave. He slowly collapsed over onto his side. He took a deep breath that was far too shallow, before slowly rolling over onto his back, taking long, labored breaths. He felt the back of his shirt soaking up from the exit wound on his back, by his expert estimation of a .45 caliber, probably the size of a half-dollar.

Horrified, Tom rushed over to him. By this time over a dozen other officers, including Graham Birdsall and

Lieutenant Mike Warner, were on the scene securing the location.

Frank lay choking on the floor. Tom attempted to apply pressure to his bleeding chest, all the while, trying to flag down medical assistance. Frank blankly gazed up at the ceiling; everything was beginning to slow down. He tried to speak but coughed up blood and saliva into the air, which came back down onto his face.

Handcuffed, with his face pressed to the cold floor, Yasmile stared at him. They looked at each other and Yasmile smirked, impressed with his own aim. Frank turned his eyes away and with much effort, pulled out Lombardo's address book, and handed it to Graham. He tried to grab Tom by the collar and pull him towards his face.

"Take this. Outside…a guy—a train guy, he's…he's been shot…" He coughed again and choked.

Teary eyed, Tom tried to remain in control. "Take it easy, Frank, please..."

Out of breath, Frank no longer had the energy or willpower to speak. Tom desperately tried to comfort him, all the while, turning his head and screaming for medical assistance. The black woman who Frank had knocked out of the line of fire just moments ago came over and knelt down beside him, gently placing her bag under his head, she picked up his hand, lightly stroking his forehead.

He looked up at her and realized it was Sparkles, his old friend, the transvestite. She wore her finest one-piece fuchsia dress that was a size too small, probably on her way to New York to party the night away at some West Village bar. Frank tried to smile at the irony but couldn't tell if his muscles moved.

He was as white as a sheet but relaxed in Sparkles' presence.

"Shhh, it's okay. It's gonna be okay, baby," she said to Frank with a warm, bright smile. She continued to stroke his head and made eye contact with Tom, conveying her worry. Frank again tried to speak but, Sparkles put her head low, so she only needed to whisper into Frank's ear. "Our Father, who art in Heaven, hallow be thy name..." Frank's lips moved, trying to repeat the Lord's Prayer. Tears slowly began to fall down Tom's cheeks while he continued to hold pressure on Frank's chest. Mike Warner turned away so no one would see a tear roll down his face, and pushed back the ever-encroaching gawkers who just wanted to see all the drama, the excitement, the blood, and the death.

Frank stared upwards, his breathing short and forced; his eyes trying to focus on something that wasn't there. Every other sound faded away from his ears. A single tear rolled down his cheek.

His muscles slowly stopped moving and his face relaxed.

The loud echoing sound of a wailing siren first stirred him from the depths of the black abyss.

Frank opened his eyes just enough to see and found himself in cramped quarters, looking up at a bright, shiny interior ceiling light. He immediately recognized that he was in a Cadillac Miller-Meteor Coach. He'd been in ambulances more times than he could count, but never from this position—on his back, looking up. He was numb and couldn't feel his body. He must have been heavily medicated because he could also perceive no pain. At least, that was what he hoped. In his head, all he could hear was Al Green's *Jesus is Waiting* and couldn't shake it. The more he tried, the more it repeated and the louder it became. Almost comical at this point, he thought.

Someone's grip tightened in his hand and Frank attempted to look up but was hindered by the oxygen mask and tube over his nose and mouth. He instead looked back up at the large, bright interior light that hung above like a blaring star going supernova. A head came into view, the face temporarily silhouetted because of the interior light behind. Frank poured all the energy he had left within to concentrate and make out whose face that was. Gradually, the face became visible, but Frank still couldn't tell who it was. He knew him but wasn't recognizing him. Why couldn't he recognize him? The head leaned in and spoke softly into his ear.

"Hey brother, I'm with you. You ain't going anywhere today."

He instantly recognized the voice. It was his best friend, Christopher Wallace. He must have not heeded Frank's edict about going home. His grip was like a vise within his own, and his emotions rushed to him at once and he didn't have the energy to keep it bottled up. Frank couldn't speak, but a tear rolled down his face.

"Shhh…it's gonna be okay, brother. I'm here. We're gonna get through this. Okay?" Chris paused, waiting for an answer. "Okay?"

Frank nodded in agreement.

Behind Chris, Frank saw the paramedics checking his IV fluids, continuing their attempts to stabilize him. Frank instantly recognized the medic. It was the older man from *The Signalman,* the Charles Dicken's story Frank was so fond of. This man was the spitting image of the face Frank so long ago conceived in his head to look like…how was this possible? Was it the delirium or the drugs or the loss of blood? Maybe he was hallucinating. He hoped so. He felt himself fading away again and hoped this wasn't it. Suddenly faced with it, he didn't want to die. He wanted to live. He prayed to God that the dark abyss he had just come out of, which he now felt himself rushing back to, wasn't death. If recognizing that man was an omen of what was to come, Frank wasn't in the position to try and figure that out. He just wanted to sleep...

His eyes closed, and he instantly fell down, down into that endless void, losing all sense of sight, sound, and touch, falling deeper and deeper into the darkness.

Frank Pasquale Suchy needed to rest.

SUGGESTED SOUNDTRACK

Bobby Bland – "I Got the Same Old Blues Again"

The Five Statins – "Downtown"

Queen – "Somebody to Love"

Syreeta – "Black Maybe"

Donna Summer – "Love to Love You Baby"

Captain & Tinnell – "Love Will Keep Us Together"

The Shangri-La's – "He Cried"

Johnny Ace – "Pledging My Love"

Frank Sinatra – "When No One Cares"

Curtis Mayfield – "Right on For the Darkness"

Jackie Gleason – "Snowfall"

The Mills Brothers w/ Count Basie – "Sunny"

Paul Williams – "A Little Bit of Love"

The Delfonics – "Hey Love"

Les Paul & Mary Ford – "It's a Lonesome Old Town"

The Beatles – "While My Guitar Gently Weeps" (Acoustic Version)

Stevie Wonder & Jeff Beck – "Lookin' For Another Pure Love"

Traditional – "Nearer My God to Thee"

Big Maybelle – "That's a Pretty Good Love"

ABBA – "Money, Money, Money"

Curtis Mayfield – "Billy Jack"

The Doors – "Backdoor Man" (live at the Isle of Wight)

Hector Lavoe – "El Todo Poderoso"

The Bee Gees – "You Should Be Dancing"

War – "Cisco Kid"

Stevie Wonder – "Maybe Your Baby"

Patti LaBelle's – "Lady Marmalade"

Stevie Wonder – "Another Star"

Stevie Wonder – "As"

Al Green – "The Letter"

The Five Statins – "In the Still of the Night"

Iggy Pop – "China Girl"

Al Green – "Jesus is Waiting"

The Doors – "Peace Frog"

ACKNOWLEDGMENTS

IT'S BEEN A long, winding road to get this story out of my head, down on paper, and out in one form or another to you, the audience. So much so that at times I felt this day would never come, and that I was just shouting in an empty room, with myself being the only one listening. My journey with this book began way back in 2002, when I commenced writing *Blood in the Streets* as a screenplay with the hopes of one day bringing it to the big screen. After graduating film school in 2001, my big idea to get into the film industry was to do it the Quentin Tarantino way: to write myself in.

When I wasn't at my day job, I split my free time between writing this and another work, a 1940s private eye opus called *Morris PI*, either working on them on the train during my two-hour (each way) commute or on late, late nights post-college after my shift, working into the wee hours of the morning, only taking the occasional break from one script to focus on the other. The idea being that I always, always needed to focus on my creative output if I wanted to realize my dreams, meaning I had to put in the time. Little did I know it would take over fifteen years to accomplish just that. I finished penning *Blood* in 2005 and the other in 2006. So, to thank all those who had a hand in all of this, I figure the best way would be to go in chronological order.

First, the biggest thanks of all might have to go to my parents, Pasquale and Clare, who fed my imagination as a child by supplying me with toys, comics, movies, books, television, and whatever else my heart desired, which kept that brain of mine working, fostering dreams of what I wanted to do with my life when I grew up. They put me through college no questions asked, always gave me what I needed, and even had a hand in getting my shoe in the door at my last two jobs post-college; at a now defunct video store called Tommy K's and at my current employer of over 16 years now and counting, Fox News Channel. I owe them the world and much, much more. A big thank you also goes to my darling sister Nicole, who's inspired me and helped shape me into the person I am today. I love you Nikki.

Next, one of the biggest thanks I can muster up would be to Robert J. Siegel, the fabulous writer, director, and producer who was my professor at film school. He and I quickly bonded when I entered his classes, and a friendship began that still lasts to this day. Not only that, but post-college he also offered to read and give me thorough notes on the first drafts of this and my other aforementioned script, reading and rereading this screenplay and offering suggestions, options, and being a real soundboard for honing this into the best story it could be. If it wasn't for his continued interest in those early years, *Blood in the Streets* and *Morris PI* would never have been finished and streamlined.

A hearty thanks to all my colleagues at work, my Fox family, a laundry list of friends on both sides of the camera who offered me friendship and support over the years when I thought this project would never see the light of day. In particular, regarding support for the book, people like Kevin P, James T, Brotha Luke, RT Machine, Dave Y, Mike Cop,

Spider, Miles W, Jim B, Matt, Joe Pic, MK (who's moved on to greener pastures), the list goes on and on and on. You all know who you are (yes, you!) and I thank you for everything. Another huge thank you goes to my former colleague John Gibson. Without his advice, this book would never have been written. In early 2012, while talking shop in the green-room before a guest spot (after venting my frustration about having, by then, three screenplays written, and not being able to get any into the right hands), it was John who made the suggestion that I turn it into a book because I'd have a better chance of getting that out to market than a script. I owe him a huge debt of gratitude because without his marvelous idea, this book may not have ever been written, and more importantly for me, this story may never have gotten out to you, the reader. I then spent the rest of 2012, while on the road with my day job, covering that presidential election cycle in lonely hotel and motel rooms after long (and I mean long!) hours at work, converting this tale from a screenplay to a novel, taking the opportunity to really flesh out and develop the story into what it is today.

There are other countless people at my day job who work in front of the camera who helped me, either by offering me a contact or perhaps making an introduction, or even passing this manuscript on to someone else, although the majority of those leads ended up being dead ends for one reason or another. Regardless, so many of them, without solicitation, offered to help me to reach my dreams, and I owe all them a huge debt of gratitude for their selflessness. Charlie G, Eric S, Dana P, Rich L, and anyone else I am blanking on now, I thank you all for that kindness.

Speaking of kindness, generosity, graciousness, and words like that, there are two people in particular that I owe huge appreciation to, which I could never begin to fully express. First would be to my dear friend, my second father, Mr. Neil Cavuto. Neil is one of the nicest, most generous men I have ever known, and he is hilarious. I owe him so much. It was Neil who decided to put me *in front* of the camera beginning in 2011, to help push his business channel on his show because he thought I was funny. After the higher-ups were unreceptive to my ideas for show and online content (it seemed I was a little too ahead of the curve), it was Neil who decided to create a segment in 2014 to help showcase me and un-can some of that talent he always said he saw in me. I have to thank him for always being my number one supporter at my day job and never treating or considering me as "the help," as I and others of my capacity on the tech side sometimes felt by others at his level.

The other person I have to thank at Fox would be the guy who jokingly refers to me as the little brother he never wanted, Uncle Sean. Aside from Neil, Sean Hannity is one of the nicest and most generous people I've ever known. It seems that outside of Fox, a lot of people get a very false picture of Sean, painted by those who do not agree with the politics of the man without even caring to tune in to see or hear him for themselves. Instead, they listen to others and make judgements, merely being told by those in the media how to think about him, and politics aside, it would be nice for once if some of the amazing things these people do behind the scenes were highlighted in stories (because you never get confidential sources telling any *good* gossip, do you? 'Cause where's the fun in that?!). Sean, like Neil, is so generous with his time. They are always there when you need them, and as I like to say, you could blindly ring Sean up at 3am and say, "*I need $10,000 for bail money,*" and his only question would be where to send it. He is amazingly generous to his staff and coworkers, especially around the holidays, which is something you can't say for a lot of the other people in this business. I cannot say enough about these two men, both of whom have been there for me when I needed it, and I will always be in their debt for it.

Now, speaking of Uncle Sean, what got this whole ball rolling was his old assistant, Elise Sabbeth, who I also owe the world to, taking it upon herself to tell her best friend about this guy who she worked with who had dreams beyond his current job title. Thank you, Elise, because if you didn't pay it forward, I wouldn't have this book published today.

So in the summer of 2014, after returning from visiting my in-laws in England, I had a voicemail from the literary agency Dupree Miller & Associates, who wanted to see my work because of Elise's recommendation. I then had Lacy Lynch at Dupree Miller & Associates suddenly taking an interest in this project, and sticking with me to cultivate this story into what it is today. So much thanks to Lacy for taking a chance on me simply because of the reference of a good friend. A big thank you to Martha Bowman for helping to get the manuscript in a good place to shop around, and thank you to Anthony Ziccardi and Michael Wilson at Post Hill Press for being willing to publish this work and sticking with the unbelievably long process it took to get all of us on the same page.

A big thanks goes to David Limbaugh, who gave his time. Little did he know he had signed up for a lot more than he bargained for in helping me get everything in order. His patience and willingness to take the lead when others didn't really saved the day, so I thank you, sir. A big thank you to Felicia A. Sullivan, who held my hand through the final editing process, really helping me iron things out and graciously showing me how everything worked on my maiden voyage, so to speak. A big shout out to Maddie Sturgeon and all those at Post Hill Press, for all their help as well.

And a big thanks to all my friends Patty Copela, Martin McHugh, Matt Garrison, Mike Copela, Chris Camputaro (and his aunts Debbie and Ann, and Uncle Chip!) and Justin Quick, for being there for me when I needed it, and doing what all good friends do to help their good friend and brother out. Thank you to Paul D'Andrea for answering my annoying questions, and a big thank you to the man, the myth, the legend, Randy Jurgensen, who I now have the honor of calling a friend. Thank you for your patience while enduring my countless interviews and conversations about the era in which this story takes place, and shedding some first-hand light on what it was like being a police officer on the front lines in the 1960s and 1970s. Thank you to John Hrabushi for his input. Also, a shout out goes to the greater Camputaro family: Phil, Nick, and Nicole, who I miss every day. Thank you also goes to my mother-in-law Christine Birdsall, for all her help and input and willingness to read my stuff.

A big thank you to my partner in crime, brother-from-another-mother, and podcasting cohost of *Saturday Night Movie Sleepovers*, J. Blake Fichera, who is always there to lend his time and energy to whatever venture we come up with and to bounce ideas off of. Heck, if we both had a dime for all the ideas we've come up with, we'd have a Scrooge McDuck money-bin full of dimes.

Lastly, but very far from least, the biggest thank you of all goes to the love of my life, my soulmate, my opposite number, my wife Helen Grace. She's endured far more than any woman should in her life, especially with all this, from moving country to be with her soulmate and putting up with me. She's also endured reading, and reading, and reading, then rereading again this novel, probably more times than me, on my request to check out new updates, rewrites, and new drafts, to proofread, and probably even to read it one more time for good measure, along with my other fictional works. Sounds like a fun idea at the time, but I have to give it to her: she's been amazing and I only wish I could pay her back for all the time she spent on all my creative endeavors. Thank you, baby. And a big thank you to our fur babies: Babe, our Yorkshire Terrier who has practically transcended being a dog, and his crazy little sister, Tofu "the Turkey" Roberta, our cat, and also to Princess Caldonia. Their unconditional joy and love is inspirational, and if the human race on a whole could be exposed to that love as I have been in recent years and open its collective eyes, the planet would be a far better place.

Also, a big thanks to you, the reader, for your support in purchasing and reading this novel. I really hope you've liked what you've read, but if you haven't, if you have found a problem with any of the content or the prose of this fictional yarn, please accept my deepest and most sincere apologies. I was just a kid with big dreams who wanted to make a good, entertaining movie.

ABOUT THE AUTHOR

DION BAIA WAS born in New Haven and graduated from SUNY Purchase College's Conservatory of Film in 2001. He immediately began working in the industry, specifically behind the camera in television at Fox News Channel, doing in-studio audio on shows like *Your World with Neil Cavuto, Hannity & Colmes, The Kelly File with Megyn Kelly,* and *Hannity,* among others.

In 2011, Dion started his podcasting career and began periodically appearing on camera, performing tiny self-written comedic vignettes on FNC to promote the newly formed Fox Business Network, encouraging viewers to call their television providers to *"Demand It"* (FBN). In 2014 he graduated to contributing weekly to panel segments on *Your World,* with ongoing involvement, and cofounded the *Saturday Night Movie Sleepovers Podcast,* a nostalgic deep-dive into the films that helped shaped his life.

Dion currently lives in Westchester, New York, with his wife Helen Grace and their son, Babe, a Yorkshire Terrier, and Tofu 'the Turkey' Roberta, their cat.